C000281292

3805301790043 7

THE DEBT

Other Five Star Titles by Thomas Brennan:

The One True Prince

THE DEBT

THOMAS BRENNAN

Five Star • Waterville, Maine

This novel is a work of fic
incidents are either the prod
real, used fictitiously.

First Edition, Second Printing.

Published in 2005 in conjunction with
Tekno Books and Ed Gorman.

Set in 11 pt. Plantin.

Printed in the United States on permanent paper.

Library of Congress Cataloging-in-Publication Data

Brennan, Thomas.
The debt / by Thomas Brennan.
p. cm.
ISBN 1-59414-276-9 (hc : alk. paper)
1. Police—New York (State)—New York—Fiction.
2. Young women—crimes against—Fiction. 3. New York
(N.Y.)—Fiction. 4. Vermont—Fiction. 5. Mystery fiction.
I. Title.
PS3602.R454D43 2005
813′.6—dc22 2004057545

THE DEBT

1

I recognized Carl Shaw's name: I'd read it on the spines of a dozen books in the store near the Precinct House, on breaks or between shifts. Maybe you build up a mental image of someone who decides to write horror novels for a living. But when I got to meet him, Shaw looked nothing like I'd expected. He looked normal. I guess you can never tell.

The duty roster sergeant had warned me and my partner, Sam Hollis, to expect company on night patrol. "Press Liaison asked the Captain for a good team. You two got volunteered. You look after the guy, give him the guided tour and make sure you don't screw up."

Now, as we waited in the squad room after the rest of the patrols had been sent out, Sam asked me, "Why us?"

I could guess why: good publicity. A few months back, me and Sam had our pictures in the newspapers after we pulled a girl of four from a burning house on Leicester and 14th. If there's one thing the Department loves, it's good publicity. I didn't say this to Sam; even though he's been in the force fifteen years against my three, he says I'm the cynical one.

Cynical? Maybe I am, these days. But I'd spent the past ten minutes looking around the squad room, with its battered desks and steel chairs, its peeling paint, and wondering if I'd miss it. If I finally decided to quit, I'd never see the Precinct again, never wear my uniform and badge. I hated to admit it, but sometimes that looked like the only option I had.

Five after ten, the sergeant walked into the squad room with a bearded guy in corduroy pants, brown leather jacket and Timberland boots. “Okay, Mr. Shaw, for your sins you got Officers Hollis and Burnett, two of New York’s finest.”

The bearded guy smiled and stuck out his hand. “Carl Shaw.”

Sam shook first. “Sam Hollis.”

“Steve Burnett,” I said, looking the writer over. About five-ten, an inch or so shorter than me. If I’d seen him on the street, I would have guessed banker or IT manager off-duty for the weekend; the leather jacket looked too new, too clean, just like the boots. Soft hands, sharp nails. His trimmed beard had traces of gray in with the black.

Sergeant Evans looked at Sam and me. “Do your regular route and check in at one and three. Any problems, call. You got that?”

We nodded. We could read between the lines: don’t take Shaw anywhere too dangerous, don’t put him on the line. Don’t bring him back in a body bag.

“Thanks for all your help,” Shaw told the sergeant. “I promise I’ll be careful. And I’ll try not to get in the way too much.”

“Glad to hear it, Mr. Shaw.” The sergeant ran his pen down a printed form. “Before you go, we need to ask you a couple of things: first off, are you carrying any weapons?”

Shaw blinked and shook his head. “No.”

“How about controlled substances?”

“Only cigarettes.”

“We’ll let you off with them, barely. Give me a minute to find you a vest and you can get out there.” The sergeant stopped at the exit. “That goes for you two as well: vests.”

Sam groaned. “Come on, Evans.”

“You want to argue it with Captain Brady?”

By the time Sam and me had struggled into our gear, Shaw had slipped a borrowed vest under his jacket. I could see the Department's logic, even though the issue vest is about as flexible as a concrete tee shirt. When you're Sam's size, six-three and two-hundred pounds plus, it's tight enough just getting in and out of the car.

"You mind riding in the back, in the pit?" Sam asked Shaw as we walked out into the parking lot. His breath hung in the cold air.

"The pit?"

Sam grinned. "It's where we stow our guests. The reluctant ones, you know?"

Shaw said, "That sounds fine. It'll give me a different perspective."

Sam winked at me.

The other patrols had long gone. October cold streaked our blue and white cruiser with condensation. You just knew that Halloween, two weeks away, would be clear and icy. Before I climbed into the car, I looked up at the wedge of night sky between the Precinct House and the tenement blocks opposite. Stars glinted like holes punched in a stage backdrop.

"You getting in some time tonight?" Sam asked, wedging himself behind the steering wheel.

I moved my nightstick to one side and slid into the passenger seat. I leaned back and looked at Shaw behind the steel mesh screen. "You okay back there, Mr. Shaw?"

"No problem. And call me Carl."

"Will do."

He held up a square of metal and plastic. "Mind if I use a recorder? I'm not too good at shorthand, especially in a moving car."

"Fine with me."

"And me."

The inside of the car glowed with lights as Sam turned the ignition. The radio crackled into life. The dash clock read 22:27. Sam rolled out of the lot and through the barrier, then pulled on to Avenue J and took a left on Bedford. Brooklyn College showed on our left, all lit up by spotlights. The Tuesday streets seemed quiet. That didn't mean anything.

"So, why pick us?" Sam called back.

"I'm sorry?" Carl leaned forward against the mesh like a suspect.

"Why this area?" Sam asked. "Why Kings and Brooklyn?"

"I've got an idea for a new novel. I need somewhere with docks and residential, not too far from an airport. And I need somewhere with a colorful history."

Sam nodded, smearing the reflections of the dashboard lights over his face. "Well, we got plenty of that around here."

"I might work Coney Island into this one," Carl said. "I've always wanted to use it."

"So this one's another horror book?" I asked.

"Not this time. I wanted to try crime, thriller, mystery—whatever you want to call it. But I need to do some research for this one. When my wife contacted your Press Office, they were very helpful."

Sam slowed at Clarendon. A handful of stores were still open, their red and blue neon lights flickering. Three guys sat on the bench outside the video store: dark, baggy clothes, hoods pulled down low over their faces. Maybe a glint of gold jewelry at their wrists. One of the sedans parked nearby could have been theirs. I tapped at the computer keyboard on the dash. None of the registrations came up with a match.

Sam glanced at me. I shrugged.

"Problem?" Carl asked.

"We'll swing by this way a little later," Sam said, heading along Bedford for Church Avenue. "See what they're up to. Probably just bored kids hanging out."

We followed our usual route. Cold rain fell, coating everything with a greasy film. The tires hissed. Carl started his tape recorder and began the questions. He started off with our backgrounds. Sam told him how he'd joined the force in eighty-nine after six years with the army. I explained how I'd applied in late two thousand and one; I didn't have to explain why.

"How about before that?"

"Before that? College, track and field, then I worked in IT for four years."

"IT?"

"Networks, communications, stuff like that."

"Tell him where you worked," Sam said, then told Carl himself: "The big banks and broker companies on Wall Street. Wall Street, man."

"From Wall Street to the police?" Carl said, smiling. "That's quite a change."

Sam shook his head. "And one hell of a drop in pay."

"The money didn't come into it, back then." I could still remember my first day in uniform. Plenty of other young guys had signed up, and some not so young. On everyone's face, determination mixed in with anxiety, maybe even fear. I'd been the opposite of cynical. Sam reckons you get cynical when you're doing something you're bored with. Me, I think maybe you get cynical when you try to do something you're not sure you *can* do.

When I didn't add any more, Carl said, "So, you were a runner in college?"

"Kind of." I shifted in my seat and stared ahead. Don't get me wrong, I'm not ashamed of the running. I just don't like to remember why I started running in the first place, all those years before. I don't like to admit it to myself.

"Kind of?" Sam half-turned to Carl but still kept his eyes on the road ahead. "He could have been up there with Johnson or Suarez. You want to see him chasing someone: he's off the mark like shit off a shovel, and he never gives in. I mean *never*. He will not stop until he gets his man."

Sam turned to me and grinned. "Like the Mounties, right?"

I smiled and shook my head. I liked Sam but he knew how to find your buttons and push them.

"It's a good quality to have, tenacity," Carl said. "Especially in the police."

"I guess so." To change the subject, I asked, "You live in the city, Carl?"

"I inherited an old apartment in Hoboken, but I spend most of my time up in Vermont. We have a house out in the hills."

"Sounds good," Sam said. "I've driven up through Windsor and Montpelier a few times in the fall, gone fishing in the Kingsbury. If I won the lottery, I wouldn't mind finding me and Donna a little place up there, maybe around Jay's Peak or Newport."

Carl leaned forward. "I'm not so far away from Jay's. You ever heard of Eastham? It's between Enosburg Falls and Sheldon."

"Can't say as I have, Carl. You close to the border?"

"Sure. If you're not careful, you could cross into Canada and not even realize it." Carl turned to me. "Have you ever been up there?"

"I used to have relatives near Rutland. Long time ago." I

remembered family trips in my uncle's beat-up station wagon, all the way from Albany to Middletown at a steady forty to make sure we had enough gas. I remembered rain and cold, a cold that gripped your bones no matter how many clothes you wore. Give me the city any day of the week.

But Carl had a different view. "It's beautiful around there, and not just in the fall. On a good day, you can see the Green Mountains and New Hampshire's White Mountains. Snow in spring, hunting in October. Lake Champlain in the summer. I wouldn't want to live anywhere else."

I almost expected him to slide some tourist brochures through the steel mesh.

"Yeah. Beautiful country up there." Sam had pulled back onto Clarendon and sat staring at the bench by the video store. Empty.

"No alarms going off," I said. "Still . . ."

Sam nodded. "Let's go take a look."

We crossed the junction and pulled up outside the video store. A convenience store stood open beside it; I could see two young, yawning Hispanic girls through the windows.

"Can I come too?" Carl asked, already sliding toward the door.

"You better wait here," Sam said, glancing at me. "We'll only be a few minutes."

We left Carl in the car and looked around. Plenty of dark shadows crowded the parking lot and the alleyways between the stores. Someone could be training an Uzi on us and we wouldn't know. I forced myself to search the area. There's a fine line between being careful and getting paranoid. A little paranoia is good, sometimes, but it can stop you from doing your job.

Sam led the way into the video store. A pierced clerk sat

behind a high counter. He had a computer game control pad on his knees. On the screen above him, angular CGI women kicked hell out of each other. They filled the store with their electronic grunts.

Without taking his eyes from the screen, the clerk told us that the kids out front were no hassle, he knew most of them from school, they were "safe". If they had money, they'd probably be down at the diner on Ditmas and Ocean. If not, they were probably just bumming around.

We walked out past racks of DVDs and videos and left the clerk to his game. We checked out the convenience store and the liquor store. The young girls and the guy in the liquor store, a wary Korean, said they'd had no trouble.

As we walked back to the car, Sam said, "What did you make of the Korean guy?"

"I saw how he kept his right hand under the counter all the time."

"Alley-clearer or alarm?"

"Why would he need the alarm for us?" I thought about a few of the grocers and owners of small stores we came across day to day. "Got to be an alley-clearer he didn't want us to see. Probably a sawn-off pump or a SPAS-12."

Sam nodded. "That's what I figured. Maybe we should pay him another visit when we don't have company?"

I knew he was right. A lot of the store owners have protection, but not all of them have licenses.

As we climbed back into the cruiser, Carl asked, "Everything okay?"

"Just some kids with nothing much to do." Sam started the car and pulled out onto Clarendon. The dashboard clock read 23:38.

"Is it always this quiet?" Carl asked.

I thought he sounded disappointed. I said, "We get good

days and bad. I guess you want to hear about some of the bad ones?"

We told him about the robberies, the rapes, the car crashes and domestics. We're nearly always the first on the scene, usually before the medics or the Fire Department. In three years, I've had four people die in my arms. I've used CPR and mouth-to-mouth. Sometimes it works. Sometimes not. I've had people shoot at me with small caliber arms and shotguns, once with an assault rifle. But my stories are nothing compared to Sam's.

After fifteen years on the street, Sam could have talked to Carl for a week and still have stories left over. Sam's delivered babies, found murder victims, gone on point in drugs busts and had more car chases than a seventies' police show. He's spent most of his time in the same Precinct and knows the pushers and the pimps, the crack houses and the fronts.

Carl leaned against the steel mesh with his recorder held up to catch Sam's words.

Outside the car, the city streets gleamed with the rain. Signs and headlights slid through the puddles. Apartment blocks showed up as grids of dark and light windows. Shadows moved behind pulled blinds.

The clock read 00:34. Sam turned up 47th toward the Gowanus Expressway. I knew he was heading for Lazzini's, a deli set back behind Sunset Park. We usually grabbed a coffee and sub before we checked in.

"You hungry, Carl?" Sam called back.

Carl yawned before replying, "And how. But if we're going to eat, the check's on me."

"We don't have a problem with that, do we, Steve?"

I didn't reply. I'd just be glad to leave behind the smell of three guys in a humid police cruiser.

Sam pulled into the curb opposite Lazzini's. Most of the

street was dark. Condensation smeared the inside of the deli's windows and blurred the fluorescent lights. Three steps led up from street level to meet a fogged glass door.

As I got out, I looked up and down the street. Rain coated the parked cars. Most of the buildings looked asleep. Somewhere nearby, a dog barked three times before whining to a stop. I stood on the sidewalk and took a deep breath.

Sam locked up and waited for a car to drift past before he crossed the street. He told Carl, "You'll like this place. Good coffee, subs, pastries. Been here for years. Gonna do great business when the new Gowanus construction guys get here."

Carl followed Sam. I followed close behind Carl. Sam reached for the iron railing at the side of the steps. He put his foot on the first step.

He started to turn back to speak to Carl. I remember he grinned. He'd probably just remembered a joke he needed to tell.

The deli's glass door exploded. Shards sliced through the air. Then the sound of a gunshot that sounded like a howitzer. Sam flew back as if yanked from the step by a speeding truck. He landed on his back, his arms spread out, one leg folded beneath him.

A dark shape stood in the ruined doorway. Hazy light framed its outline. The guy looked huge. His right arm swiveled toward me and Carl.

Everything moved too slow. I think I yelled. I pushed Carl to one side with my left hand. My right reached for my automatic, had it out of the holster. Then the second shot took me in the chest.

The same truck that had pulled Sam back now slammed into my body. I spun as I fell. I landed on my face. I saw my

Glock 9-millimeter skid along the sidewalk.

My chest didn't hurt yet. I tried to move but a massive weight pushed me down. I listened for the third shot, the one that would split my back.

I saw Carl crouch down. One hand reached under the hem of his pants and pulled a revolver from an ankle holster. Still crouching, he fired twice toward the deli's entrance. I couldn't see his target. Then, with three steps, he crossed to my fallen gun.

I tried to move my head. I saw Carl stand up and point my gun toward the steps. He fired another shot from the Glock.

Then a hand pulled my radio from my belt. I heard Carl's voice. "Hello? Anyone? Dispatch? Look, I need assistance. Two officers have been shot . . . Lazzini's delicatessen off . . . ah, it's Forty-Seventh. Sure. Officers down. They need help . . ."

I saw the blood pooling beneath Sam's body. Glass splinters caught the streetlight. Rain slanted down in gray sheets, mixed with the blood and washed it toward the gutter. I might have heard sirens but I couldn't be sure. The weight on my back, sharp and hot and increasing, stopped me from breathing. Then darkness reached out and pulled me down.

White. Everything white. I stared at the white wall, white bedclothes, white furniture. My hands rested on the top sheet, their tanned skin the only shot of color. For a moment, I wondered if they were really my hands. I tried to tell them to do something: make a fist, give the finger, anything. They lay there like things that had crawled up from the Hudson.

The second time I woke up, a nurse smiled at me from the foot of the bed. She set down the clipboard she'd been reading. "How are you feeling?"

"Not too bad," I lied. I could move my hands now, and feel the stabbing pains in my chest, so I guessed whatever drug they'd given me had worn off. "How's Sam?"

She reached for my right hand and gazed at her wristwatch. "Was that your partner?"

I didn't like the way she said that. "Was?"

"Oh, don't worry, he's okay." She counted my heart rate and nodded. "I'll tell the doctor you're awake. Everything's fine. You just rest."

Before I could ask any more questions, the door had closed behind her. After a few minutes, it opened again, but instead of the doctor I saw Marie. She stood beside the bed and looked down at me, shaking her head. Her eyes glistened with reflected light. "What the hell have you been up to?"

I tried to smile. "Long story. Well, no, short story, I guess: we got ambushed."

Marie sat on the edge of the bed and took my hand.

"How's Sam?" I asked.

"I think he's okay. He's just come out of surgery. I saw Donna in the waiting room."

I struggled to sit up but gasped when knives sliced into my chest and sides.

"Hey, none of that," Marie said, pushing my shoulders back. "You've got three broken ribs, last I heard. If you hadn't been wearing a vest . . ."

We had a lot to thank the duty sergeant for, me and Sam. I remembered how close Sam had been; that first shot must have been from six, maybe seven feet. Hell, I'd been a good fifteen feet away and still felt like I'd been through a car crusher.

"Did they get the guy?" I asked.

"What guy?"

"The one who shot us?"

Marie tilted her head to one side. "He's dead. You shot him."

"I did?"

"Well, you and then that guy you had with you, the writer—"

"Carl?"

"That's right," Marie said. "I guess the drugs are still in your system. They doped you up pretty good."

I had hazy memories of the scene, but nothing about shooting the guy. I wanted to ask Marie more questions but the door behind her opened and a doctor in a blue cotton smock and pants walked in. His Nikes squealed on the slick floor. "I'm sorry, no visitors."

Marie stood up and kissed me. "I'll be back tomorrow. Well, later today. You take it easy."

"I will." I waited until the doctor, a guy a little younger than me but with a tired, lined face, had finished reading my chart. "How's my partner, Sam Hollis?"

"Oh, he's fine." The doctor took my pulse. "We sent him up to the operating room but the bullet—a .45—came out nice and clean. He's lucky: another inch to the left and it would have hit artery. And the vest took most of the impact, of course."

I breathed out and sank into the bed. It had been one hell of a night.

"You've a slight concussion and three cracked ribs, but no obvious internal damage. I'll keep you in until morning, then send you home with painkillers if you have a good night, or what's left of it. You'll need to take it easy for a few weeks. Get plenty of rest."

The doctor turned off the overhead fluorescents as he left. Only the illuminated panels beside the bed glowed with soft light. I closed my eyes and tried to piece together what had happened. I opened my eyes when I heard the door creak. "Marie?"

"Hey." Carl stood beside the bed, with his hands deep in his pockets. He smiled. "I heard you and Sam are going to be okay."

"It looks that way." I didn't know what to say, but the first thing was, "We owe you."

He shrugged. "I was in the right place at the right time."

"Lucky for us."

We stared at each other. I remembered the duty sergeant asking if Carl had any concealed weapons, and Carl saying he didn't. And I could see that ankle holster as if I was choosing it from a catalogue: pale brown leather, single strap over the revolver, a Smith and Wesson .38.

Carl stared at me. "I told the officers that took the call that the .38 belonged to the robber. I said you shot him in the shoulder as you went down, making the robber drop the .38. Before he could shoot you again with the .45, I grabbed the .38 and shot him twice. Self-defense."

The drugs that the hospital had pumped into me started to pull me down in to the bed. One part of my mind knew that Carl shouldn't have been carrying that gun. But the guy had saved our lives. It was too complex. We'd have to work it out later. Before I faded away again, I repeated, "We owe you."

Carl stepped forward, a darker blur against the white, and said, "Look after yourself."

The next morning, Marie helped me to pull my clothes over the bulky dressings around my chest and lower ribs. The skin had already started to bruise. The vest had taken most of the bullet's impact and spread it out, but the result wasn't pretty.

"Stop squirming," Marie told me. "You're worse than a child."

She should know. She works across town, in a pediatric unit at Mercy. She's four years older than me, another point she reminds me of when I'm behaving like a kid.

"Won't they miss you in work?" I asked, wincing as she slid my arms into my shirtsleeves.

"I swapped with Veronica, earlies for lates." Marie reached down and started lacing up my boots. I felt like an invalid, not something I enjoy. But I appreciated her help and the fact that she'd collected some spare clothes from the apartment I share.

I followed Marie through to Sam's room. He lay asleep, swaddled in bandages. A heart monitor beeped above the bed, next to an IV drip. The nurse said Sam had had a good night and seemed fine. As we left the ward, I saw a tall guy in a dark blue suit walking toward me. I thought I recognized him.

He called out, "Steve Burnett? Tony Mendez, Homicide."

I shook hands and winced. "This is my girlfriend, Marie Doran."

"Marie. How are you?"

Marie glanced at me, then back to Detective Mendez. "You need to talk?"

"Just five minutes."

She nodded. "I'll grab a coffee. Don't grill him too hard; he's still woozy."

As Marie walked over to the vending machines, Mendez led me to a horseshoe of chairs set between two ward entrances. A middle-aged woman in gray stared straight ahead and ignored us.

"This is just to touch base," Mendez said, leaning toward me. "No big deal. I've got the case and I wanted to check you and your partner are okay."

"I'm fine. With luck, so is Sam."

Mendez nodded. "Glad to hear it. We got a name for the robber: Tyrone Cursell, with two years in Riker's and smaller stuff going back four years. I guess you were lucky, though it mightn't look that way from where you sit."

I remembered the glass door exploding with the gunshot, and the way Sam flew back. "It could have been worse."

"That's right. If you hadn't winged Cursell, he could have finished off all three of you. Shaw showed quick thinking."

Again, I thought of the ankle holster and Carl's .38. I looked at Mendez and hesitated.

"What is it?" Mendez asked.

"I . . . I wondered what happened to the deli owner?"

"Cursell whipped him with the .45 and locked him in the back room." Mendez shook his head. "All for sixty-seven bucks. From the old tracks on Cursell's arms and legs, it has to be for drugs, but it's still pathetic."

My head started to ache. The lights and sounds in the hospital, the ringing phones and bustle, made me wince. The antiseptic smell made my stomach turn over.

Mendez continued, "Shaw told us all about it before he went back to Hoboken, how he picked up Cursell's .38 and shot him. Good thing he was there, I guess."

I rubbed my temples. "Do you need a statement off me?"

"Not yet; you look beat." Mendez stood up. "We can wipe this off our shoes anytime. Come and see me when you're back off leave."

"I'll do that."

As Marie walked back toward us, Mendez said, “One good thing came out of this: at least we took a murderer off the streets.”

“Murderer?”

“Sure. That .38 was used in a killing last year. It came up straight away on the ballistics database.” Mendez nodded to Marie and went to leave.

My insides turned to ice. I caught Mendez’s arm. “Who was murdered?”

“A young woman, last November. But it wasn’t around here. It happened up in Vermont, some place called Eastham.”

2

I started running young, eight or nine, back on the projects outside Albany. After dad died, we had to move into a development of identical two-story houses that looked like Army barracks. Either the local kids resented any and all newcomers or I wore a sign, invisible to me, that said: *kick me, kick me now*. Either way, I learned to run away from kids bigger and stronger and meaner than me.

In hindsight, I should have stopped running and stood my ground. But hindsight makes everyone a genius. At the time, I ran, and I ran *quick*. I'm not that proud of it, but the school coaches liked it. My hundred- and two-hundred-yard times were the best in my grade. Not so good on the long distances, the five- and ten-thousand. I collected a bunch of medals at track and field meets and started to think about serious competition, maybe even making a living from it. But life didn't work out that way.

I thought about Albany a lot after leaving the hospital. The Department told me to take off whatever time the doctors said, so I had a month to myself. Sam would be off a lot longer. I wondered if he'd come back at all. He wasn't too far from early retirement age, or maybe medical retirement on a good pension. It might be tempting, especially if he saw that bullet as a warning.

I didn't know what to do with myself. I had to rest, but daytime TV got stale quick; I get enough of people yelling and screaming at each other during the day. Thanks, but I gave at the office. I tried listening to music, the Pumpkins and REM, but my mind kept sliding back to the shooting and to the dead woman in Vermont.

Detective Mendez had told me the bare details: Sarah Westlake, a postgrad student studying at Burlington but working in Eastham, had been found dead in her car on the shore of Lake Champlain. Single bullet wound to the head. Personal effects scattered on the lake, and some of them missing, so robbery as the presumed motive. No sign of sexual attack. An opportunistic crime carried out for quick money. It fitted.

Still, I stared out of the window at the passersby and thought about calling Mendez about ten times a day. I paced the apartment and circled the phone like a bear in a cage. I'd pick up the receiver, then set it down without dialing.

What could I tell Mendez? Hey, here's a weird thing: that .38 really belonged to Carl, the writer who doesn't live in Hoboken but who just happens to live in Eastham, Vermont, where the gun was used to murder a woman. Mendez would roast me, that's for sure, but that wasn't the reason I didn't call.

No, we owed Carl, me and Sam. Mendez and the Department would tear into Carl for carrying the unlicensed gun in the first place and using it in the second. They'd crucify him.

And what if they tried to connect him to the woman's death? That bothered me. I doubted that Carl had anything to do with the murder. Not so much out of loyalty as out of logic: if he'd shot someone, he'd get rid of the gun, right?

If I told Mendez the truth, what would be the worst that could happen to me? I'd drop Carl into the shit, but I wouldn't personally suffer that much (except maybe a shared reprimand for putting a visitor in danger). The Department would probably fire me, but the idea of leaving had been at the back of my mind anyway—they'd just be making the decision for me.

If I lied when I gave Mendez my statement, and told the detective the edited version of events, nobody would know except me and Carl. And, like I said, we owed Carl.

So I should agree with the story that Carl told Mendez: the robber dropped the .38 and Carl picked it up. Easy. No problem. After all, he'd done everyone a favor by taking Cursell off the street, a young druggie who'd already seen the inside of Riker's Island for knifing a girl. Carl would probably get a commendation.

But I remembered my day on parade in front of the Police Commissioner and the Mayor, with all the other new officers. I'd stood to attention in my dress uniform and white gloves and smiled at my mom and sister watching. I'd sworn an oath that day, and I didn't like going back on it. If I was going to leave the force, I didn't want it to be this way.

And I kept wondering about Sarah, the murdered woman. So I kept circling the phone.

I'd been home four days when Marie asked, "What the hell's wrong with you?"

"Sorry?"

"I've been talking to you for ten minutes and you haven't said a word."

We sat on the couch with our feet up on the coffee table and the lights on low. Marie had banked cushions behind me so I could sprawl out. We had the TV on, mute. I laid my right hand over hers. "I was miles away."

"I could see that." She stared into my face. "What is it? Sam?"

"No, he's okay." I'd been to the hospital that afternoon. Sam had given me a feeble grin and said he felt fine. The doctors said he'd be back home in another week or so. Sam didn't remember anything after the deli's glass door erupted in front of him and the sidewalk slammed into his back. But he'd heard the story about Carl saving our lives, and he wanted to thank the guy. I didn't tell him any different. Not yet.

"If it isn't Sam, what is it?" Marie asked. "Are you worried about going back to work?"

I thought for a moment, turning Marie's hand over in mine. "No, I don't think so. Before I joined, I used to wonder what would happen if I got shot. You know, would I lose my nerve? But it hasn't got to me like that."

"Good. Keep it that way."

I smiled. "You don't want me to pack it in and go back into the banks?"

"No way."

"The money's a lot better . . ."

"So?"

"You must have insured me for a hell of a lot."

"Not until we're married." Marie laughed, then her face became serious. "I just think you've found your niche in life, what you were meant to do. That means a lot. And I don't like to see you running away from something."

That took me right back to Albany. I pulled my hand from Marie's and stared into the silent TV. A wildlife documentary showed a blond guy in safari clothes prizing apart the jaws of an alligator.

"What?" Marie sat on the edge of the couch and stared at me. "What did I say?"

I wanted to tell her about Carl and the gun. I wanted to ask her what I should do. But I knew what she'd say. Marie has always done the right thing; I guess you have to when you're dealing with children's lives every day. No room for debate—do it right or not at all.

"I'm just on edge," I told her. "Give me some time. I'll start to relax."

She hesitated, then curled up with her head on my stomach. "I hope so."

Over the next two days, I tried to put Carl out of my mind. I played cards and drank beer with John, my roommate. We'd met when I started work at a big financial securities firm in Manhattan: good money. Stupid money, looking back. I'd been trying to find a place to rent and seen John's message on the firm's e-mail. It was supposed to be a temporary fix, but I'd moved in five years before and stayed.

With the money John earned, he didn't need anyone to share, not anymore. But I think he liked the company. And he said he was doing his bit for charity by subsidizing a poor cop. I told him he should pay me for being an on-site alarm system and security officer. It worked out even.

Almost a week after the shooting, John looked over his cards and asked me, "You want to talk about it?"

"About what?"

"What's bothering you."

I moved the cards in my hand, sliding them into a different order. "I'm okay."

"You reckon?" John gulped beer from the bottle and pointed the base at the pile of colored plastic chips in front of him. "If we were playing for real, I'd own everything, including the clothes on your back. For what they're worth."

"Maybe you're just a sharp player."

"Could be. Or maybe your mind's on something else."

I set my cards down and pushed my chair away from the table. From the window, I could see red taillight blurs snaking along the street below. Cold air drifted from the glass and washed over my face.

"Is it your ribs?"

"No, I feel fine." And I did. Most of the time, there was hardly any pain, although the bruising had turned purple and black. I couldn't turn without wincing, and I wouldn't be running anytime soon, but I was getting there.

"So what is it?"

I spoke to his reflection in the glass. "What would you do if you knew that someone at work was . . . I don't know, skimming money off an account?"

"I'd report him. It's happened, too."

No surprises there. John comes from an old family of Dutch Reformed Church followers, straight and upright as they get.

I turned from the window. "What if the guy had done you a favor in the past? More than a favor: he'd saved your job, he'd put himself out there for you. If it wasn't for him, you'd be dead."

John stared at me, then shook his head.

"So, what would you do?" I asked.

"I guess I'd have to think about it. Maybe I'd speak to the guy, find out what was going on . . . I'd want to know the background. Wouldn't you?"

I nodded. "Thanks."

The next day, I rode the subway three stops and walked through Prospect Park. Clouds pushed down low on the Bay, hiding the coastline of Jersey City and Bayonne. The wind pushed around drifts of wet leaves and made the mothers pushing strollers cling to their hats. I put one foot in front of the other and kicked at the leaves like a reluctant kid.

I didn't aim in any particular direction. I just needed the fresh air. At least that's what I told myself. Carl and the gun had become a dull ache that beat at the back of my mind and wouldn't go away. I kept juggling my two options: tell Mendez the truth or go with Carl's story.

Then, as I stepped onto Parkside Avenue, I knew I had to accept the third option, the one that John had hinted at: try and find out the truth for myself.

I started walking as fast as I could toward Marie's hospital, ignoring the tightness around my chest and the dull stabs from my ribs. I'd been worrying because I didn't have enough information to work on. Maybe Carl bought the gun; maybe he found it in the road; maybe Cursell had been in Eastham and the whole thing was a total coincidence. Or maybe another robber had murdered Sarah and then sold the gun on to someone else, the old firearms barter network.

I wasn't trying to solve the woman's murder, but I could find out enough to help me decide what to tell Mendez.

As I waited at the Clarkson intersection for a break in the traffic, I had to lean against the traffic light post. Sweat trickled down my back and the breath scraped through my chest. I'd thought I'd had enough rest, but maybe I was wrong. Then the lights changed and I crossed over and headed for the hospital.

Through the automatic doors, I followed the signs for Pediatrics. I found a short, heavy nurse behind a counter. "Can I see Marie Doran, please?"

"Visiting someone?" The nurse didn't look up from her computer keyboard. "Are you family?"

"I'm her boyfriend. Could you tell her Steve needs to speak to her."

The nurse looked up and gave me a big smile. "The cop, right? Sure. Take a seat and I'll page her."

I sat beneath colorful cartoon animals chasing each other

across the pale blue walls. Every time the doors opened, I looked up. After five minutes that felt like an hour, Marie hurried through the doors and toward me in her blue and yellow uniform. "Are you all right? Has something happened?"

"I'm fine." I held her by the shoulders and smiled. "I just need to disappear for a week or so."

"Where?"

"Eastham. It's a little town in Vermont."

One thing that survived from my high-salary days was my car, a three-liter Grand Cherokee. It spent most of its time in the parking garage under John's apartment block; usually I took the train into work, or accepted a lift from Sam if he swung by.

Once I'd decided to go up to Vermont, I piled warm clothes into a bag and threw it into the back of the Jeep. I left a note for John and locked up the apartment. Marie had offered to try to get some time off and come up with me; I managed to change her mind. I would have liked her company but this wasn't a vacation, even if I used that as an excuse. I could tell she wasn't too sure about it. Even so, she'd kissed me and told me to keep in touch.

I took the Expressway to FDR Drive and hit rush-hour gridlock. I ground my way up Manhattan and took the GW Bridge to the Palisades Parkway. As the forest of New York's lights faded into the darkness behind me, I had a cold sensation in the floor of my stomach, almost like childhood homesickness. Except for short family visits, I hadn't been outside New York in more than three years. And I hadn't driven this far for a long time.

I settled into the seat and watched the slick road unroll under the headlights. I'd worked out my route and planned to break my journey around the halfway mark, maybe somewhere near Glens Falls on Route 87. That meant driving around Albany; I could have dropped by my sister's place and used her couch, but I didn't want to explain why I was traveling.

I hadn't told my family what had really happened outside Lazzini's. I'd told my mom and sister that I'd been hurt, no big deal, and I'd need a few weeks' rest. I didn't want to worry what was left of my family. And, to tell the truth, I didn't want to hear the same old lectures.

Before I left the apartment, I'd powered up John's laptop and entered the words *Sarah Westlake murder Eastham* into a web search engine. Only a few hits had come back, mostly pointing to local newspapers like the *Burlington Times* and the *Eastham Courier*. But they referred to archived copies, nothing online that I could read. I found plenty of sites for Carl Shaw: the writer had a lot of fans.

A little after eight, I pulled into a gas station north of West Point and filled up with gas, coffee and stale Krispy Kreme donuts. I hadn't had much of an appetite since the shooting but I needed fuel. I wanted to check my voicemail, but when I opened my cell phone I saw a blank display; I could picture the charger still back at the apartment, in its usual home next to John's laptop. The gas station had a bank of pay phones along one wall. I hesitated, wondering whether to call my family in Albany, Marie, or maybe even Carl. Instead I climbed back into the Jeep and headed northeast.

I started yawning into the glare of trucks heading south. Local radio stations sprang to life for a few miles and filled the cab with rock, news, traffic reports and God's Word. One by one, they died in a hail of static. I stared at the road.

Why didn't I just come right out and ask Carl? Because so long as there was a chance, even the smallest chance, that he was a murderer, I couldn't afford to tip him off. If I asked him, what would he say? He wouldn't admit to it unless he was psycho. No, the question would warn him, let him know that the police—or at least me—knew something.

I passed the off-ramp for Albany without looking at it. I swallowed a couple of painkillers and pulled into a motel near Wilton, just south of Glens Falls. As I signed in, snow replaced the rain and smeared down the office windows. I spent the night twisting and turning on the thin mattress, listening to the wind pulling at the roof.

I wondered what the hell I was doing up here. After all, for the past six months I'd been thinking about quitting. Why should I worry about Carl or even Sarah?

Because I'd still have to face myself in the mirror each morning. And I wanted the final decision to be mine, not some Disciplinary Hearing's.

I got up at six. After a shower and shave, I had coffee and silver dollar pancakes in Glens Falls and crossed the state line. Rutland, Vermont, lay due east, but I checked the map and dog-legged up, heading for St. Albans.

Carl was right: the countryside was beautiful. The mountains' shoulders wore snow. The trees had kept enough color to distract me; my uncle—the one that used to drive us over to Middletown every Memorial Day—reckoned there was real money to be had running a garage recovery service in Vermont. A good percentage of rubbernecking tourists ended up in the roadside ditches.

I didn't have many cars for company. A few late vacationers headed south with bikes and canoes strapped to roof racks and Winnebagos. Soon I could see water to my left. Lake Champlain glimmered through the trees.

Eastham didn't appear on my map, so I drove through Burlington and St. Albans and asked for directions at Enosburg Falls. The owner of a knitwear store told me how to find the town and said I wasn't too far away. Twenty minutes' drive showed me a scene I thought only existed on postcards: white clapboard church with steeple, main street shops with bow fronts, a town green supporting a cannon and a flagpole. Red barns dotted the hills above the forest. Too good to be true.

I parked on Main Street, climbed out of the Jeep and stretched, nice and slow. My ribs burned and my lower back throbbed like it had been kicked by a quarterback. I looked around and saw clothes stores and a bakery, signs pointing to a school. A diner with *Shirley's* painted on the plate glass front in peeling gold letters. The local police station stood about thirty yards up on the right, a fieldstone building with an engraved block of slate embedded in the grass in front of it. Two white sedans with red and blue light-bars stood at the curb.

I could walk into that station, introduce myself and tell the Police Chief why I was here. I might get all the way to the end of my spiel before he called New York and had me hauled back there. I was an off-duty policeman on medical leave, sniffing around a year-old, unsolved case. In the Chief's jurisdiction. Not good.

Instead, I pushed open the door of the diner and found a seat at the counter. A middle-aged couple sat in a booth reading newspapers while three of the eight counter seats supported kids, teenagers with magazines and portable CD players. More baggy denim and grungy tee shirts, but fewer pierced body parts than the kids I usually spotted on the City's streets. And these Eastham youngsters looked freshly scrubbed.

The waitress, an elderly woman with coiled, steel-gray hair, wiped the counter in front of me and set a glass of water down. "Hi, honey. Coffee?"

"Please." The diner reminded me of one of the retro fifties places that spring up every so often in New York, all red vinyl and chrome. But this place looked real.

"How about a piece of pie?"

"What do you have?"

"Apple or peach. Made the apple myself."

"Apple, then, thanks." I saw the kids glance over at me for a moment before they went back to their magazines. One of the boys wore a pair of bulbous headphones that leaked a tinny, repetitive beat. The counter in front of the kids had a line of grinning Halloween pumpkins. More plastic pumpkins decorated the cash till.

"Here you go, honey."

When I'd almost finished the pie, I told the waitress, "Pretty town you have here."

"We like it."

"A bit remote, though."

She smiled, revealing perfect teeth, probably dentures. "Nice and quiet. Apart from high season. Then you can't turn around without falling over a townie."

Before she turned away, I asked, "You get many townies buying places up here?"

"Some, why?" She paused, with my plate in her hand, and stared at me. "You looking?"

I thought fast. "That's right: we're hunting for a weekend place."

She glanced at my left hand. "You and your wife, maybe?"

My face started to burn. I reached for my coffee cup. "I'm not married."

The waitress tilted her head to one side as if examining something strange on the sidewalk. "Good-looking young guy like you, not married? You gay or something?"

I laughed so hard I spluttered coffee all over the counter and the nearest teenager, who reached for napkins and said, "Gross!"

"No, I'm not gay," I told the waitress, still not believing she'd actually asked the question. "I'm looking for a place for me and my girlfriend. Marie. Marie Doran. She's a nurse."

She nodded. "Well, you walk down the street and look into the windows of Devane Real Estate on your left. You tell them that Shirley sent you. They'll set you up right."

I finished my coffee and left some bills on the counter. The teenager I'd sprayed glared at me as I left. Outside, I checked my watch: eleven-twenty. I found the real estate office where Shirley had told me it would be. Most of the houses and cabins in the window would have cost us ten years' salary, presuming we never ate or went out. The woman beyond the glass saw me and waved me inside.

I didn't have a clear plan. I was just fishing, seeing what came up. "Hi. Shirley from the diner sent me along."

"You're looking for a property in the area? I'm sure we can help." The short, stout, blond woman offered me her hand. "Andrea Devane."

"Steve Burnett."

"Take a seat, please. Have you driven up from New York?"

"Just this morning." I sat across from Andrea at a neat desk.

"Well, you picked a good time: it gets quiet toward the end of fall." Andrea folded her hands on her desk, settled down and began to interrogate me about where I worked, how much I earned and what I expected to pay. She didn't come out and ask; she was pretty subtle, but I knew what she wanted.

Lying like a weasel, I told her I was an IT manager working in the SEC in New York. I earned good money and was due to get married in three months' time.

In return for these assorted lies, Andrea showed me photographs of houses I couldn't afford and promised to take me out to any I liked, six percent commission with the very small possibility of negotiation. I shuffled the laser-printed information sheets in my hand and asked, "We were looking for somewhere really quiet. Do you have any trouble up here?"

Andrea frowned. "Trouble?"

"Well . . . do you have any 'townies' that cause you problems?"

She smiled. "No, nothing like that. We have a good Police Department."

I took a risk. "I think Shirley mentioned there was a writer . . ."

"She must mean Carl Shaw. He's been here for years—one of our most successful citizens. There's even talk of his wife running for the council."

I opened my eyes wide. "Carl Shaw? Really? I had no idea."

"Well, I shouldn't really say, but . . ." Andrea looked left and right, then leaned her heavy bosom on the desk and said, "He lives just outside town, off Route 108."

I nodded as if the secret was safe with me, then stood up to leave. I waved the sheets. "Thanks for these. I'll take a look at them tonight."

"My number's at the top," Andrea said. "Call me any time . . ."

Outside the store, I folded the sheets into my coat pocket and looked around. I'd forgotten to ask where the offices of the *Eastham Courier* were, but when I looked east along Main Street I saw a faded white wooden sign with scrollwork edges. The *Courier* building was set well back from the street. A sixties' concrete cube, it didn't match the rest of the stores with their antique fronts.

A beat-up Chevy Impala, probably a seventy-seven, had been parked at an angle in front of the newspaper office's entrance. I squeezed past it and stopped at a high counter loaded with dusty local pamphlets and a laminated chart showing various advertising rates.

A woman looked up from one of the three desks and smiled at me. "Can I help you?"

"I hope so. I was looking for information on a murder last year. Sarah Westlake."

The smile slipped from the woman's face. She stood up and crossed to the counter. "Can you tell me why you're asking?"

I had a choice: to tell the truth or come up with another version of the "homebuyer" story. I compromised. "I'm an investigator looking into the case. I've just come up from New York."

The woman looked at me and gave me the chance to guess her age: around forty or so. She had a single streak of silver in her untidy black hair, and tiny crow's feet around her eyes. Her rumpled business suit and blouse didn't hide her figure.

"I suppose you can't tell me what's behind this?" she said.

"I'm sorry. But I could offer to give you any fresh information I find."

"Offer or promise?"

"You'd be the first to know, after the police."

She chewed her lip and then nodded. "It's a deal. Fran

Dutroux. I'm editor and owner of the *Courier.*"

I shook her hand. "Steve Burnett."

Fran lifted a hinged part of the counter to allow me through to the rear of the office. She said, "I keep the old copies and stories in the archives."

The archives turned out to be a large cupboard lit by a fluorescent ring light. Fran pushed boxes out of our way and read along the shelves. I couldn't see any logical order to the arrangement, but she must have. Her hand stopped at a blank space between two overflowing lever-arch files. She frowned.

"Something wrong?"

"Probably not." Fran spent another ten minutes checking through the assorted boxes and files on the floor, then shook her head. "It's gone."

"The story or the old issue?"

"Both. I keep one copy of every weekly issue; that's missing. But I also keep all the relevant notes and jottings in the files. That's gone, too."

The old paranoia resurfaced but I pushed it down. "Could someone else have borrowed them?"

"Not without me knowing about it. Unless . . ."

"What?"

"Back in January, I had another guy asking about Sarah."

"What sort of guy? Police? Press?"

"He said he was an investigator. I was pretty busy at the time, so I let him read the back issues."

"That was trusting of you."

She stared at me. "It's how I work: *quid pro quo*. Just like with you, I expected some return for my trust. Maybe I'm making another mistake."

"Not with me. Did the investigator have a name?"

"Henry or Harry. Harry. Balding, heavy, late forties maybe."

That wasn't much to go on. "You think he's got the notes?"

Fran led me through to the main office. "Don't worry about it. I keep backup copies at the offices of the *Berkshire Times*, in case this place burns down. I'll call them up, but it won't get here until tomorrow at the earliest."

"No problem," I said. "I appreciate the help. Can you remember anything about the case?"

"Sure. We don't get that many murders around here." Fran sat on the edge of a desk and swung her long legs. The left calf of her pantyhose had a run up the side. "One night in November last year, postgrad student Sarah Westlake drove up to the shore of Lake Champlain, near to Cardford Springs. Someone shot her once in the head and stole her purse, laptop PC and suitcase."

"Suitcase?"

"Apparently she was on her way back home to Burlington."

I thought for a moment, trying to picture the scene. "They took luggage but left her car?"

Fran looked away. "The inside was pretty messed up."

I could imagine how much damage a .38 could do at short range, especially a head shot. "So the robber must have had his own car."

"That's what the local Chief and the State Police thought."

I had a hundred questions: forensic details, tire tracks, witnesses. But I'd have to take this one step at a time.

"Thanks for your help," I told Fran as I walked to the other side of the counter. "One thing, though: what was Sarah doing around here if she was studying at Burlington? Vacation? Temporary job?"

Fran stared at me. "I would have thought you'd know. She was working for a writer that lives near here. Have you ever heard of Carl Shaw?"

3

On my way into Eastham, I'd noticed signs for the Mill Hotel. I left town and drove back west. I turned from the main route and followed more signs down winding, narrow roads. Trees arched overhead and almost touched; shadows collected in the roadside ditches. I had to flick on my lights even though it wasn't yet two.

I found the Mill Hotel, a squat brick building with white-painted windows, and parked out front. Next to the lot lay a massive water wheel maybe twenty or twenty-five feet across; the new owners had embedded it in concrete and set wooden benches alongside to make an enormous picnic table. The stream that must have once fed the wheel circled the parking lot and poured white water into a lake bordered with forest. It probably looked like a million dollars in the summer.

I sat for a moment in the Jeep with my forearms resting on the wheel and my chin on top of them. The pains in my chest and ribs had faded to a low heat but my lower back complained. I wondered how Sam was doing, stuck in a hospital bed back in New York. Probably goosing the nurses and cracking jokes. That made me feel a little better.

What would Sam have said, if I'd told him? He probably would've told me I was crazy for haring up to Vermont. He would have either confronted Carl right out or he would have kept quiet and let it ride. Maybe I was just fooling myself, trying to avoid confronting the truth. Maybe I was just putting off the inevitable.

Either way, I was here and I had to go through with it. I slipped my dead cell phone into the glove compartment, collected my bag and headed for reception. Inside the hotel, bare brick walls, faded carpets and furniture in dark wood. The desk clerk told me they had plenty of rooms free; they were winding down until the skiers arrived. She gave me a key to room three-ten and told me dinner started at seven. I found my room, dumped my bag and started running a bath before doing anything else. By the time I'd unpacked, the tub was ready. The journey had turned my ribs into rusty metal hinges. I slipped into the warm water very slowly and let it take away the pain. I lay back and closed my eyes.

So Sarah had worked for Carl. I didn't like the news. I'd guessed there might be some connection between the two, but I hadn't expected such a strong link right from the start. Maybe I should just go home now and tell Mendez everything? I would have done, but the idea that me and Sam owed Carl our lives wouldn't go away. It meant something.

I needed more information. Much more.

I lay there, half-asleep, until the water turned cold and made me move. I showered and dressed, then went downstairs. The lobby clock said seven-twenty. Out of habit, I reached for my cell phone, then cursed and used the pay phone set behind the stairs. I dialed Marie's number and heard hundreds of miles of white noise and the distant ringing. I left a message on her answering machine and went in to eat.

I'd forgotten that Marie had swapped shifts. Sometimes, when the great god of lousy timing butts in, Marie and me end up on opposite shifts. We see each other for half an hour a day, or at weekends. But sometimes it works the other way, and we have three days to ourselves. We're pretty happy with that. It would be different if we had kids, but that wasn't an issue, yet.

The Mill Hotel was part of a chain, so I felt as if I'd already visited the red-carpeted, dimly-lit restaurant, just as my bland room upstairs had been no surprise. I took a window table and looked out into darkness. Somewhere out there lay the lake. I saw only my own reflection staring back at me. When the young waitress came over, I ordered steak, well-done, salad, potatoes and a beer. I had the restaurant to myself except for a whispering, elderly couple and a silent family of five near the exit. The Muzak made the atmosphere weigh down on us, heavier than silence; it took a lot of effort to make "The Girl from Ipanema" sound like a funeral dirge, but the session musicians had managed it.

I'm not that used to eating alone. I don't much enjoy it. Even when I was at college and often away on track meets, I was always part of a team. We ate together, trained together, drank together. I guess a part of me liked it that way and saw something similar in the police. I wasn't disappointed. It can be great, so long as you get in a crew with like-minded guys. If not, it's hell.

But that hadn't given me any problems. No, my doubts went a little deeper.

I finished eating and walked through to the lobby. I flicked through the courtesy magazines and brochures on a table and thought about phoning Marie again. This felt like dead time, the gray intervals you get between stuff happening, like dentists' waiting rooms or standing in line for a clerk.

I decided to waste some of that time on another beer. I walked through to the Wheelhouse bar and found a stool. Strange pieces of metal and varnished wood had been fixed to the walls and ceiling; I guessed they were relics from the previous life of the Mill, something to do with textiles. They could have been instruments of torture for all I knew.

A woman came into the bar and chose a stool two down from me. She ordered a glass of red wine, a Shiraz. In the mirror, I watched her playing with the stem of her glass. She smiled when she caught me looking. “Quiet night in here.”

“It’s the end of the season,” I said, echoing the desk clerk’s words. I noticed the gray-haired bartender slide away to the other end of the counter as if he had important business there.

The woman turned on her stool and leaned one elbow on the polished bar. Her jeans and boots looked expensive. Her white silk shirt and black leather jacket hadn’t been cheap, either. She could have been around the mid-forties; if her long chestnut hair had been dyed, it had been by someone who knew what they were doing.

“You’re a little early for the skiing,” she said, still smiling.

“We’re thinking about a holiday home up here.”

“We?”

“Me and my girlfriend. Marie.” I seemed to have the need to repeat Marie’s name.

“I suppose she’ll be down to join you?”

“No . . . she stayed in New York.”

“Really? What do you think of the property up here? It can be pretty expensive.”

I nodded, remembering the realtor. “Seems quiet, though. A good place to bring up a family.”

The woman turned back to her glass for a moment. She twisted the gold ring on the third finger of her left hand. “Yes. Yes, it can be. You have kids?”

“Not yet.”

We chatted for a few minutes, with me gently pushing

the topic of marriage and kids out of sight. It's not a subject I run away from, but I try not to give strangers my life story. Every so often I get the lecture from my mom, back in Albany, about marrying Marie. I try to think of it like I used to think of promotion: it's out there and it'll happen to me one day. No way am I avoiding it.

The woman signaled for another drink and nodded at my almost empty glass. "Another beer?"

"Well, I guess . . ."

"Marie needn't worry—you're safe with me," she said, grinning. "I just enjoy a little company while I'm drinking. My husband isn't much of a drinker any more."

She turned to the bartender. "Bob, another wine and a beer, please. On my tab."

The man nodded. "Right away, Mrs. Shaw."

I froze. I couldn't have heard that right. "Mrs. Shaw?"

She tilted her head to one side. "Problem?"

"I just . . . it's weird, but I recently met someone from up here: Carl Shaw. The writer."

Her smile slid. In a thin voice, she said, "He's my husband."

The bartender put the fresh drinks on the counter, took away the empty glasses and retired to a safe distance. I stared at Mrs. Shaw; she stared back. I reached for my beer first.

"You're Steve Burnett, aren't you?" she asked.

"How did you know?"

"Carl told me what happened." Mrs. Shaw reached into her bag for a packet of Dunhills and a gold lighter, then glanced at the sign above the bar and thrust them back into the bag. "He said you were almost killed."

I wondered if he'd told her the full version or the edited one. "We were. All three of us. We owe him, me and Sam."

"I suppose you do." She looked around the empty bar and then back at me. "You're not up here to look for holiday cottages."

"Well . . ."

"Can you level with me?"

I didn't want to tell her the truth. I doubted she knew about the .38 that Carl had used; he'd probably left that part out. Even if he had told her, she had no reason to connect it to Sarah's murder.

"The department gave me a month off," I said, "and I needed somewhere to rest. Your husband—Carl—really went overboard on how beautiful and quiet it was in Vermont, and especially around Eastham."

She nodded. "He loves it up here. We both do."

"Sure, we could see that when he talked. So I thought, why not spend a week or so just relaxing? No big deal." I smiled and opened my hands on my thighs. "I'm not stalking him or anything."

"No. You don't look the type." Her smile looked a little uncertain, as if she truly wanted to believe me.

My story sounded shaky even to me. I'm not used to lying, and I really hadn't expected to run across Carl's wife.

"Were you scared?" she asked.

"It happened too fast for that."

She leaned forward. "How about afterward?"

I swirled the beer in my glass. "Yes. Yes, I was. I guess I should give you the old line, say it's all part of the job. Maybe it would be, one day. But not yet."

Maybe not ever. Maybe I wasn't up to the job. That particular doubt had been whispering in my ear for too long already. The shooting had just made it louder.

I remembered seeing Sam all bound up like an Egyptian mummy in the hospital bed. Another inch higher and the bullet would have hit artery. I could have been first at that door. If the robber had fired sooner, or fired again . . .

"It's all chance," I said. "But if you dwell on it, I guess you wouldn't be able to do your job."

"Fate," Mrs. Shaw said, more to herself than to me. She looked up. "Thanks for being honest with me. Men don't like to admit that they're afraid."

I shrugged. I had no reason to lie. At least, not about how I'd felt. "How did your husband take it? Was he okay, afterward?"

When she didn't reply, I thought either she hadn't heard the question or she hadn't liked it. Then, "Carl's a very private person. It's difficult to know what's going on in his mind. Even to me, and we've been married fifteen years. Sometimes he looks at me and I hardly recognize the person behind his eyes. I think the shooting did scare him. But he's good at dealing with pressure."

The image of Carl reaching for the .38 returned. He hadn't fumbled, hadn't panicked.

"Have you spoken to Carl?" she asked.

"I didn't want to bother him."

She hesitated. "Do you want me to tell him I met you?"

Good question. I didn't want to tip him off that I was here, but he'd find out eventually. "Not yet, if you don't mind. I'm sure I'll run into him in town."

She thought for a moment, then finished her drink and stood up. "I won't tell him."

"Thanks. And thanks for the drink, Mrs. Shaw."

She smiled. "You're welcome, and it's Elaine."

I stood up. "Elaine."

She called out, "Bob, add the usual for yourself."

"Thank you, Mrs. Shaw. Goodnight."

From the bar, I could see her walk through the lobby toward the cloakrooms. I sat down and asked the bartender, "Is she a regular?"

He shrugged. "Three, four times a week. Nice woman. Never any trouble."

"How about her husband? Does he ever come in?"

Bob the bartender stared at me for no more than two seconds. "Mr. Shaw doesn't visit the hotel. He likes to keep himself to himself, what I hear."

I took the hint and finished my beer in silence. When I left the bar there was no sign of Elaine in the lobby or the parking lot. I used the pay phone and got through to Marie, telling her that I'd got here safe and sound and was relaxing. On top of that smaller lie, I didn't mention Elaine. I hung up and told myself I had nothing to feel guilty about. Nothing had happened or would happen. It didn't help.

Back in my room, I set the alarm clock and lay back. My body wanted to sleep but my mind wouldn't slow down; it fastened onto fragments of the day's events and mixed them with the shooting. There was one point I could focus on: I figured the chances of running into Elaine on my first night in Eastham were small. It could happen, since she was a regular, but it seemed like too much of a coincidence.

I must have slept because the alarm dragged me awake at six-thirty. I felt I'd only just closed my eyes. I drew the drapes back on a cloudless day. I could see out across the lake to a solid wall of tree trunks and ocher leaves. The surface of the water looked like rippled steel.

I needed coffee. I went downstairs but I couldn't face breakfast in the empty hotel restaurant that still carried last night's food smells. I remembered the coffee at Shirley's Diner and decided to drive into town.

My Grand Cherokee was dead. I turned the key but nothing happened. I lifted the hood and stared at the engine.

It didn't mean that much to me. But there were no obvious loose wires or hoses, no pools of liquid under the car. I tried again for luck. The starter motor didn't even turn. I'd let my Auto Club membership lapse, but the hotel's morning desk clerk told me that Eastham's only garage had a tow truck. She offered to call the owner, Ross Willard, and get him out. I thanked her and said I'd walk into town.

It was a good morning for a walk: cold, clear and dry. The high blue sky had vapor trails and small V-shaped wedges of ducks or geese. I could smell damp soil and decaying leaves. Only two cars passed me, a battered green Chevy Suburban aiming for town and a minivan heading the other way. I thought I'd seen the Chevy in the hotel lot. Probably another late vacationer.

The walk gave me time to think. I had to congratulate the great god of lousy timing for choosing this exact moment to trash my Jeep. With luck, it would only be a flat battery or loose contact, but it was still a pain.

The thought of coincidences led me straight back to Elaine. There was no way she could know I'd be in Eastham on any particular day unless she was psychic or had been following me. I didn't believe either. Like I said, paranoia can fasten on to you before you know it. No, despite the odds, it must have been coincidence the previous night. Just coincidence.

A handful of Bed and Breakfast signs announced the start of Eastham. Set well back from the road, the neat clapboard houses looked empty and cold. Not neglected, just forgotten. A gleaming Subaru dealership, private houses, then a garage with two brand-new pumps outside. The workshop's doors were locked tight and a sign in the office window said the garage opened at eight. Another sign told me that Ross Willard was a member of the local Volunteer Fire Department.

As I walked on into town, a few more cars passed me. The streets were waking up. Men filled half of the booths in the diner, hunched low over plates of bacon and pancakes. The smells of coffee and syrup hit me. I took the same seat I'd had the day before.

"Morning, honey." Shirley set a glass of water down and moved a pencil from behind her ear and into her hand. "What can I get you?"

I looked at the menu board. I knew I should order cereal and toast, but the smells worked their magic. You couldn't come to Vermont and not eat maple syrup, I told myself. "Pancakes, please. With syrup."

I drank the coffee and tried to plan my day. I'd be stuck without the car. But if Willard could get it going, I had a list of people I wanted to talk to: Sarah's friends and teachers in Burlington, any witnesses around Cardford Springs, people who might have known her in Eastham. But Fran stayed top of my list; she'd promised she'd have the backup copy of her *Courier*, the one with news of Sarah's murder.

"There you go." Shirley slid a plate of small, crisp pancakes in front of me, then reached for a bottle of caramel-colored syrup. "You need anything else, just yell."

Before she moved away, I asked, "Do you know the garage owner?"

"Ross? Sure. You having car trouble?"

I said that I was.

Shirley looked at the clock above the menu board. "He's usually here about now, unless he's had a call. I'll grab him when he gets in."

"I'd appreciate it."

I started in on the pancakes. About halfway through, I knew I'd ordered too much. My body remembered the low-fat, high-carb diet from my running days, and it still expects a long workout after refueling. Sometimes it argued with my new lifestyle.

"Hey, honey. Meet Ross Willard, owner of Eastham's only garage and Chief of the Fire Brigade." Shirley handed a cup of coffee to a tanned, wiry man of about fifty who'd just walked in and pushed him forward. "He won't rip you off too much, not unless he can get away with it."

Willard shook my hand, took a gulp of coffee and asked, "You got trouble?"

I explained what had happened.

Willard nodded. "Sounds like your battery. I could take a look, I guess; not much on this morning. You want to ride up with me?"

I thought about Fran Dutroux in the *Courier* office. "Thanks, but there's someone I need to see. I'll follow you up there."

I gave Willard the Jeep's keys and paid for my breakfast. As I walked down Main Street, I saw most of the stores open and waiting for business. Cardboard skeletons and pumpkins hung in a few of the windows, ready for Halloween. I could imagine the town in high season, filled with tourists and sightseers. I wondered how the locals felt, living in a goldfish bowl. Maybe you could get used to it. You could get used to most things if you had to.

The glass door to the *Courier* office was locked but I could see Fran moving around the back. I tapped on the window and waved.

"Hi. Nice and early." Fran let me through into the office. "Find anything last night?"

"Only that the beds in the Mill Hotel have seen better days. Any luck with the old copy?"

Fran started shuffling mail. "I was just going through this stack. Mainly bills. Or complaining letters to the editor, which is me of course . . . This looks promising."

She extracted a fat envelope from the pile and set the rest down. She slit the envelope to reveal a folded, faded, off-white newspaper. "Let's check the date . . . excellent. I knew I could rely on them. And the mailman."

I reached for the newspaper but Fran pulled it away and said, "Remember our deal? If you find anything—"

"You'll be the second to know."

Fran offered me the newspaper and made a clear space on one of the unused desks. "Used to have a staff of three in here. Well, me and two part-timers."

"What happened?"

"I couldn't match the salaries down south," Fran said. "Hell, I can't even afford mine. Holler if you need me."

I started leafing through the newspaper. The masthead gave the date as November nineteenth the previous year. The *Courier* seemed to be mainly news of local events, sports, awards, low-level politics and photographs. Plenty of photographs. Cheerleaders, football and soccer teams, bake sales, fund-raisers.

Sarah's murder took up the top half of page two. The story looked as though it had been shoehorned into the paper at the last minute. The black and white photograph showed a smiling woman with long, pale hair and sharp features. The article beneath it told me that Mr. Edward Petchey, an inhabitant of Cardford Springs, while out walking his dog, had found Sarah's body at eleven-twenty p.m. State Police confirmed that the victim had died from a single gunshot wound to the head. The family had been informed and had identified the body.

I hoped that I'd never have to go through that.

The rest of the article referred to the growing number of roadside attacks in the state, and compared it to the spate of tourist shootings in Florida: "A Deadly Trend?"

The very last paragraph said that Sarah's employers, Mr. and Mrs. Shaw of Eastham, were devastated by the news and had offered a ten-thousand-dollar reward for the murderer's conviction.

I searched for the name of Tyrone Cursell but couldn't find it. I waited for Fran to finish a phone call before I asked, "Was anyone ever arrested for the murder?"

Fran looked away. "Not that I know of."

"How about the reward? Didn't that jog people's memories?"

"What reward?" Fran crossed to the desk and skimmed through the article. "Ten thousand? I'd forgotten about that."

"So, no takers?"

"I guess not." Fran hesitated, then continued, "The State Police picked up a local man and held him for a few days, but nothing came of it. No arrest."

"When did they take him in?"

"A few weeks after this. But they never charged him." While she said this, Fran shuffled the papers on the desk in front of her, moved the pens around, shifted the blotter an inch to the left. Anything except look me in the eye.

"Any idea of the name? Maybe Tyrone Cursell?"

"Cursell? I've never heard of him."

I noticed she only answered the second half of my question. I didn't make an issue of it yet. "Could you search for the name in the later editions?"

She laughed and pointed to the back room. "You've seen my archive. It would take weeks to go through that lot. If I remembered right in the first place."

"Don't you have anything on computer?"

"Sweetheart, I don't even have it on microfiche."

In IT, I'd been used to companies spending hundreds of thousands, sometimes millions, of dollars to record their information for posterity. Stuff that nobody would ever read: sales figures, statistics, indexes. Here, Fran had a room full of news and no time. I could ask to wade through the past copies, but I left that as Plan B.

Fran said, "I wish I knew what happened to all my notes—they'd have interviews with witnesses and a hell of a lot more detail."

I guessed they were probably sitting in the desk of the investigator who had paid Fran a visit in January.

"What about this Cardford Springs?" I asked. "What kind of place is it?"

"An old town, mainly fishing and tourists, basically a few houses and a store set next to the lake. Small. Quiet. Self-contained. Close."

I smiled. "How many ways can you describe the same thing?"

Fran shrugged. "What can I say? They didn't like all the interest last year. They keep themselves to themselves."

That's what the hotel bartender had said about Carl. Maybe they had that on their license plates.

"You thinking of going up there?" Fran asked.

"Next on my list."

"Good luck."

"Can I use your photocopier?"

"Sure, if it works." Fran pointed to a squat machine in the corner.

I made two copies of the article and left Fran with the original. I promised again to keep in touch and started walking back toward the Mill Hotel. The hands of the clock on the Town Hall pointed to fifteen after eleven, more or less. I walked past the police station. I didn't hesitate.

Even before I walked into the Mill Hotel parking lot, I could see a bright red and yellow truck. For a moment I thought it was a fire engine, then I saw a flat cargo bed with my Jeep sitting on it. When I got close, I saw Willard clamping the Jeep's wheels to the steel bed.

"How's it looking?" I asked, trying to sound optimistic, like a relative asking a hospital doctor.

"Not too good. I had to winch her on board," Willard said, snapping shut the clasp. "She'll need to go into the shop."

"So it wasn't just the battery?"

Willard looked at me.

"How long before I get it back?"

He scratched the side of his head and stared out over the lake. "I'll need to send over to Burlington; there's a Jeep dealership down there. If he's got the parts, a day, maybe two. If he hasn't, and has to send off, I'd say best part of a week."

I shook my head. This was all I needed. Then I wondered if Willard was jerking me around: maybe lots of stranded "townies" had helped to buy his new red recovery truck. "So what's the problem?"

Instead of answering, Willard asked, "You piss anybody off recently?"

"Not that I know."

"No angry husbands after you? People you owe money to?"

I almost laughed, but the sight of my disabled Jeep stopped me. "What happened?"

"Well, someone reached up and sliced through your wiring. They knew what they was doing." Willard spat into the lot. "And it wasn't an accident."

4

As Willard drove me back to his garage, I asked him where I could rent a car. He told me there were rental places in St. Albans and Waterbury, but he had a pickup I could use if I wasn't too fussy. When he said this, I saw him look into his rear-view mirror at my Grand Cherokee standing on the flatbed.

The pickup, an old white Ford with wide tires, stood behind Willard's workshop. Its roof reached a foot higher than my head.

Willard patted the deep, ridged tires. "Good mud-pluggers, them. Get you out of anything. What do you say?"

"How much?"

"Fifty a day."

I could probably rent a suburban compact for slightly less than that in the city, but I needed transport now. "It's a deal."

"Gas extra," Willard said.

"No problem."

Willard laid a hand on my shoulder. "One last thing: you're responsible for it. If someone starts trimming the wires like they did on your Jeep, or they decide to rearrange the fenders, I expect you to make good the damage."

I nodded. "You got it."

While he checked out the pickup and filled it with gas, I sat in Willard's office and wondered who had cut the wiring on my Jeep. If someone wanted to steal the car, they could have. Disabling the Jeep meant inconvenience but it wasn't terminal. No, to me it looked like a warning. But from who? Who else had an interest in Sarah's murder?

Carl?

"She's all ready," Willard said, wiping his hands on a piece of old plaid shirt. "Take it easy until you get used to it."

I grabbed my road map from the Jeep and climbed into the pickup. I settled myself in the seat. The engine bit on the second try and made the whole cab vibrate.

"She'll calm down soon enough," Willard yelled. He gave me a thumbs-up sign as I pulled out of the garage and headed west. I aimed for St. Albans until Sheldon Junction, then turned north and headed for the border with Canada. After a few miles, the pickup did settle down. I began to enjoy the drive. My ribs hadn't given me any grief, the day was high and clear and the roads were empty. I could have been on vacation.

Then I saw a sign for Cardford Springs and I remembered Sarah.

I pulled over and found the photocopied article, then followed the road down toward the water. Lake Champlain showed between low clapboard houses like poured steel. When the trees opened up, I could see angular white sails and a few motor cruisers. The road passed a handful of houses and a jetty before it petered out in rocks and water.

I parked up and walked to the shore. Somewhere around here, Sarah had sat in her car and waited. For what? She'd had her suitcase and laptop with her. Had she been meeting someone? To give them a lift or to say goodbye?

Either way, someone had approached her and shot her. I looked back to the houses and the jetty a hundred or so yards back. The spot was a long way from the road. Opportunistic shootings with robbery, like the ones in Florida, revolved around turn-offs or parking spots close to roads. Tired drivers, usually tourists who were lost and didn't know the area and its dangers, would pull over for a rest. The next thing they knew, they'd be staring at a gun.

To me, this spot looked too far away from passing traffic. The robber must have known she was there or must have followed her down. Had it been Cursell? Maybe, but he would have been a long way from home.

I started walking back toward the houses by the jetty. A couple on jet bikes carved circles in the bay, throwing up white plumes. I wondered just how cold that water was. I stopped at the first house and knocked. I didn't see any reason for holding back.

The door opened and a young girl peered up at me.

"Hi, is your mom or dad home?"

The girl yelled over her shoulder, "Mom!"

A tired-looking woman walked through from another room. She set down the basket of laundry in her hands and pushed the little girl behind her. "Yes? What's the problem?"

I smiled. "No problem, ma'am. You might remember an incident last year, near here: Sarah Westlake."

Her eyes opened wide. "The murder."

I nodded. "I'm investigating the case and wondered if—"

"Are you State Police?"

"Not exactly, ma'am, but—"

She reached for the door. "Look, I'm sorry but I'm very busy."

"I'd only take two minutes of your time . . ." I stopped talking to the closed door. I tried another two houses but nobody else opened their doors. It looked like Fran was right: they didn't like anyone prying. Or maybe they had something to hide.

I stood on the shore for a while and threw pebbles into the hard water. I wondered what the hell I was doing up here. Maybe, deep down, I did have some crazy idea of solving Sarah's murder. I needed to find out about Carl, of course. But was I using that as an excuse? Even if I was, I still had to face Detective Mendez in just over two weeks. I needed to know whether Carl was involved.

I started walking along the road to a cluster of houses at the bend. Then I saw an old man with a limp walking a sagging Labrador whose coat looked almost white. I scanned the article again and called out, "Mr. Petchey? Mr. Edward Petchey?"

The man put his head down and walked faster, almost dragging the poor old dog. The man's limp looked almost comical, as if he were practicing it for a joke.

"Sir? Could I just ask you . . ." I crossed over and walked up behind the man. "I wanted to ask you about the murder victim you found last year."

The old man stopped and turned around. I'd taken another two steps before I saw the gun pointing at my stomach. I stopped and kept my hands at my sides.

"Stop bothering me." Petchey's voice trembled, just like the gun in his hand. His eyes below his woolen hat focused on my chest. The dog scratched itself and then looked up at us and panted.

"I don't want to bother you, Mr. Petchey."

"Then why the hell won't you leave me alone?"

I could see the gun wavering in his hand. Small, a .32. Enough to cause me problems. I wondered if I could cross the five feet or so and knock it away. That wasn't going to happen.

"I've only just arrived up here," I said, my voice quiet and calm. "I read that you found the car. Now, I wonder if you know there's a reward attached to this case?"

"Oh, I know."

"Well, if you could help me—"

He stepped forward, jerking the dog's lead. "I helped last year. This is the reward I got."

Petchey folded his woolen hat in his fist. The hair had started to grow around the thick scars above his left ear. The bone looked swollen and misshapen, as though someone had squeezed it while warm, like dough.

Before I could say anything, Petchey pivoted and hobbled away. The limp made him swing his left leg wide. In less than a minute, he'd disappeared around the bend where I'd parked the pickup.

I let out my breath and uncurled my hands. My shoulders felt as if I'd just bench-pressed a ton. I thought then about climbing into the pickup and driving straight back to New York. Instead, I walked toward the jetty, where I could see a storefront facing the lake and a handful of small boats. I sat on one of the stanchions and looked out across the bay. Directly opposite me lay a forested headland I took to be Gander Bay. Somewhere to my right, to the north, Canada hid behind low cloud and mist.

I wondered how many boats crossed the invisible border. Cardford Springs had probably been a riot during Prohibition. I could have used some of that liquor right now.

"Old Petchey give you a scare?"

I turned around and saw a woman leaning in the doorway of the store. She wore a long green apron over jeans and plaid work shirt. A pair of half-moon glasses had been pushed back to sit on her graying hair.

"He doesn't mean anything with it," she said. "I don't even think it's loaded."

"I wouldn't like to take the chance." I walked up to the

doorway and looked back to the road. The woman would have had a good view of Petchey and me. I stuck out my hand. "Steve Burnett."

"Louise. You looking into that young girl's murder?"

"How did you guess?"

She waved me inside the store. " 'Cos it's the only thing that's happened round here in years. And you were talking with Petchey."

I looked around at shelves of canned and dried food, fishing tackle, ammunition and kids' toys. Duck decoys stared back at me with the most realistic painted eyes I've ever seen. I was going to ask if Louise sold liquor when I saw her fish a bottle from beneath the wooden counter. She poured a single measure into a mug. "It's good for shock."

The whisky burned. "Thanks. I needed it."

She set the bottle back beneath the counter. "So. You another investigator?"

"How many have you had up here?"

"Two that I know of," she said. "If you don't count the Chief from Eastham and the State Police."

"Anybody recent?"

She shrugged. "Depends what you mean by recent."

"Past few weeks?"

"Only you."

A sudden growl of petrol engines made me look outside. The jet bikes were chewing up the water off the jetty. They looked out of place in the old bay with its leaning houses.

"Idiots," Louise said, making the word sound like my old Aunt Mary would have, with *e*'s instead of *i*'s. "They don't know what they're stirring up."

"I bet it was a big deal, last November," I said.

"Sure. Police everywhere. News crews for a day. But it blew over. Poor girl."

"Did you see anything?"

"Only her car."

"Nothing on the night of the murder?"

Louise shook her head. "Nobody did."

"Not even Petchey?"

She didn't answer that.

I asked, "Do you get many robberies around here?"

"Not really. Fishermen, tourists mainly, sometimes get their cars opened up."

"So there wasn't a history of robbers picking on people in cars?"

"You'd have to ask the police about that. They've got all the figures, I bet."

The more I dug into the murder, the less I could be certain of. But I knew that it stank. "What happened to Petchey?"

Louise rearranged some of the stock on the counter, moving spools of fishing line and hooks. "Oh, he had an argument with a car. The car won."

"When did this happen?"

She hesitated. "January."

Not too long after Sarah's murder. Was there a connection? I could think of one. "He found the body, didn't he?"

Louise nodded.

"Maybe he told the police he saw someone else around here that night," I said, talking low as if to myself. "Maybe he saw a car or a boat."

"It could happen."

I continued, "Maybe the police picked someone up and asked Petchey to give evidence . . ."

Louise looked at me.

"Petchey never gave that evidence, did he?"

"The car accident sort of distracted him," Louise said.

"After that, his memory wasn't so good."

A man's deep voice called from above and behind the counter. Louise said, "That's my Derek waking up; he works nights. He wouldn't like me talking to strangers."

I dropped a bill on the counter. "Thanks for the drink."

Louise waited until I was at the doorway before she called out, "That reward still out there?"

"As far as I know. Interested?"

Louise stared at me, then called upstairs, "I'm coming, Derek, don't yell."

As I walked back to the car, I looked at Cardford Springs and wondered how many people knew what had really happened that night in November. And how many of them would admit to it.

I left Cardford Springs, checked my map and set out for Burlington. Willard's pickup sounded smoother now, although it pitched through the bends like a top-heavy sailboat.

Who had scared Petchey off? Fran remembered that the police had pulled someone in for questioning but nothing came of it. That fitted in with Petchey's change of heart.

Could Carl run over an old man just to stop him testifying? It was possible, if Carl had already killed Sarah. Witness intimidation was nothing new; it happened all the time at the Precinct. We'd take down an initial interview after an incident, when the witnesses were usually willing to cooperate. Then the case detectives would go back and find the witness couldn't exactly remember what had happened. They couldn't swear to it. Sometimes they just refused point-blank.

The detectives knew the score. Witnesses had families, wives, husbands, kids, parents. Everybody had their weak spot. All it took was someone ruthless—or desperate—enough to apply the right pressure.

I would have paid good money to read the witness statements. Instead, I had to work between the lines, pick up what I could. I hoped Sarah's friends and teachers at the University would be able to help. At least I should get a clearer picture of the murdered woman.

I'd noticed the Chevy Suburban in my rear-view mirror for the past few miles. Thousands of them had been made and sold. Many of them would be green, just like the one behind me and the one that passed me on the way into Eastham that morning. Again, it could be coincidence.

I pressed down on the gas and saw the Chevy shrink in my mirror. Another mile and it reappeared. I gripped the steering wheel harder and took a deep breath. I stared into the rear-view mirror so hard I didn't see the slow-moving motor home until I'd almost slammed into its rear. I hit the brakes and dropped my speed. When I looked back, the Chevy had disappeared.

Burlington reminded me of a slimmed-down Albany: old and new alongside each other; developments of identical suburbs; winding streets and lots of plate glass. I left the pickup on Delamere Street and found the main Public Library. An hour's research delivered three newspaper articles about Sarah. She had been studying Psychology at the University; her teachers were sorry to lose such a promising talent. One in particular, Professor Alex Crosby, was mentioned in two of the three articles. I took down details and asked for directions to the University campus.

Outside the Library, I had to stop and dry-swallow two painkillers. My chest and ribs didn't like all the activity. Not for the first time, I wondered whether coming up to Vermont had been such a good idea. But I couldn't cut and run. I'd started something.

The University campus stretched across six or seven

blocks in the city center. I found the Psychology building and followed the signs to the front desk. I'd hit the tail-end of lunch hour and a few students ambled through the corridors. A receptionist who looked younger than the students took my name and asked me to wait. I took one of the hard, orange plastic chairs lined up beneath notices for rock groups, meditation classes and what to do if you caught an STD.

After ten minutes, I saw a tall, bearded man watching me from behind the desk. I walked over. "Professor Crosby?"

"Correct."

He didn't fit my expectation of a professor. He wore jeans and a faded cotton shirt. His gray hair touched the collar of his tweed jacket. "If you have five minutes to spare, I'd like to ask you about Sarah Westlake."

The receptionist glanced at me, then Crosby, who gave no reaction.

"I'm investigating what happened last year," I said.

"Did Sarah's parents send you?"

"No. I've never met them."

Crosby stared at me and then came around the reception desk. "This way."

I followed him along a short corridor to an office crowded with books and journals. Shelves sagged beneath the weight of paper. Crosby sat behind a desk and pointed to the chair opposite. Pale sunlight came through the slatted blinds and fell on the desk's PC and overflowing ashtray.

"I should have asked Security to throw you out," Crosby said.

"I'm sorry?"

"We had a lot of trouble over the case," he said, lighting

a cigarette. "We were being harassed, even though we had nothing to do with it."

"Sarah's parents?"

"Among others." He checked his watch. "I've a class in twenty minutes. So, who do you work for?"

I could have told him a variation of the truth I'd told Fran or Elaine. I didn't think he'd fall for either version. Instead, I told him the truth. "I'm a police officer from New York. Ten days ago, a thief held up a deli and shot me and my partner before he was killed. One of the guns used in the incident was the same weapon that killed Sarah."

Crosby blew smoke away from me. "You think the thief killed Sarah?"

"I don't know. I do know that I have to trace the gun's past history."

Crosby reclined his chair and looked up at the ceiling. "You know, I enjoy language. I enjoy what's not being said even more than what is. You said 'one of the guns used in the incident,' not 'the gun he used.' "

"So?"

He turned to me. "So, I think there's more to this. Are you looking into the case officially?"

"No." I shifted in my chair, trying to ease my chest and ribs. "I'm just a patrol officer."

"So what brings a patrol officer all the way up here for a dead case?"

I almost walked out at that point. I didn't want to play word games with the professor; for one thing, he'd win. And I didn't want to tell him everything. "Will you just accept that I have an interest in Sarah's murder? I think there may be a connection between the two cases. I need to know."

"It's personal?"

"It's personal."

He leaned forward, stubbed the cigarette out and said, "Okay. Try me."

"What was Sarah like?"

"What kind of question is that? Physically? Mentally?" He shook his head. "Be more precise."

I felt like one of Crosby's students. "Well, was she a good student?"

"One of my best. She had a great future."

"She was doing post-graduate studies?"

"She was. She'd decided to concentrate on addictions, their causes, morphology and selective treatments."

"Do you know why she went to Eastham?"

Crosby reached for another cigarette. "Of course I do. I helped to arrange it."

I waited.

"Sarah needed to interview people in the various stages of addiction. She met drug addicts, alcoholics, patients with food dependency problems. She worked through the treatment processes with them and monitored their progress. Some did well; others fell back. Near the end of her studies, one of the people in the alcohol program offered her a job, three months' secretarial work."

"Carl Shaw?"

"Yes, it was Shaw."

So Carl had been an alcoholic. It didn't necessarily make him a murderer.

Crosby continued, "Sarah accepted. She didn't need the money. I think she wanted to observe Shaw's progress after the end of the treatment."

"Did she ever tell you how he did?" I wondered if Carl had gone back to the bottle.

"He did very well," Crosby said. "The last I heard, he was completely dry."

So Sarah had been studying Carl for three months before she died. "Did she keep any notes about Carl?"

Crosby shook his head. "Even if I had access, I couldn't let you see them. Patient confidentiality."

I understood. I chanced a long-shot. "Was Sarah sleeping with Carl?"

Crosby's laugh turned into a cough. "Jesus, no."

"How can you be so sure?"

"Because she wasn't into men," Crosby said with a brief grin. "She liked women."

I left Crosby's office with the names of Sarah's old roommate and the investigator that Sarah's parents had sent up to Vermont. Crosby described Harry Braid as a fat greaseball with bad breath and a comb-over. And Harry drove a beat-up green wagon. The investigator had appeared for the last time in August, but Crosby had thrown him out. From the way Crosby spoke about Sarah's parents and their investigator, there must have been no love lost. Did her parents blame Crosby for her being in Eastham? Or was there more to it?

I had to wonder why Crosby had cooperated with me in the end. Maybe he just wanted the whole thing to go away. Or maybe he carried a little guilt about what happened. I think I would have.

I grabbed a sandwich and used the deli's pay phone to call up the numbers Crosby had given me for Sarah's roommate. Alison Tate had moved on from the last address and they wouldn't give me her new number. I had more luck with her work contact, a doctor; she'd interned for a local hospital for six months before transferring to Boston. She was off-duty but I left a message at the Boston hospital, asking her to call me at the hotel number. I had no guarantee that she'd return my call; she might have had enough of the whole deal. But it seemed like I was making progress.

As I turned the key in Willard's pickup I had that split-second of doubt—had someone got to this car, too? But the engine roared to life first time. I left Burlington behind and headed back for Eastham through gathering darkness. I had plenty to think about on the way. I had connections between Sarah and Carl, and if Crosby could be believed, those connections didn't include sex.

So what motive would Carl have for killing her? If I tried, I could come up with a handful of possible reasons right away: he'd made a play for her and she'd bounced him, hard; he'd started drinking again and lost control; perhaps Carl had other vices beside the alcohol, and Sarah had found out. Hell, maybe Sarah had gone for Elaine.

But I still didn't want to see Carl as the murderer. I could see him as an alcoholic—half of the guys I worked with could be called that if you wanted to be strict about it. And alcohol does warp your view, the way you react to things. That could be a part of it.

I pulled into the Mill Hotel parking lot without seeing the green Suburban. The desk clerk told me I had one message: Willard said my Jeep should be ready in three days. On my way up to my room, I could already feel that hot bath working on my aches. I slid my key into the door and flicked on the switch.

Someone had enjoyed trashing the room. You could see it in the way they'd ripped the sheets and emptied the torn pillows onto the floor. The cheap, corporate artwork on the walls had been smashed, leaving jagged glass embedded in the mattress. My clothes lay like crime-scene outlines on the floor. I could hear running water.

I closed the door and picked my way through the mess.

In the bathroom, the contents of the cabinet had been dumped in the toilet. All the faucets had been left running, spewing clouds of steam into the air. Someone had tried to wedge the bathtub overflow shut with toilet paper, but it had disintegrated. I turned off all the faucets and imagined the damage that the overflowing bathtub would have caused.

I stood in the center of the bedroom and shook my head. Hotel thieves wouldn't go to this much trouble. They wouldn't want to attract the attention. Like the sliced wiring in my Jeep, this had to be a personal message for me.

The loud knock made me jump. I hesitated, then stood back from the door, my left hand ready at my side. I opened the door and stepped back.

A heavy, crew-cut blond man smiled at me. The etched nametag on the pocket of his uniform shirt said "Chief Petersen." He looked past me, into the room, and rested his hands on his belt. "Mr. Burnett? I think we'd better have a little talk."

5

The Police Chief slid past me, into the room. He looked at the wreckage and then at me. "You lose something?"

I didn't reply. I left the door slightly ajar.

He started to reach for the cell phone at his belt, then picked up the hotel phone and pressed zero. "Sue? Hi, it's Gary. Sure, I found him. Can you send the manager up to three-ten? Thanks."

Through the window, I could see the surface of the small lake. Despite the last of the light fading away, two dinghies were chasing each other, their sails pushed out by the wind.

"Did they take much?" Chief Petersen asked.

"I don't think so. There wasn't much to take."

"Looks like they had fun finding out."

I heard the bell of the elevator down the hall. Someone pushed at the open door and knocked at the same time. "Hello?"

"Come on in, Tony," Petersen called out.

When the hotel manager opened the door, the smile disappeared from his face. "Oh, my God. What happened?"

"Burglars," I said.

The man turned to me, his eyes narrowed.

"I just got back," I said. "The door hadn't been forced."

"Will you get this cleaned up?" Petersen laid a hand on the manager's shoulder. "It looks worse than it is."

The manager shook his head. "Don't you want to check for fingerprints or anything?"

"Not this time; I don't think we'll find anything."

Petersen turned to me. "You can buy me a cup of coffee downstairs, Mr. Burnett."

We sat by the windows in the echoing restaurant. I watched the waitresses set up the tables for dinner. One of them waved at Petersen, who nodded back. I sipped bitter coffee and tried to settle into the chair.

"You okay?"

"A few bruised ribs," I said.

"Sounds like you're having a rough time, lately."

I reached into my pocket for the painkillers, then pulled back. "How did you find out about me?"

"Oh, me and Fran go way back," Petersen said. "And Shirley said you'd been in the diner a few times. Small town like this, strangers stand out."

I smiled. "Too early for skiing, right?"

Petersen looked me over, slowly. "You know, it's considered good manners for a private investigator to drop by and say hello to the local officers. I mean, it's not legal, nothing set down in the statute books. But I'm an old-fashioned kind of guy; it would have been nice if you'd dropped in and let me know you were working around here. I might have been able to help you. I don't bite."

I hesitated, then said, "I'm not an investigator."

He leaned forward. "Then who are you?"

Again, I didn't know whether to tell the truth. Petersen might have contacts in New York; he might know people who knew someone else, who knew . . .

I told him the same as I'd told Crosby. I didn't mention Carl's name.

"You're a patrol officer? And you came all the way up here just to chase up a possible link? Are you trying a shortcut to detective?"

I smiled. "Nothing like that. I just wanted to satisfy

myself that there was no connection."

"What about the .38? That's a connection right there."

"The gun could have been through a dozen people since last November," I said. "It's barter."

Petersen stared at me. "I don't buy your story. Leastways, not all of it. There's something personal in this."

"Don't forget the reward . . ."

"I haven't."

I tried again. "Let's just say I'll sleep better when I know more about Sarah's murder."

"And what about your fans?"

"How do you mean?"

He pointed at the ceiling. "Your room's trashed and your car is taken out. What do you want? An engraved invitation to go home?"

I guessed that Willard had told him about the Jeep.

"I have no idea who's behind it," I said. "But doesn't it prove that someone else is interested in the murder?"

He didn't look convinced.

"The case was never solved, was it?"

"Not yet," he said. "State Police took it over."

"Would it interest you if someone was leaning on witnesses?"

"Go on."

"A guy called Ed Petchey found the body at Cardford Springs."

"I know."

"He identified someone, didn't he?" I asked. I was fishing here, but not without good reason. "He placed someone at the scene."

Petersen nodded. He didn't take his eyes off my face.

I went on, "In January, a car ran over Petchey and messed him up. He dropped his statement."

"People get hit by cars all the time. Especially with crane-necked tourists everywhere."

"Maybe so, but Petchey didn't see it that way. When I asked him about Sarah, he pointed a gun at my stomach and told me he'd had enough."

"Is that right?" Petersen looked over to the doorway, where a family with squawking children had just arrived. In a low voice, as if talking to himself, he said, "There's no law against you coming up here and asking people questions, I suppose. So long as you don't harass them or threaten them."

I waited.

"Of course, I could always put a call through to New York, see what your Precinct Captain thinks of your little trip up here."

"You could do that," I said, trying to keep my voice neutral. I've never been very good at poker, and I was glad Petersen wasn't looking at me. He looked like the kind of guy who could spot a bluff.

He turned to me. "When is your Jeep ready?"

"In three days."

"Whatever happens, I want you heading back for New York then. No matter if you found what you're looking for or not. Understand?"

"Thanks."

Petersen stood up. "Anything you find, you come to me. I don't want you screwing things up if there's a chance of getting the guy that killed Sarah."

I followed him to the exit. "One thing. Can you tell me who the police picked up after the murder? The one that Petchey identified?"

Petersen hesitated, then said, "Petchey never identified the guy, just his car."

"And?"

He scratched his jaw. "What the hell. Leon Mathers. He used to look after families' houses out of season."

"A caretaker?"

"And plenty more besides."

"Who was he working for last November?"

Petersen paused at the lobby door. "A local couple."

I could already guess the answer, but I asked, "The Shaws?"

"The Shaws."

I went back up to my room and found three maids cleaning up. They didn't look too happy about it, and I couldn't blame them. My clothes lay in a neat pile on the dresser. I tried to remember if I'd seen anyone hanging around the hotel or the corridors. Nothing came to mind. Then I thought of the green Suburban. Maybe he'd had time to tail me until he was sure I was on my way to Burlington, then drive back to the Mill Hotel and trash my room.

I thanked the maids and set down three ten-dollar bills. It wasn't much, but this trip was proving to be expensive. I left them to their work and grabbed my coat. The woman at the front desk called me over to let me know they'd given me another room. I wondered if the manager had wanted me out. If it had been high season, or if Chief Petersen hadn't been involved, I think I would have flown out of the door.

I drove into town on the off-chance that Fran's office might be open. The *Courier* building was dark, with no car out front. I sat in my pickup and went through the facts. It had been a hell of a day and it wasn't over yet.

Everything seemed to come back to Carl. I didn't like it, but it made life easier in a way: if he was connected with

Sarah's murder, I'd front up to Mendez right away. Carl might have saved me and Sam, but if he had any part in the killing, it had to come out. I was just about ready to call Mendez right then.

I hoped the hotel had my new room ready; my ribs, chest and back felt like I'd been through a cement mixer. As I pulled out of Fran's parking lot my headlights washed over the front of the Tavern over the road. A green Suburban stood outside the doors, in between a dark sedan and a shiny new pickup. There might be ten Suburbans in the state, all beat-up and rusted. Hell, maybe twenty. This one didn't have to belong to Harry Braid, the so-called investigator hired by Sarah Westlake's parents.

I sat with the engine idling. I should go back to the hotel. I was tired and sore. I should rest.

Instead, I pulled in front of the Tavern, braked, then reversed into the Suburban's rear lights. I heard glass shatter. I parked and inspected the damage: the caged tail lights on Willard's pickup had smashed the Suburban's passenger-side indicator and sidelight. Nothing too bad, but it would be polite to go inside the bar and confess my careless driving to the owner.

I took a few breaths and flexed my hands. My heart beat a little faster. Jukebox guitar music drifted through the frosted glass. I pushed at the door and stepped inside.

A long bar lined the wall facing the windows. Bottles crowded the glass shelves behind the bartender. Men hunched over six or seven tables arranged on the bare floorboards; I could see more tables through an open doorway opposite. A waitress in jeans and halter top slid beers onto the nearest table. I almost expected honky-tonk music instead of Alanis Morissette.

None of the drinkers looked up. I walked up to the bar

and told the young guy behind it, "I just smashed into a car in your lot: a green Suburban."

He looked at me for a moment, then yelled above the music, "Hey! Anyone own the green Chevy Sub outside?"

By that time, I'd slipped out of the doors. I waited in the shadows outside until a big, balding man in a parka strode out. He walked around his Suburban until he saw the damaged lights. "Oh, frigging great!"

I stepped out of the shadows. "Sorry about the damage, Harry."

He whirled around pretty quickly for a big guy. "Hey, how did you know—"

Then, as I stepped into the pool of light, he stopped. His whole face went slack.

"I guess we can call this quits," I said. "My trashed hotel room for a couple of bulbs."

"I don't know what you're talking about."

I kept my distance. I put his weight around two-fifty, and my ribs and chest still hurt. But I pushed a little further. "Sarah's parents send you up here?"

He moved toward his car. Maybe he had a gun in there. Maybe he just wanted to drive away. I stepped between him and the car door.

His whole body went tense beneath his parka; I could see his silhouette shift like a bear. He took a step forward, then relaxed. "Look, bud, I was here first. This is my territory."

"That gives you the right to trash my stuff?"

"I don't know anything about that."

"How about my Jeep?"

Harry licked his lips. "Yeah, well, okay. I just wanted to give you a hint. I'll make it good."

I looked at the patches of rust on the Suburban, and at the tattered edges of his parka. "I doubt you could afford to."

He grinned. "I'm as good as my word. I got money in the bank, practically."

"The reward?"

"And the rest."

The cold and exhaustion suddenly swamped me. "Buy me a drink, Harry."

Inside the bar, I drank half my beer in one gulp and looked at Harry Braid, private investigator. His comb-over had disappeared along with most of his hair. His skin looked pasty and the whisky in front of him wasn't his first.

"So how'd you know my name?" he asked.

"A guy called Crosby described you. And I noticed you tailing me. Maybe all the way from New York."

He drained his drink and waved for another. "You're paranoid."

"Maybe. Anyway, you're not up here for Sarah's parents, so I guess it's personal?"

He nodded. "You guessed right. How about you? Who's paying your bills?"

"Just me. Like you, it's personal." The beer on top of no food made me yawn. I get slow when I'm tired, and now would be a bad time for that. "You heard about Petchey?"

"You mean his car accident? Old news."

"Who do you think did it?"

He glanced at me and tried to make his face go blank. "No idea. Who do you think?"

"Me? I've just arrived. You know all the ins and outs, the stuff between the lines."

He nodded his stubbled chin at me. "I know what's what."

"That's what I thought: clever guy like you must know the background to all this. Me? I'm not even interested in the reward."

Harry looked into his drink, then at me. He chewed his lip like a schoolboy with a difficult math test. Eventually he said, "The cops know nothing."

"No?"

He leaned in close. "The cops said it was a chance thief. But kids found her suitcase and clothes washed up on the shore of Gander Bay, three days after the murder. Then her empty purse showed up in Long Marsh Bay, just around the headland."

"So the thief rifled her suitcase, took her money and ditched the empty purse."

"You reckon?" Harry grinned like a fat cat we used to have back in Albany. "Then explain how the suitcase and purse showed up after the police had already searched the area."

I couldn't.

Harry continued, "The Crime Scene boys swept the lake and the coastline the first and second days. The suitcase and purse showed up on the third."

"Maybe the tide had carried them in?"

"They'd already searched the lake."

I sipped my beer and thought for a moment. "If Petchey found the body but not the suitcase and purse, maybe he wasn't the first on the scene."

Harry toasted me with his glass. "Smart boy."

"What about the laptop?"

Harry drained his drink and stood up, swaying a little. "If you can find that, you're looking at serious money. But that's for another day."

I followed him out to the lot, still keeping a little distance between us.

"We're even, right?" Harry said. "My lights for your Jeep's wires."

It wasn't much of a bargain, my Grand Cherokee's

wiring for a rusty Chevy's lights, but I let it go. "We're even. But you're sure you didn't trash my room?"

He raised two fingers, palm forward. "Scout's honor."

"Then who was it?"

Instead of answering, Harry climbed into his car and said, "See you, Burnett."

Maybe I should have stopped him, but I watched him drive away; he followed Main Street, back west toward the hotel and the main route to St. Albans. Cardford Springs lay out there, too. I wondered which of the local inhabitants had first found the car and Sarah's body. They must have been pretty desperate to take Sarah's purse, suitcase and laptop. Then, when the police started investigating, they must have ditched the suitcase and empty purse. But why not the laptop?

There might be a couple of hundred bucks for a stolen laptop if it was a top brand. But you needed to have a buyer, someone you could trust to keep their mouths shut. No, that laptop was probably at the bottom of Lake Champlain, with whatever notes Sarah had kept gradually decaying as the water and silt ate away at the connections.

I drove back to the hotel and found my clothes in a new room, four-twenty. Before I got into bed, I locked the door and jammed a chair under the handle. That's when I remembered about calling Marie. I cursed myself for leaving my cell phone charger back in New York, but I couldn't face going down to the pay phone. I used the bedside phone and tried not to think about the hotel's long-distance charges.

"Hey, how are you?" Marie sounded warm and relaxed, as if I'd just woken her.

"I'm fine," I lied. "Just relaxing, taking it easy. You?"

"Watching TV. I miss you. It's no fun by yourself."

"Watching TV?"

"Anything," she said. "When are you coming back?"

I remembered Petersen's advice. "Another three days. Maybe sooner."

We talked for a few more minutes. Before Marie hung up, she said, "John called me today; someone wanted to get in touch with you."

I sat up in bed, and winced. "Who?"

"Detective Mendez. Wasn't he the guy we met at the hospital?"

"Sure. It's just about the shooting," I said, amazed at how normal my voice sounded. "Did John say what Mendez wanted?"

"Not to me. Is there a problem?"

"I'll call him tomorrow. You take care."

"You too."

I lay back and wondered what Mendez wanted. Had Petersen decided to get in touch with the Precinct anyway? I almost rang John, but it could wait. News, bad or good, could wait until morning.

I thought I dreamt of bells ringing, then woke up and grabbed the bedside phone. "Burnett."

The front desk told me they had a call from Boston, a Miss Tate. I asked them to put her through.

"Mr. Burnett? I had a message asking me to call you."

"Thanks for getting back to me." I sat up and almost dropped the phone.

"Are you all right?" she asked.

"Just a little disorganized. I wanted to ask you about Sarah Westlake."

"Yes, I guessed that. Are you with the State Police up there?"

I hesitated, then said, "No, I'm an officer investigating a

recent shooting in New York which may be related."

"New York? Right. How can I help?"

"Just any background about Sarah. How long were you roommates?"

"Three years. We got to know each other very well."

I remembered Crosby's comments. "Excuse me asking, but were you . . . I mean . . ."

"No, Mr. Burnett. We were just friends. I wasn't Sarah's type."

Alison went on to describe Sarah as quiet, intelligent, independent and hard-working. "She would have made an excellent psychologist. When she spoke to you, she made you feel . . ."

"Go on, please."

"Oh, it's stupid. It was as if you were the most important person to her. Maybe she was just focused. I don't think it was manipulation. She hated manipulation."

"Did she say anything about the family she worked for in Vermont? The Shaws?"

"She'd left our apartment by then, but we ran into each other a couple of times; I saw her in late September, I think. We had a good talk."

"Was she having trouble with the Shaws?"

"No, not at all. She seemed happy with them. She said the couple would make her dissertation a bestseller."

So Sarah had been observing the couple, not just Carl, as material for her work. I wonder how they had felt about that.

"I'll have to say goodbye," Alison said. "I'm due at work."

"Thank you for your time. If there's anything else, please call me."

"I hope you find the murderer. Sarah deserved better."

Right then, I wished I'd told Alison the truth. "I'll do what I can, Miss Tate."

I went to put the receiver down but heard her call my name.

"I almost forgot," she said. "Someone else was asking about Sarah. About two months ago, but I'd seen him before that."

I took a guess. "Harry Braid?"

"That's right."

"Can you tell me what he asked?"

"Well, he wanted to know how Sarah recorded her notes. I told him she put everything onto her laptop. Then he asked me if she'd sent me anything, any disks or printouts, backup copies. I told him no. But the timing was really weird."

Two references to the missing laptop had to be more than coincidence. I asked, "Weird in what way?"

"Well, the week after he questioned me, someone broke into my apartment, ripped it apart and stole my PC."

After Alison had hung up, I lay back in the dark room and went over her information. Too many coincidences. Rooms being trashed. Laptops going missing and then being hunted. It made no sense, not yet.

I had no idea of the time, since my travel alarm had been doused in the toilet. I flicked on the TV and an anchorwoman told me it was six-twelve. I wondered what kind of shifts Alison had to work at the hospital. Almost as bad as being a cop.

I got myself together and planned my day. I had to call Mendez at some point. I wasn't looking forward to that. Even if he only wanted to know where I was, what could I say? He'd put it all together.

I realized that I'd lost track of why I'd come up to Vermont in the first place. I'd focused so much on Sarah's murder that I'd almost forgotten Carl and the .38. I had to say that everything I'd learned so far pointed to Carl being the killer, or at least involved in Sarah's death. Maybe I should just tell everything I knew to Petersen and Mendez, let them make the final connections.

I didn't like giving up. Just like the Project house back in Albany, or getting the scholarship to college. If I hadn't pushed and pushed, I'd never have achieved anything. And I still had two days to gather more information. That would be my cut-off point.

As I took the chair away from under the door and reached for the latch, the phone rang. "Burnett."

"Petersen." The line crackled with static. "Can you get over to Cardford Springs?"

"Well, I haven't had any breakfast and—"

"Let me rephrase that: get your ass out to Cardford. Now."

I gripped the receiver. "What's happened?"

"We just fished a body from Lake Champlain. It's carrying an expired PI license in the name of Harry Braid."

6

Harry lay on the wooden jetty and stared into the blue sky. His mouth hung open and slack, his lips the same pale gray as his face. I knelt beside him and focused on the swelling behind his right ear. When I stood up, the State Trooper drew the white tarpaulin back over Harry.

"A single blow," Petersen said, "but I don't know if that killed him or he drowned."

"How long has he been in the water?"

"What time did you leave him?" Petersen asked instead of answering my question.

"Around nine. And it was the other way around: he set off first."

"Did he say where he was headed?"

I shook my head. We stood on the jetty where Harry's body had been laid out. Birds circled above us and split the air with their cries. The only other people in sight were the Crime Scene Team standing beside their white panel van on the road, and another Trooper writing on a clipboard. To enter Cardford, I'd had to get past one of the Chief's officers parked close to the highway.

I saw a figure move behind the dusty window of Louise's storefront. It could have been Louise or her husband looking out.

"Did anybody see Harry leave you last night?" Petersen asked.

I looked at him. "You think I did this?"

"I don't think anything, not yet."

I tried to remember if anyone had passed us by while we spoke in the Tavern's parking lot. "You'd have to interview the guys in the bar."

"We will."

A long, dark sedan pulled up next to the white van of the Crime Scene Team. A sandy-haired man in slacks and a hunter's jacket got a small leather case out of the trunk and walked down to the jetty. He shook hands with Petersen. "What have you got for me?"

Petersen nodded to the State Trooper, who pulled back the sheet. The Medical Examiner knelt down and started examining the body.

"What did you two talk about?" Petersen asked me.

I looked across the bay to the handful of houses facing us. Nothing moved in their windows. "He wanted to warn me off. He thought he was close to something, some part of Sarah's case that everyone had missed."

"He came out and told you this?"

"Not in so many words. It was more . . . you remember at school, where the kid that always gets picked last for teams suddenly has some luck? Harry looked like that. As if he'd finally got lucky."

Petersen glanced at me, then at Harry. "He wasn't working for Sarah's parents. I checked."

"I don't think he was working for anyone except himself."

"Gary?" The Medical Examiner stepped forward. His latex gloves snapped as he peeled them off. "He's all yours. Dead around ten hours."

"Cause?"

"I'll let you know, but I'd say drowning. I think the blow to the head put him out first."

"Thanks, Chris."

As the ME walked away, the Crime Scene Team approached with their white all-in-one suits and their equipment cases. Petersen called out to the woman in front, "Who got the call?"

"Stanton, I think."

"Great." Petersen spat into the water.

"Who's Stanton?" I asked.

"Detective Stanton is one of the State's finest," Petersen said. "About your age and looking for promotion like a pig digging for nuts. He's all we need."

I watched the Crime Scene Team get what they could from the body. Harry had wanted to drive me away; he hadn't liked the competition. He'd cost me a couple of hundred bucks by snipping my Jeep's wiring. But I didn't want to see him stretched out on that jetty. "Who found him?"

"One of the fishermen, Ralph Simmonds. He was coming back from Missisquoi Bay when he spotted something in the water. He reeled in this guy."

"How come Harry hadn't drifted out?"

Petersen lifted the lower part of the sheet. He pointed with the toe of his boot at Harry's left leg; a thick blue nylon rope had been sliced with a clean cut. "The killer tied him to the jetty on a long line. Simmonds had to cut him loose."

I looked up. Three electric lamps stood along the jetty, about ten feet apart. "Somebody must have seen what happened."

Petersen scratched his neck. "You'd think that, wouldn't you? But I've found that people around here aren't all that observant."

When one of the CST technicians opened Harry's mouth with a probe, I asked Petersen, "Mind if I look around?"

"Don't get lost; we need to talk."

As I left the jetty, I thought I saw movement behind the store's window. I walked past the closed door and headed for the trees around the bay. I stopped where the road ran out. I could taste the lake's water in the air, acrid and cold. The trees behind me whispered in the breeze, the same breeze that made me zip up my jacket and thrust my hands deep into my pockets.

Whoever killed Harry had wanted to make a point. He could have weighted the body down and dumped it. He could have left it to drift. Instead, he'd tethered it to the jetty to make sure someone saw it. But who? I couldn't believe it was just for my benefit.

The ME had estimated ten hours. Harry must have driven straight to Cardford Springs after leaving me. To meet someone? Or to cover something up?

A white shape slid through the undergrowth to my left. Leaves rustled. I watched the old Labrador pee against a trunk. He took his time.

I knelt down and stretched out my hand. "Here, boy."

The dog trotted up as if we'd known each other all our lives. He sniffed my hand and then stared at me, his pink tongue lolling.

I looked around for Petchey. Only the wind moved among the trees. "Where's your master got to, eh?"

The dog blinked at me from milky eyes.

I walked toward the trees, then changed my mind and headed for the nearest houses. The dog stood up and followed, then overtook me. I could see the technicians still kneeling beside Harry on the jetty. Petersen had disappeared. The dog led me past the first few silent houses. He turned left and went down a rutted track between clapboard walls. At the steps of a peeling, blue-painted shack, he stopped and looked back as if to make sure he still had company. Then he climbed the steps.

I knocked at the torn screen door. "Mr. Petchey?"

The inner door stood open a foot or so. I pulled the screen door open and stepped inside. The dog brushed past me. I could see a kitchen at the end of the passageway, and the hard white outlines of stove and fridge. Mud had been tracked across the linoleum floor and left to dry. The dog headed for the kitchen.

"Mr. Petchey?"

A clock ticked somewhere. Stairs led up to a dim landing. Coats had been slung across the bottom stair post. I found the small .32 in the outer coat's pocket. It wasn't loaded.

I didn't close the door behind me. I thought about calling Petersen but I wanted to see if I'd guessed right. I took two steps along the hall passage and listened at the door on my left. I stepped to one side and pushed the door open with my left hand.

Old, dark furniture crowded the room. A chair had been overturned. Some light made it past the dust on the blinds and rested on a shoe pointing to the ceiling. I found Petchey lying on his back behind a heavy horsehair sofa. Blood encrusted his face. He looked like a marionette after someone had cut his strings. But when I felt at his chill neck for a pulse, I found one; weak and out of step, but there.

The Labrador came in and lay beside its owner. It rested its head on its paws and closed its eyes. I peeled off my coat and threw it over Petchey. Then I ran toward the jetty. "Chief!"

Petersen looked up from Harry's body, saw me and started running, holding on to his gun belt. He checked Petchey's body for a pulse and then used his radio to call for paramedics. He looked up at me. "How did you know where to look?"

"I saw the dog by itself and followed it."

"You know who this is?"

"Petchey."

"That's right." Petersen checked out the fallen chair and the disarranged carpet. He didn't touch anything.

His sergeant, a tall, sallow man with acne, walked in. "Jesus, Gary. Another one?"

"Almost, Phil." Petersen turned to me. "The front door was open?"

"By about a foot."

"So you just ambled in?"

"It seemed like a good idea." I waited. If our roles had been swapped, and I was Petersen, I'd be suspicious. "I'd guess those injuries happened not too long before Harry's murder."

Petersen scratched his neck. "You think Harry did this?"

"You know I don't. Whoever killed Harry had something to settle with Petchey here, too."

Petersen reached down and patted the Labrador, then told the sergeant, "Send a car out to Mathers' trailer. If he's there, bring him in."

The sergeant frowned. "And if he isn't?"

"Put a call out for him. And tell them to be careful."

As the sergeant jumped down the steps, flashing blue lights appeared in the window. Van doors opened and slammed. A man and a woman in green coveralls ran in and knelt beside Petchey. The woman spoke to Petersen without looking at him, "Hell, Gary, two in one morning's pretty good going. At least this one's got a chance."

"How's he look?" I asked, leaning over.

The woman pushed me back. "Give us a minute."

As Petersen knelt beside the paramedics, I slid out of the room. The kitchen looked clean, with no overturned furniture, no signs of any struggle. A single white plate, chipped, and a white mug stood upended on the sink's drainboard. A gray enamel coffee pot stood on the stove. From the window, I could see the jetty and the Crime Scene Team carrying Harry's body away in a black plastic bag. They had to stop for a moment and rest.

As far as I could tell, the kitchen door hadn't been forced. Two new bolts had been fitted at the top and bottom of the wooden door. Neither had been opened.

It looked like Petchey had had time to eat and wash his dishes. He hadn't started to get ready for bed; he'd been wearing what looked like the same clothes I'd seen him in the day before. He must have let the dog outside. Then someone had come in and attacked him. Had they wanted to kill him? And had Petchey seen Harry and the murderer on the jetty? There must be a connection, but it might not be that obvious.

I climbed the stairs. The house had two small rooms on the first floor. The front one, facing the road, held bedroom furniture. The room at the rear, facing the lake, looked like a storeroom. I saw boxes and chests, old clothes and fishing poles. An enormous dollhouse filled one corner, its front white, its roof red.

"Burnett?"

I heard heavy steps on the stairs. Petersen filled the doorway. "What the hell are you doing?"

"Wondering why Petchey became a target."

"You touch anything?"

I looked at him.

"Okay, okay." Petersen walked around the storeroom. "Any ideas?"

I didn't have to lie. "Not yet. After seeing me, Harry came back last night for something or someone. I'd guess he was followed."

"You didn't see anyone?"

"I'd tell you if I had."

From out front, the sound of van doors slamming, then tires spinning on gravel. I asked, "Where are they taking him?"

"Why do you care? You don't know him, do you?"

I didn't reply.

"I don't want you going near him; there'll be a man outside his room from now on."

"I don't know what's going on here," I said. "Don't you believe that?"

Instead of answering, Petersen said, "I want you to give a statement in my office."

"No problem. When?"

His radio crackled on his belt. He waved me down the stairs. "Let's say four this afternoon."

The paramedics had left my coat draped over the sofa. Some of Petchey's blood marked the collar. I left the house and then remembered the Labrador. "What about the dog?"

"You can leave him with me." Petersen closed the front door.

I walked back toward the jetty, then stopped. Louise's store was still shut. I had questions I wanted to ask her, but now wasn't the right time. I had the feeling that Petersen was watching every move. I couldn't blame him.

I climbed into Willard's pickup and left Cardford Springs. A dark blue sedan passed me, heading for the settlement. I guessed Detective Stanton would soon be taking charge. I wondered what had happened in the past between Stanton and Petersen. Maybe Fran would know.

I headed back toward Eastham. The trees and fields looked beautiful even in the dull gray light. Sawtooth mountains towered in the distance, indistinct with haze and low cloud. Violent crimes couldn't happen up here. This was a place for vacations, for families gazing at nature and enjoying hard-earned time off. Skiing and sightseeing. Eating too much and relaxing. But people did the same things to each other wherever they lived. They had the same passions, the same failings. Statistically, New York had more crime; pack as many people as that into a small space and it's no surprise. But even Vermont wasn't exempt.

Had Tyrone Cursell ever driven on these roads or visited Cardford? The more I learned, the less likely that seemed.

In Eastham, I drove along Main Street and noticed the empty spaces in front of the police station. I wondered how many officers had gone to collect Mathers. I parked outside the diner and walked up to the *Courier* building. I saw Fran in her office and pushed open the door.

"I was wondering when you'd show up," she said.

"I've been busy. And so has someone else."

I told Fran about Harry's murder and Petchey's injuries. She jotted down notes on a pad. When I'd finished, she stared out of the dusty window. "Poor idiot."

"Who?" I asked. "Harry or Petchey?"

"Both, I guess. Harry wouldn't take no for an answer; he just had to keep sniffing around."

"Any idea what for?"

She looked up at me and made her eyes big. "No. Have you?"

"Not yet." I didn't want to mention the laptop, not until I had more information. "Petersen told me that Mathers worked for the Shaws not so long ago."

"You've been busy," Fran said, without smiling. "Leon worked for a lot of people over the years."

"He ever work for anyone out at Cardford Springs?"

"They work for themselves. Why?"

I thought about Petchey. "I wondered what Mathers could have been doing out there last November. Petchey thought he saw his car there on the night of Sarah's murder. He even told the police. His recollection changed after someone drove into him."

Fran still had the pen in her right hand. She started tapping it against the pad. Her eyes weren't focused on anything I could see. Eventually she said, "I suppose every town has someone like Leon Mathers. Trouble. But useful trouble, to some."

I waited.

"He used to take care of properties in the winter: check the pipes, roofs, shingles, whatever. He'd be in the Tavern most nights, until they barred him for fighting. Hunting out of season, drunk driving, speeding, accidents; Gary must have pulled him over a score of times. Leon has spent time in prison, a year or so. For assault."

"Doesn't sound like the kind of guy you'd want looking after your property."

"Oh, he was clever. Whenever someone from out of town bought a property, he'd turn up and just . . . take over. He set himself up as the only caretaker in town, and nobody argued with him." Fran drew circles on the pad and stared at them. "He can be very forceful. Even charming."

I wondered what kind of relationship Fran had once had with Mathers. I wouldn't have guessed she liked that type, but what I don't know about women could fill a library. But I did know you couldn't legislate for attraction.

I didn't push the point. Instead, I said, "Petersen sent his men to collect Mathers."

Fran looked up. "Why? Harry or Petchey?"

"You'd have to ask Petersen."

As if she intended to do that right then, Fran stood up and collected a camera and hand-held tape recorder. I waited until she'd pulled on her coat before I asked, "Any idea where Harry was staying?"

"I don't think it was in town," she said. "You could ask at the diner."

"Shirley?"

"She knows what's going on before I do." Fran held the door open for me and then locked it behind us. She climbed into her Impala and pulled onto Main Street.

I walked down to the diner and went inside. A few tourists and men in work clothes sat inside. The young waitress stood at a booth, taking an order. I slid onto a stool at the counter and waited for Shirley. The older woman appeared from the kitchen with plates in each hand. "Patti! Eggs over, pancakes!"

Then she turned to me and poured out coffee and water. "Morning. What'll it be?"

"Just the coffee, for now. And maybe some help."

Shirley didn't seem surprised when I told her I was investigating Sarah's murder. "Gary told me."

"Gary? You mean Chief Petersen?"

"That's right. I brought him up when his mom passed on. It's like having your own son but without the pain and the whining husband."

I smiled. "What did he say about me?"

"Oh, nothing I'd repeat." She leaned on the counter. "Now, what were you after?"

I looked around. The nearest customer was four seats away and engrossed in a paperback book. "Did you know Harry Braid? He was looking into Sarah's murder, too."

"The big guy? Sure, I know him."

I told her what had happened to Harry, but left out Petchey.

Shirley shook her head. "It's all changing, up here. One time, the worst piece of news you'd hear was a car in a ditch or someone caught out in a blizzard. What the hell's going on?"

I didn't have an answer for that yet. "Have you any idea where Harry was staying?"

"Sure. He was renting rooms over in North Sheldon." Shirley pointed to a corkboard hanging by the restroom entrance.

I walked over and read some of the notes pinned to the board: three by five index cards, scraps of writing paper, yellow sticky slips. I read about puppies for sale and someone looking for a car-share to St. Albans weekdays. Junk cleared. Garage sale. Rooms for rent.

"Near the bottom," Shirley said. "Anne Calwell."

A typed slip at the bottom advertised B&B accommodation, hot and cold, reasonable rates. I made a note of the address and returned to my coffee.

Shirley returned from the kitchen with another plate, then rested her arms on the counter before me. "Harry liked his food. Sometimes I'd see him two, three times a day. He wasn't one for diets, you know?"

"When was the first time you saw him?"

She chewed her lip. "Last December, I reckon. About a month after the girl's murder over at Cardford. He was talking to everybody, asking if they knew her, what she was like, who she ran with. Seemed even sadder, talking about killing when you're supposed to be getting ready for Christmas."

I guessed that the year's rhythm still meant something to the town: Easter, Thanksgiving, Christmas. In the city, the holidays meant more shopping days or a chance to get drunker for longer. Maybe Sam was right when he called me cynical.

"Did Harry ever talk to you about the case?"

Shirley grinned. "He was a great one for dropping hints. He'd look around the diner, then lean toward you and talk low, almost whisper, as if the walls had ears. But he never came right out and said anything definite. He was just a kid that wanted to impress."

So Shirley had the same impression. In the short time I'd known him, Harry had reminded me of a child. But had he discovered anything solid about Sarah's murder? His words at the Tavern, the night before he died, suggested he had. And someone else must have thought the same.

"Did Harry ever talk about the Shaws?" I asked.

Shirley glanced over at the young waitress and then at me. "First time he was up here, he asked a lot of questions, sure. But you could understand that, right? I mean, the murdered girl used to work for them. It made sense."

We turned as the street door opened and a bunch of men in hunting clothes, camo and orange, walked in. They took up two booths. When Shirley returned, I asked, "What did you make of the Shaws?"

"They keep themselves to themselves." Shirley grabbed mugs and swapped the coffee pots, empty for full. "Look, if you want to know about them, come back when we're quiet and talk to Patti. She gets off at one."

"Patti?"

With the empty jug, Shirley pointed at the waitress. "She used to work for them."

I finished my coffee and dropped a bill.

"You not having anything to eat?" Shirley asked.

"Maybe later. I appreciate your help. Really."

Shirley nodded. "Gary did some checking up; he says you're okay. And I liked Harry."

As I left the diner, I wondered who Petersen had spoken to in New York. And that reminded me that I had to speak to Mendez. I'm not usually a great believer in putting off something that needs to be done. I decided this time could be an exception.

I parked opposite number Thirty-seven Water Street, a second-floor apartment in a line of fading white clapboard houses in North Sheldon. A narrow flight of stairs led up from street level. On the first floor, a small laminated sign gave Anne Calwell's name. I pressed the bell but nobody answered. I rapped on the screen door with the same result, then climbed the stairs.

Someone had kicked open the door to Harry's place. It hadn't been too difficult. Behind the screen, the open inner door had black marks where the guy's boots had hit. The cheap lock hung out of the frame. I could see papers and furniture strewn over the floor.

I listened but heard only the rustle of the trees behind the houses. Then a dog barked nearby.

I walked down the stairs and found a pay phone half a block away. It had no graffiti or surprise offerings from passing dogs, and it worked when I dialed. Still watching Harry's apartment, I asked the operator for the police station in Eastham. A woman's voice answered on the first ring. "Can I help you?"

"Is Chief Petersen in?"

"Not right now. Is this an emergency?"

I hesitated. "Would you tell him that Harry Braid's apartment has been ransacked. Thirty-seven Water Street, North Sheldon. He'll know who I mean."

"Harry Braid . . . North Sheldon . . . and your name, please?"

I took a breath. "Steve Burnett."

"Okay . . . got it. I'll let him know."

I hung up and returned to the apartment. I should wait for Petersen and the Crime Scene Team. This wasn't a coincidence; I guessed the same guy that had trashed the apartment—and probably my hotel room—had a hand in Harry's murder. I should sit here and let the local police do their job. But what if the guy that did it was still inside?

I pushed open the door and stepped inside. The smell of decaying food hit me. The curtains hadn't been opened and it took a minute for my eyes to adjust. I walked around the upturned dark furniture and the stack of newsprint and papers. A copy of the *Courier* faced me. The masthead date was November in the previous year. Layers of lined paper, filled with precise, tiny writing, covered the rag rug. I knelt down and read what I could without touching anything. They seemed to be witness statements. Harry's labored writing made them look like school essays.

I caught a flash of fluorescent yellow book cover. *The Jerk's Guide to Computers* lay face-down, its pages spread like an injured bird. Next to it, a copy of the Lake Champlain ferry timetable. Burlington, VT to Port Kent, NY; Grand Isle, VT to Plattsburgh, NY. Dates, times, fares. None had been underlined or highlighted.

The bureau's drawers had been pulled out and emptied. I looked into the kitchen but didn't enter; the contents of the refrigerator had been emptied onto the floor. Coagulated TV dinners leaked juice onto cooked meat. Milk cartons had been emptied. I couldn't see any reason why.

Same with the bedroom: sheets pulled off the bed, drawers emptied, clothes pulled from the open closet. I stood on tiptoe and looked on the closet's shelves. Dust stared back at me. I checked out the bedside table and found Tylenol and a pack of gum. A small, framed photograph lay on the floor, its glass shattered. It showed a big woman in a swimsuit on a beach. The sun must have been in her eyes; her left hand shielded the upper half of her face but not her smile.

I returned to the main room and stared at the mess. Left to myself, I would have rooted through the papers on the floor. But I had to leave everything untouched for Chief Petersen. And I didn't really expect to find much.

I dropped down the stairs and knocked on Anne Calwell's door again but got no reply. I climbed into Willard's pickup and hesitated, my hand on the ignition key. Petersen wanted to see me at four o'clock. No point in waiting around here. I couldn't see the guy that trashed Harry's apartment returning any time soon. Even if he didn't have what he wanted, he wouldn't risk coming back. That wouldn't make any sense.

I started the engine and looked up at the curtained windows of Harry's apartment. From what I'd found, he hadn't been a very good investigator. He might not even have been honest. But I didn't think he deserved to die like he did. Very few people deserved that.

7

I had just pulled up outside Shirley's Diner when I saw Patti, the waitress, walk out. I leaned over the seat and rolled down the passenger window. "Patti?"

The girl glanced at me, looked away and went to walk on. Then she paused and took a step toward the window. "Hey, you were in this morning. Shirley said you wanted to talk to me."

I opened the passenger door. "Can I give you a lift?"

She checked her wristwatch, then glanced back to the diner. She smiled. "Okay. I guess."

She climbed into the pickup and slammed the door.

"Where to?" I asked.

"Straight on, then head for Enosburg. So, you're a cop? All the way from New York?"

"It's the truth." Her short skirt revealed good legs the color of honey. I concentrated on the road ahead. "Shirley said you worked for the Shaws for a time?"

"That's right. For almost six months."

"When did you leave?"

"December, after that girl got killed."

The signals at the end of Main Street stopped me. "What did you do for them?"

"Oh, cleaning up, mostly. Helping out with the laundry. Easy stuff." Patti wound her dark hair around one finger as she talked. "Isn't this Ross Willard's truck?"

"I'm renting it." I pulled away when the lights changed and looked for signs for Enosburg. I glanced over. "How come you left the Shaws?"

She stared out of the passenger window. "I guess . . . my mom and dad argued a lot before Dad disappeared, so I didn't mind that so much as the bad atmosphere. Some ways, with the Shaws, the arguing was better. At least you knew where you were."

A sign pointed to Enosburg down an avenue of trees. I followed it. "The Shaws argued? What about?"

"Stupid stuff: what to eat for dinner, what to watch on TV, who took the dogs for a walk." Patti crossed her legs and turned to me. "They eased up for a while, like they had a truce or something. Then that girl got killed; I couldn't take the atmosphere anymore. Plus, my boyfriend, Jeff, and my mom both wanted me to quit. So I quit."

The avenue of trees ahead broke up to reveal glimpses of neat fields either side. Red barns stood at the junctions of white fences. One part of me took in the surroundings while another wondered why the Shaws had argued so much. "Did Carl drink?"

"Carl Shaw?" Patti shook her head. "Not a drop while I was there."

That fitted in with his recovery program. Could Sarah have caused the tension in the house? I only had Professor Crosby's word that she wasn't interested in men. Maybe she just wasn't interested in Crosby.

"Did Sarah get on with the Shaws okay?" I asked.

"I guess."

"You're not sure?"

"It's not that, it's just . . ." Patti did that thing with her hair again, winding it around her fingers like a child. "She just sort of faded into the background. You'd be cleaning up or helping out in the kitchen, turn around and there she was. I used to call her the ghost."

Patti realized what she said, and winced. "Sorry."

"It's okay." I wanted to phrase the next question just right. "Do you think there was anything between Sarah and either of the Shaws?"

"Like, sex?"

"Well . . . yes."

Patti thought for a minute. "I don't think so. I never really thought about it before. Like I said, she just wandered around, watching everyone and everything."

That would have been Sarah studying the Shaws, her pet project. Probably studying Patti, too. "Did Carl ever come on to you?"

She stared at me as if I'd just propositioned her myself. "Are you kidding? He's got to be fifty, at least. Gross!"

I smiled. "It happens."

"Not with me it doesn't." Patti grabbed my arm. "Take a left; I live up there."

I left the roadside clapboard houses behind and drove up a narrow lane of poorer houses with peeling porches and cars standing in weeds. Lines of pumpkins, plastic and real, waited on top of steps like suspects waiting to be picked out. I saw a new black pickup outside a neater single-story house. The pickup had Blackford Contracting on the side in yellow.

"Just here, thanks. Jeff must have stopped by."

I parked up and left the engine running. "Can I ask you a couple of final questions?"

Her hand on the door handle, Patti said, "Shoot."

"Did you see much of a guy called Leon Mathers?"

"You mean the Hulk?"

"Sorry?"

"Mathers is short but wide," Patti said. "He works out, I guess. His chest and shoulders look like Schwarzenegger.

But short guys can be mean, you know? Like they got something to prove."

"Did he come out there often?"

She tilted her head to one side. "He lived there. Oh, sure, he started out just doing odd jobs. But then, when someone started stalking Carl, they kept Mathers on as security."

Nobody had mentioned a stalker before. Another piece to try and fit together.

The front door of the house opened. A crew-cut blond guy in jeans and tee shirt watched us from the top step. He folded his muscled arms and stared.

I had plenty more questions to ask. I needed to work out the relationships between Mathers and the Shaws and Sarah. But it would have to wait for tomorrow. "Are you in the diner in the morning?"

"Seven till one, home afternoons, then college," Patti said. "Anything else?"

"Do you know why Mathers left the Shaws?"

"He didn't leave."

"But, I thought—"

"He got fired." Patti stepped down, revealing her legs to the guy on the porch, and to me. He didn't look happy about it. Patti leaned in through the window and said, "I heard that Carl found him with his wife. Maybe he did. See you!"

"Wait!"

Patti, halfway up the path, turned.

"When was it? When did Mathers get fired?"

"End of October: Halloween." She grinned. "Trick or treat."

I found a post office in Enosburg and checked the area

phone directory for an *L. Mathers*. There were two Matherses listed, one *Mrs.* and one *Mr. Mr. Mathers, L.*, lived on Larrabee Road. I asked the clerk, who pointed back the way I'd come and gave me directions. I turned the pickup around and checked the clock. I still had time before meeting Petersen.

As I drove, I thought about what Patti had said. I tried to picture Elaine, Carl, Sarah and Mathers all living together. Had Sarah started observing Mathers? Maybe he hadn't liked that. Maybe the Shaws hadn't been so keen on her watching them, either. I wondered if Sarah had been up front with them about it when she accepted the job. The only way I'd find out would be to ask Elaine or Carl.

I followed the clerk's directions and found a steep, winding lane with deep ruts either side. The pickup skidded a little on the damp surface. I slowed down and looked out for signs of houses. Mailboxes leaned at the entrances to dark driveways. I could make out names on some of them. I slowed right down and hoped nobody enjoyed racing through the back roads.

One mailbox leaned out so far it defied gravity. Somebody, long ago, had written on it in white paint. I read what was left: *Math*. I'd started to turn up the drive when I saw the trunk of a police car jutting out ahead of me. I turned back onto the lane and drove up a hundred yards or so. I could just walk up and try my luck, but I thought Petersen had probably seen enough of me at crime scenes. And he'd want to know why I hadn't waited at Harry's apartment after calling in the burglary.

I looked around. Narrow tracks either side of Larrabee Road twisted away through the trees. From the patches of golden sawdust and the few discarded trunks, I guessed the loggers used them. I hesitated, then pointed Willard's pickup into the nearest track to my left. The track should come out above Mathers' trailer, or near enough. Halfway along the narrow track, I wondered how I'd turn around and get out. Hell, if the loggers did it, I'd find a way.

Trees crowded in and blocked most of the light. I felt the pickup brush the track's grassy central ridge. Either side of the ridge, deep ruts held brown rainwater. But the pickup's wide tires clawed through and over everything.

The track climbed through the forest. Other, even narrower, tracks led off at right angles. I stuck with the low gears and tried to make as little noise as I could. Ahead of me, the track opened up into a wider passing place. Two rusting metal drums stood to one side.

I parked next to the drums and jumped down onto the wet ground. Shadows collected between the tree trunks; I couldn't see more than twenty yards. Below me, the ground dropped away. I hoped Mathers' trailer lay somewhere down there. I started walking.

My shoes slid on the wet leaves and mud. Soon, I had streaks all down my legs and my ass. I wiped my hands on my jeans and listened. Nothing except rustling noises from the forest, and the flapping of wings. I looked back. I could just see the roof of the pickup.

The trees thinned out. I saw more and more trunks cut off at the base. The chainsaws had left neat, golden stumps that reminded me of horror films. I slid down a slope and grabbed the nearest standing tree to stop myself from falling.

The white and blue double-wide trailer lay in a clearing below me. A bent TV aerial and a chimney jutted from its rusting roof. No smoke came from the chimney. A chopping stump stood to one side, next to an old Ford pickup with no wheels or glass. A police car waited in front of the trailer, blocking the drive I'd seen from Larrabee Road. I thought I recognized the sergeant I'd seen at Cardford Springs; he sat in the driver's seat, head back, smoking. I couldn't see anyone else with him.

I sat on a tree stump and waited. The light began to fade, or I imagined it did. Creatures scurried through the forest around me. My ribs and chest ached from the cold and the exercise. The doctors had told me I should take things easy. My body told me they had been right.

After what seemed like hours, but was probably only thirty minutes or so, I saw the sergeant throw his latest cigarette from the window and lean forward. He grabbed the radio from the dashboard, listened, spoke into the mike and then started the car. He did a quick three-point turn in the clearing and headed out toward Larrabee Road. I gave him a few minutes, then skidded down the last few yards to the clearing.

Up close, Mathers' trailer looked worse. Crumbling cinder blocks supported the base. Paint peeled to reveal rusting metal. One of the windows facing the lane had been smashed and replaced with metal mesh and plastic sheeting. The sheeting blew in and out with the draft, like an animal breathing.

I reached out for the door, then drew back. It wasn't a crime scene, far as I knew. But even if I got inside, Petersen wouldn't appreciate me looking around. Still, it did no harm to try . . .

I tried the door. Locked tight. As well as the trailer manufacturer's cheap lock, I counted two mortise lock holes, top and bottom. Mathers hadn't wanted any company.

Then the dog inside the trailer barked and threw itself against the door. I stepped back. Any dog with a bark like that, and enough mass to make the whole trailer shake, was one to avoid. I circled the trailer and found a boat hiding under a seal-gray tarpaulin. I hauled the cover back and saw a brand-new rigid-inflatable on a wheeled trailer. At the rear of the boat, two big outboard motors with Evinrude painted on their sides. The boat looked fast and efficient. I wondered how much time it had spent on Lake Champlain, or near the Canadian border.

I had to admit that I didn't know what I was looking for. Three years before this, I'd been tapping keys and taking calls from irate computer users. How could I expect to turn into some kind of detective overnight? It was crazy. Having chutzpah was okay, but I wondered at what point it became self-delusion.

The light was failing. I looked up from the bottom of the clearing and saw color bleeding from the sky. I scrambled back up the hill toward Willard's pickup. I guessed Mathers wouldn't be back soon. That Canadian border lay pretty damned close to here. And to Cardford Springs.

The forest closed in. I slipped on the dank ground and ended up on my knees more than once. I grabbed branches and hauled myself up the slope. I wanted to get out and back to Eastham but I had to stop and rest. I wrapped my arms around my chest and ribs and gulped deep breaths. Sweat trickled between my shoulder blades. I couldn't see the pickup. I told myself it had to be close by. All I had to do was find the loggers' road. I set out again, climbing the slope.

After ten minutes, I knew I was lost. Shadows had swamped the forest. The road had disappeared. I swallowed and pushed down on the rising panic. I must have taken the wrong direction. Easily done. All I had to do was drop down to the clearing and start again. I'd get my bearings.

I stumbled on the road by accident. God knew what

direction I'd taken. I walked back and saw the rusty metal drums first, then Willard's pickup beside them. I smiled and shook my head. I was glad nobody had seen me flailing around. I climbed into the pickup, fastened my seatbelt and started the engine.

As I turned the key, another engine started up. I had time to look through the window. Then the truck roared from the shadows and slammed into the pickup's tail.

My head snapped back. The seatbelt pulled me into the deep seat. I tasted blood.

The truck reversed, then plowed into the rear of Willard's pickup again. Some part of me knew what he wanted: to push me down the slope. The discarded oil drums had already disappeared into the darkness below.

I struggled to find a gear, any gear. As the truck pulled back for another strike, I floored the gas. My tires spun, spat mud and then bit. Willard's pickup leaped forward and skidded along the loggers' road.

Tree trunks streamed toward me and headlights filled my mirrors. Branches thrashed the windscreen. I heard an engine's howling. I remembered to change gear before my transmission burned out. Willard's pickup slithered all over the road and missed trees by inches. The steering wheel bucked and twisted in my hands.

The truck rammed the back of the pickup, making it jump like a rodeo rider. It hit again and again. I heard only the roar of engines and the crash of metal on metal.

Then, ahead of me, the road disappeared. Two choices: down a sheer drop or up a steep, forested slope. I yanked the wheel hard to the right and chose the slope. Most of the trees had been chopped. I weaved between trunks and hoped the pickup had enough clearance over the stumps. If I stalled or got stuck, I didn't like my chances.

The truck shrank for a moment in my mirrors, then leaped forward. I dropped a gear and aimed for a gap between trunks. I started slipping back. I hit the pursuing truck at an angle. My head slammed into the cabin roof. Bright lights that weren't headlights filled my eyes.

I shook my head and dropped another gear. The pickup clawed mud. I heard myself yelling. I couldn't make out the words.

The slope looked vertical. I wasn't going to make it. The pickup slid back into the truck again. We both started sliding back towards the bottom. I dropped down to my lowest gear, gripped the wheel and hit the gas.

Willard's pickup slewed over the wet ground. The tires spun, then gripped. The pickup roared up the slope like a cork from a bottle. The front wheels crested the slope and chewed air. Then all four tires crashed onto the level ridge. I'd made it.

I looked down the slope. The truck tried again and again; its tires whined and churned mud. It bucked and skidded, but couldn't climb the wet slope.

I leaned from the driver's window and yelled at the truck's driver. I grinned like a madman. I think I gave him the finger.

The first shot took out the side mirror next to my head. The second thudded into the roof. I didn't stick around for the third. I ducked down and aimed the pickup along the ridge. I found a loggers' track, switched on the headlights and raced along it as if the Four Horsemen chased me.

I skidded out onto a road and drove like a man possessed. I wanted to put distance between the truck's driver and me. A lot of distance. Not for the first time, I swore at myself for not having my cell phone. As the signs announced Eastham, I saw my hands, knuckles white, clenched on the wheel. I forced them to relax.

As the adrenaline faded, pain hit me. My back, my chest and ribs, my head. When I wiped my mouth, blood smeared my hand. By the time I pulled up outside Willard's garage, I just wanted to crawl into a bed and sleep. I slumped over the wheel and killed the engine.

Willard walked out of the workshop, wiping his hands on a cloth. He saw the pickup. Very carefully, he folded the oily cloth into quarters and slid it into his pocket. His eyes went to me, then to the back of the pickup. He walked around it like a museum curator checking out a piece of modern art.

He saw the bullet holes and nodded. He leaned on the open window. "You're trouble."

I couldn't argue with that.

"I didn't think it, first time I saw you, but that's the way it is." Willard sighed. "Trouble."

"I'll make it good," I said, surprised at how thin and tired my voice sounded. "I know it looks bad, but . . ."

"Drive her round back where I can take a look."

After parking the pickup, I waited in Willard's office. Whichever way I sat, my body hurt. My hands shook. I could still see the massive truck with its blinding headlights and tinted windows. I hadn't seen anyone in the driver's seat. I couldn't even remember the license plate.

Willard walked in and sat at his cluttered desk. On the wall behind him, a calendar advertising tires showed a tanned girl in a bikini. Willard stared at me. "The frame is out of whack. Exhaust shot. Body's shunted."

I said nothing but started counting dollars.

"What do you do for a living, son?"

It had been a long time since anybody had called me that. "I'm a patrol cop. New York. But I'll make good the damage."

Willard toyed with a small, toothed wheel on his desk, spinning it like a gyroscope. Then he nodded and said, "I'll see what I can do. I'll call the distributor down in Burlington, see if we can get your Jeep's part in any sooner."

I stood up. "Thanks. I appreciate it."

"Don't say that until you've seen the bill."

I left Willard's garage and took my time walking into town. I had to stop a few times and catch my breath. Most of the afternoon light had gone by the time I reached the police station. I glanced over to the warm yellow windows of the diner, then entered the station.

A low wooden counter separated the public area from the private. A young, uniformed woman with short blond hair looked up from a desk. "Can I help you?"

"I'm Steve Burnett. Chief Petersen told me to come in."

The officer walked through to a back office and leaned inside the doorway. Petersen followed her back to the public counter. He lifted a hinged section to let me through. "I thought I said four o'clock?"

"I got distracted," I said, touching my swollen mouth.

He looked at my face. "You can tell us what happened."

"Us?"

But Petersen didn't answer until we walked into his office. A tall, slim man lounged against the wall, his arms folded. His suit hadn't been cheap.

Petersen closed the frosted glass door and said, "Burnett, this is Detective Stanton, State Police. He's come all the way from Waterbury Headquarters just to say hello."

I went to shake hands but Stanton didn't unfold his arms. "We got plenty to talk about. For a start, you can tell us exactly what the hell you're doing up here."

I took a deep breath and told them.

8

"I don't buy it."

I looked up at Stanton from the visitors' chair in Petersen's office. I shifted, trying to get comfortable, and hugged my ribs.

Stanton continued, "I know you were shot at in New York, and you killed the guy."

"It was a . . . member of the public that killed him."

Stanton ignored me and said, "So this Tyrone Cursell died; no great problem there. He won't be missed. The case is practically closed. Why are you here?"

"There was a connection between Cursell and Sarah's murder."

"I know: the .38. But what's your problem? Sarah's killer could have sold the gun on or ditched it. Or Cursell could have been the perp."

I hadn't heard the short form of "perpetrator" since watching old cop shows on TV. I wondered where Stanton had picked it up.

Stanton asked again, "Why are you here?"

I hesitated. I wanted to tell them that Carl had shot Cursell with the same gun that had killed Sarah. The more I discovered about Carl, the more it looked like he was involved, maybe even the actual killer. But I remembered the deli's glass door exploding, and Sam lying on the sidewalk. I couldn't do it. "I thought there was a link. Cursell almost killed me and my partner. That's what made this personal. I had to know."

Stanton glanced at Petersen. The Chief sat back in his chair, his hands resting on his stomach. He looked as if his thoughts were far away. He didn't register Stanton's gaze.

Stanton turned back to me. "And you'd never met anyone connected with Sarah's murder before? Never met Harry Braid or Sarah herself?"

"Nobody," I said. "I met Harry for the first and only time last night."

Stanton nodded. "Just before he died."

I fished around in my pockets but couldn't find the pain-killers. They must have fallen out in Willard's pickup.

Petersen focused on me. "Lost something?"

"Nothing important. Is there any chance of a cup of coffee?"

Stanton snorted.

Petersen opened the office door and called out, "Evie? Would you get us a pot of coffee from Shirley's?"

I asked, "Did you find anything at Mathers' place?"

"No sign of him," Petersen said, returning to his chair. "Neighbors reckon he's up in Canada."

I took a deep breath. "I don't think so."

Stanton and Petersen stayed silent until I'd finished telling them about the truck that had trashed me. Officer Evie came in with a glass jug of coffee and three mugs, then left.

"So, you were spying on Mathers' trailer from the loggers' road?" Stanton said. "Would you say that was normal behavior for an off-duty patrol officer?"

Before I could answer, Petersen asked, "What did the truck look like?"

"Big, powerful, dark body," I said, gulping coffee. "I think it had steel bars over the front grille."

"Most do, around here," Stanton said.

"Make? Model? License?" Petersen asked.

I looked away. "It happened too fast."

Stanton poured himself some coffee and shook his head.

Petersen left the office and closed the door behind him. Stanton looked at me. I concentrated on blanking out the pain in my chest, ribs and neck. The coffee helped.

After a few minutes, Petersen returned. "Phil is checking out the area for a damaged truck. But Mathers knows those woods; he could hide out for weeks, months maybe."

Stanton reached for his cell phone. "I'll get my boys on the roads. You need a good, tight cordon for something like this."

Petersen glanced at me and shrugged. When Stanton had finished his call, I asked, "Did Mathers kill Sarah?"

"Go home," Stanton said, heading for the door. "We don't need amateurs up here."

My hands tightened around my coffee mug. "Since I've been here, my room's been trashed, my car put out of action, a man killed and another almost beaten to death. And I've been shot at. I'm part of Sarah's case now, whether I like it or not."

Stanton stared at me. "You interfere in my investigation, you screw things up for me, and I'll throw you inside and then bounce you all the way back to New York. Personally."

The door slammed shut behind him. I turned to Petersen. "I don't think he likes me."

Petersen reached into his desk, uncorked a bottle and added bourbon to my coffee; the bottle didn't go near his own mug. "Detective Stanton is one focused individual. He doesn't have much time for anyone that can't help him."

"Does he think I have anything to do with all this?"

Petersen shrugged. "It looks like you're the type of guy

that things happen to. You're in all the wrong places: Cardford Springs, Mathers' trailer. And Harry Braid's apartment."

I waited.

"You should have hung around." Petersen leaned forward and rested his heavy arms on the desk. "Why didn't you?"

"Well, I could see that the place had been ransacked—"

"So you went inside?"

"The door was open. I wondered if the guy might still be there. He wasn't."

"But you didn't touch anything, right?"

"Right," I said. "I guessed that the guy that trashed Harry's place wouldn't leave anything useful."

Petersen leaned back in his chair and watched me.

I thought for a moment, then said, "Harry was after something at Cardford Springs. I think he'd been chasing this . . . something for a long time, ever since Sarah's parents first put him on to the case."

Petersen let me talk.

"Harry told me he was coming into serious money." I sipped my drink. "Even more than the reward. Unless he expected to get his hands on a stash of bills or drugs, or something similar, I don't see how the thing he was chasing could be so valuable."

"You know what it is?"

"I think so. It's the laptop, isn't it?"

Petersen nodded. "We never found it in the car. Sarah's professor and roommate said she carried it everywhere, used it all the time. Stanton sent divers down into the lake but they never found it."

"But Harry thought it was still at Cardford . . ." I went over the possibilities in my mind and came up with a name and a face I didn't want to share yet. It was only a suspicion, and I didn't want to make a fool of myself in front of Petersen. No more than I had done already.

"Harry thought you'd get there first," Petersen said. "You scared him into going to Cardford Springs."

"I had no idea. But what's on that laptop? What's so important?"

"I don't know, but someone thinks it's worth killing for." Petersen stood up. "Come on, I'll give you a lift back to your hotel."

I didn't tell Petersen the word that had appeared in my mind: blackmail. Harry thought that laptop contained information he could use against someone. And it looked like that someone had agreed with him.

Petersen dropped me off outside the Mill Hotel. I thanked him and walked inside. Fran stood up from one of the lobby's couches. "I've been looking for you everywhere. What happened to your face?"

We sat while I explained the day's events. Fran took shorthand notes. I told her about Stanton but didn't mention the laptop. If someone at Cardford Springs still had it, I didn't want to warn them off.

"So, you think Leon tried to kill you?" Fran asked.

"Either that or he really wanted to scare me." I smiled. "He did a good job."

Fran looked away.

I hesitated, then asked, "It's none of my business, but . . . you and Mathers . . ."

She nodded. "Couple years back. Only for a few months. We all make mistakes."

When she didn't continue, I stood up and said, "I could really use a bath and about a week's sleep. If there's nothing else—"

"You're invited to dinner."

I smiled. "Thanks, Fran, but maybe some other night."

"Not with me, stupid. With the Shaws."

I showered, changed my clothes and was back downstairs in fifteen minutes. The shower helped. There have been times when I've felt more awake, but you play the hand you've been dealt. I climbed in beside Fran and opened the window a crack. Cold air washed over my face.

Fran explained while she drove. "I went out to Cardford Springs but everyone was imitating clams, as usual. Then I tried the hospital at St. Albans; the State Police moved Petchey to Burlington, which is not a good sign. Anyway, he's out cold and won't be talking to anyone for quite a while."

Her headlights showed a slick, narrow road edged with tall trees. A sign declared this as Route 108.

Fran continued, "I thought about calling up Sarah's parents and asking them what Harry had been up to, but I didn't think they'd know. Then I found Elaine waiting in my office."

I turned in my seat.

"She'd heard about Harry and wanted to know what I'd found. I couldn't tell her much more than you'd told me. So she asked us both to dinner tonight."

"To pick my brains, right?"

Fran grinned. "That's right."

I didn't like this but I knew I had no choice. I knew I'd have to speak to Carl at some point and I was running out of time. I just didn't know how to react when we met again. Play dumb? No, that wouldn't work. Act as if meeting him in his home town was the most natural thing in the world? That would take confidence.

"How well do you know the Shaws?" I asked.

"Him, not so well." Fran concentrated on the road. "He's pretty reclusive these days. There was a time he used to hit the bars in Eastham; we had three, few years back. Now there's only the Tavern. Carl got himself barred from all of them."

This was news to me, but it fitted in with his rehab program. "For what?"

Fran glanced over. "Fighting, mainly. I think he was one of those men that turns into an angry drunk, you know?"

The more I learnt about Carl, the less I liked him. I still owed him, but that debt was being eaten away. "What about Elaine?"

"A good woman," Fran said. "That's what they call her type up here. Does a hell of a lot for charity, especially the children's hospitals in St. Albans and Montgomery. Organizes bake sales, fund-raisers, sponsored runs, that sort of thing."

I remembered Elaine sitting in the bar at the hotel. "I can't imagine her as Lady Bountiful."

Fran looked at me as if weighing me up for the first time. "She helps a lot of people. And she does a lot anonymously; I only know because I run the paper."

We didn't speak for a while. I tried to imagine the relationship between Elaine and Carl: he a reformed, possibly violent drunk, she a hard-working supporter of charities and the local community. I couldn't build a picture. I still didn't know enough about them.

Then Fran said, "I guess Elaine wanted to pay the hospital back."

"For what?"

A moment's hesitation, then, "St. Albans' ER saved her life about a year and a half ago. Close call. I heard she lost so much blood on the drive over, they thought they'd lost her and were calling in DOA. But she pulled through."

Before I could ask for details, yellow windows appeared through the trees. Between brick piers, a massive iron gate illuminated by floodlights.

"Here we go: Maison de Shaw." Fran opened her window and pressed a buzzer on a control pad set at waist height beside the gates. After a moment, the gates swung open on silent runners.

Gravel crunched beneath the tires. The driveway led through tall trees and ended in front of a wide, low house. Brick and clapboard walls. Gray shingle roof. White windows. The whole thing lit by white floodlights set into the front lawn. The sharp light cut over the rooftop and caught wisps of smoke drifting from the chimney.

If I had a couple of million and wanted a bolt hole, I thought, it might look something like this.

The front door opened as Fran drew up. Elaine waited, framed by warm yellow light. She waved and called out, "Come on in."

I let Fran enter the house first. I didn't know what to expect. It reminded me of the first time I'd had to chase a suspect down a dark alley at night; hunched down and alert, I hadn't known where the attack might come from.

"Steve, how are you?" Elaine took my coat. She glanced at the dried red stain on the collar, then said, "Carl will be down in a minute. He wanted to finish a scene before he got ready. He doesn't like to leave something halfway through."

I followed her into a split-level living room. Two leather couches faced each other in front of a banked fire. I sat next to Fran and looked at the paintings on the walls. I knew nothing about art but they went well with the area: landscapes in shades of ocher, gray and blue. A dining table stood to one side, set with crockery, glasses and napkins for four people.

Elaine stood beside a cabinet. "What would you like to drink?"

"White wine, please," Fran said.

Right at that moment, I don't know why, I really wanted a beer. Instead I said, "Wine for me, too, thanks."

Elaine returned with two glasses. She had a drink already on the table between us. She took a sip and smiled at me. "You look like a child about to see the dentist."

"I'm just waiting for the interrogation," I said, returning her smile. "That's why I'm here, right?"

"Partially. But I thought it was about time you said hello to Carl, too. He was pretty surprised to find out you were up here."

Before I could say anything to that, a voice called out from the doorway, "I certainly was."

I set my drink down and got to my feet. For a moment, I didn't recognize Carl; he'd shaved off his beard and looked maybe ten years younger. He smiled as he crossed the room and held out his hand. "It's good to see you, Steve."

I shook his hand. "Carl."

And there we stood, looking at each other and not knowing what the hell to say. Had he killed Sarah? It made sense. But the gun that had murdered her had saved my life. Could the same man be responsible for both?

Elaine saved us. She gave Carl a soda and walked toward the dining table. "I'm sure you have a lot to talk about but it can wait until after dinner. Let's eat."

I don't know who had cooked the food, but Elaine brought it to the table and it tasted good. Clear soup, roast chicken with potatoes, blueberry cheesecake. I'd forgotten how hungry I was. I bent my head down and hardly spoke a word during dinner. I looked up when I heard my name mentioned.

"It's good to see someone enjoying my food," Elaine said, smiling.

I felt my face burn. "Sorry. It's been a long day. I'm not very good company."

Fran said, "I was just talking about Cardford Springs. It seems to be a pretty unhealthy place to live, lately."

I glanced over at Carl. He was moving the food around on his plate and didn't look up. He'd hardly touched his glass of soda.

"I just got here," I said, "but I think you're right. Cardford wouldn't be top of my list of vacation destinations. Although it must be popular with fishermen."

"Why'd you say that?" Elaine asked.

I took a sip of wine. "It's only a small place, right? Twenty-odd houses? But I'd guess there must be fifty or sixty boats in the bay. Maybe more. Fast ones, too."

"You've got to remember how close that Canadian border is," Fran said. "One side Vermont, the other, Quebec. Just a patch of water between."

"Drugs?" I asked.

"People, mainly," Carl said.

We looked at him.

"Some of them probably bring drugs through as well, but people are the latest contraband. Then again, Vermont has a history of people-smuggling; the old Underground Railroad went through here, carrying slaves to safety. Cardford has always been important."

I wondered how Carl knew so much about it. Before I could find out, he said, "Perhaps that's what poor Harry Braid was doing up there: chasing someone who wanted to disappear?"

I saw Fran and Elaine watching me. I asked Carl, "Anyone in particular?"

He gulped his soda. "The guy that killed Sarah, I'd guess. The last time we saw him, Harry hinted to us that he had a lead. Maybe he told you more?"

I felt like an exhibit in a museum as they stared at me. I didn't want to give too much away. "He mentioned he had something important, some new information. But he died before he could share it with anyone."

I pushed my plate away. I'd lost my appetite.

Elaine stood up and reached for the plates. "Would you like to give me a hand clearing up, Fran? Maybe Carl would like to show Steve around his study and have a cigar . . ."

Carl took the hint and led me to the doorway. I looked back and saw Fran watching us. I gave her a small wave behind my back. Carl led me through to a compact room at the back of the house. On a dark wooden desk, two computers and a laser printer. Books lined the walls and stood in leaning piles on every surface.

"It's not usually this messy," Carl said, lifting books from a leather armchair. "When I'm working on a new story I develop tunnel vision. Nothing else matters."

I sat down and saw my reflection in the dark picture window. There was probably a hell of a view during the day. Carl could probably see Canada. Comforting.

He closed the door and reached into his desk. "This is the only place Elaine allows me to smoke."

When he opened the flat box of cigars, the rich tobacco smell flooded out. "Thanks, I don't smoke."

"You don't mind if I . . ."

"Go ahead." I watched him trim the cigar and hold it over a Zippo lighter. The blue-gray smoke went with the study atmosphere, a kind of gentleman's club/library ambiance. It wasn't unpleasant. The smell reminded me of my uncle Frank sitting at the kitchen table with my dad, playing cards and talking fishing.

I waited.

Carl sat in the other armchair, facing the wood fire, and blew smoke to the ceiling. After a couple of minutes, he said, "Just over a year back, someone started stalking me. Phone calls in the night, letters, e-mails, dead animals on the doorstep. It got scary. I wondered what drove someone to . . . persecute me and Elaine. I wondered what I'd done. I began to suspect everyone around me."

"I'm not a stalker," I said.

Carl focused on me. "Then why did you come up here?"

I hesitated. As far as I knew, only two people knew about the .38 used on Sarah and Cursell: me and Carl. If he hadn't made the connection already, he soon would. To play for time, I had to come up with a logical, alternative lie. Or as little of the truth as I could get away with. "There's a connection between Sarah's murder and the robber that you shot."

He leaned forward. "What connection?"

I didn't want to give him everything, not yet. "The detective in charge of Cursell's case linked him to Eastham. I wanted to find out if there was anything to it. Simple as that."

Carl looked into the fire. "Did you tell Mendez what really happened with Cursell?"

"He doesn't have any version except what you told him," I said. Not yet, I told myself.

I knew I might be endangering myself here: if Carl had killed Sarah, the only one who knew the link was me. I'd have to watch my back.

"I got that gun almost a year ago," Carl said. "When the stalker got personal."

"How do you mean?"

"He started threatening me and Elaine. He said . . . he said we'd both end up at the bottom of Lake Champlain. In pieces. He described exactly what he'd do to us, like someone from one of my books. He sounded psychotic."

Again, a link to the lake. "What did the police say?"

Carl glanced at me. "Gary Petersen, the Chief, did what he could. But the letters never came through the mail, and the calls were made from an unregistered cell phone."

To me, that suggested an inside job. Unless Carl had been sending them to himself.

"What about Sarah? Did she have any ideas?"

"Sarah," Carl said, as if the name was an answer complete in itself. He breathed out. "Sarah developed quite an interest in the letters and calls. She took them seriously even before I did."

"Did you ever think that maybe Sarah could be sending the letters?" I asked. "That she might be your stalker?"

Carl smiled as he shook his head. "No, it wasn't Sarah. It crossed my mind; all kinds of crazy ideas crossed my mind back then. But I know it wasn't Sarah. She had other interests."

I didn't want to admit that I'd spoken to Professor Crosby about Sarah and Carl. Or that I knew Sarah's interest was observing Carl and his path to recovery. I waited for Carl to tell me himself, but he didn't volunteer.

"Was there anyone else you suspected?" I asked.

"No, not really. I didn't have any enemies, far as I knew. But I must have upset someone, mustn't I?"

I wanted to ask about Mathers, and about how Carl had got hold of the .38. Before I could ask, he stood up and set his cigar in an ashtray. "How about another drink? I could use some coffee."

I'd left my wine on the dining table. "Sure, thanks."

Carl left me alone in the study. As soon as the door clicked shut, I started looking around. There might be a nanny-cam hidden in the room, but I was happy to take that chance.

The papers on his desk looked like sections of his latest book. Red and blue notes had been scrawled across the text. The bottom right drawer was pulled out slightly, but instead of checking it first I went in sequence. The top two drawers of his desk held yellow adhesive memo notes, pens, general stationery. Two appointment books, unused. A selection of batteries.

The bottom left drawer had maps and guidebooks of the US, Canada and Europe. Passages had been highlighted in fluorescent markers. Map routes picked out in pencil and red pen. Three old copies of *Playboy*, one of which had a short story by Carl.

I found it in the bottom right drawer: the top front page of a stack of newspapers. The *New York Times* photograph had started to fade and the newsprint looked brittle. Most of the text had been ripped off, leaving ragged edges, but I could still read, ". . . two police officers commended for bravery for their part in rescuing a three-year-old girl from a burning crack house on Leicester Street . . ."

The photograph showed two officers in dress uniform accepting framed certificates from the Chief of Police. They looked uncomfortable. I remembered that we had been.

It was me and Sam.

9

I let Fran drive me back to the hotel. I almost offered to take the wheel, but I wanted to think. Fran chatted away in the driver's seat. I didn't hear a word.

When Carl had returned to the study with the drinks, I'd told him I had to leave. He hadn't tried to stop me. On the way out, he'd promised to look me up at the hotel the next day. I'd jumped into Fran's car before I'd had to shake Carl's hand.

"You two have much to talk about?" Fran asked.

"Sorry?"

She shook her head. "You promised to let me know what you found out, remember? So, spill."

What could I tell her? That it looked like Carl had set me up? She'd never have believed me. The *New York Times* photograph made another connection between Carl and New York, between Sarah's murder and Cursell's shooting. Coincidence could only stretch so far. "Carl told me that somebody started stalking him."

"That's right. That was when Leon moved in with them." Fran gave a short laugh. "He called himself their security officer."

"What did he do before that?"

"Odd jobs, gardening, general caretaker stuff," Fran said.

I had a thread running through my mind: the stalking looked like an inside job. Both Mathers and Sarah had been close to the Shaws; Sarah had lived with them. What motive could either of them have had for persecuting the Shaws?

Either the night air or dust made me sneeze. I searched my pockets.

"There's tissues in the glove box," Fran said.

I found the box of tissues mixed in with crumpled papers, wrapped candy and an unopened pair of stockings. I also found a small-caliber automatic. It looked like a .22. I didn't touch it.

Fran glanced over. "For self-defense. You never know what might happen on these country roads."

I couldn't argue with that. As Fran turned into the hotel parking lot, I said, "I realized tonight that there's more than one connection between New York and Sarah."

"How about between Sarah and the Shaws?"

"I think it's all the same thing."

Fran pulled up in front of the lobby and turned to me. Her eyes reflected the green instrument lights. "I'm helping you out because I can smell something going on. There's a big story here, and I want in."

I nodded. "I promised that you'd be the first to know. I haven't forgotten."

"So. What's next?"

It was a good question. "If Willard can get my Jeep going, I'll go and visit Sarah's parents in Burlington. If not, I'll sniff around Eastham and Cardford, see what I can find."

"Keep in touch," Fran said. Then, as I climbed out of her car, she added, "Be careful."

I watched her taillights make for the road and disappear. I had to wonder about the relationship between her and Mathers. Attraction is a strange thing, but my mental image of Mathers didn't fit with Fran at all. I'd have to ask Mathers when I met him.

I'd put off one question I wanted to ask Fran: did she think Mathers could kill someone? Could he have killed Sarah? Perhaps she wouldn't want to answer that one. I guessed she must have already thought of it. In her position, I would have.

I collected my key from the front desk and made for my room. I dragged the phone across the bed and called Marie. I got her answering machine again. She probably had to cover for someone else. They needed more staff. Maybe they needed a fund-raiser or benefactor like Elaine; Fran said she'd done a lot for charity. Particularly children's charities.

I dialed another number, one I knew by heart. Evans, the Precinct sergeant back in New York, answered on the third ring. "Jesus, Burnett, where the hell are you? Mendez is after you."

"I'll call him soon as I can," I said. "Look, can you tell me something? Remember when you first told me and Sam that we'd be having company on one of our patrols?"

"Sure I remember."

"How come you picked us?"

"What do you mean?"

"Why me and Sam? Why us?"

I heard conversation in the background, and the everyday bustle of the basement admin area.

"What does it matter?" Evans asked.

"It matters."

"Well, I was told to pick you."

I took a deep breath. "By who?"

"Press Liaison said Shaw's people wanted you and Sam in particular," Evans said. "They must have heard something good about you, right?"

I pulled a chair up to the window and looked out into

darkness. A handful of lights showed the few houses on the opposite shore of the lake. They looked very small and very far away.

I'd expected Evans's answer but it still bit deep. Why had Carl asked for me and Sam? I don't think I'd ever met him before the day of the shooting. The same went for Sam. That left the photograph: Carl had seen news of the girl's rescue and decided he wanted those particular two guys. He'd wanted it enough to rip out the item from the newspaper and bring it back home with him. Later, he'd called Press Liaison and asked to take a ride with us.

It could be innocent. Maybe he just liked the positive publicity. Maybe he wanted to share in it. Or maybe he'd set us up right from the start.

I thought about calling Mendez. It could wait until tomorrow. I brushed my teeth and climbed between cold sheets. I had time to picture the newspaper's photograph and to wonder what the missing text had said. Then sleep dragged me down.

Marie's call woke me up just after seven. "Hey, sleepy, how's it going?"

"Hi, sweetheart." I sat up in bed and rubbed my eyes. I'd left the bedside lamp burning all night. I could smell hot dust and sweat.

"Sorry I missed you last night," Marie said. "I had to cover for Lim Kee. Flu again."

We chatted for a few minutes about nothing in particular. I enjoyed hearing her voice. I almost forgot about Sarah, Harry, Petchey and the Shaws. Then Marie said, "John told me that Detective Mendez rang again. Is something wrong?"

I had to admit the truth. "I don't know. I'll call him today, I promise."

"You should do. Remember, if you put something off . . ."

"I know, I know," I said, smiling. "Look, maybe you could help me: your place has plenty of people raising money for charity, right?"

"The hospital? Sure. We've got committees for a new scanner, new wards, play areas, family rooms, everything. Why? You volunteering?"

"Maybe. I ran into someone up here who does a lot of charity work, and I wondered why."

Marie's voice cooled. "You don't think people do something for nothing? You think everyone's selfish?"

"No, it's not that. It's . . . what are their motives? Why this charity and not that one?"

Silence for a moment, then, "I guess I've met two types so far: families that have seen their kids saved by the hospital, and families that have lost kids, maybe not even in our hospital. Does that make sense?"

It did. "Thanks. You've helped. As usual."

"Finally, you've realized," Marie said. "So, how are you enjoying your break? Feeling any better?"

"Sure I am." I twisted in the bed to ease the pressure on my back and ribs. "I'll be home soon. I promise."

We said goodbye and I thought about Elaine. I didn't know how her charity work might fit in with the other information. It probably didn't. But I hadn't heard anything about her and Carl actually having children.

I showered and dressed and bundled my laundry for the hotel to clean. I ate greasy waffles and coffee downstairs and used the lobby phone to call Willard. He hoped to get the new parts for my Jeep by lunchtime. I thanked him and hung up.

I had time on my hands. I fished in my pockets for the number of Sarah's parents in Burlington. I tapped in three digits, then stopped. I walked down to the lake in front of the hotel. A beach of smooth gray pebbles bordered the water; they crunched under my feet as I followed the shore.

Should I visit the Westlakes? My gut instinct told me it was selfish. I'd stir up memories that might have only just settled. I remembered Harry, then Petchey lying in his own blood. Since I'd come up to Vermont, I'd screwed up people's lives: Harry, Petchey, even Willard in a smaller way. And for what? To try and make things easier for myself; so I wouldn't have to lie to Mendez. How could I face Sarah's parents and lie?

I sat on a rock and watched small sailboats skimming over the choppy water. Whatever had originally brought me up here had changed forever. I saw too many connections between Carl and New York. I had to follow it through as far as I could, and that meant talking to Sarah's parents. But I wouldn't lie to them.

Back in my hotel room, I called their number, introduced myself and got as far as Sarah's name. A woman's tired voice said, "Thank you, but we're not interested in hiring a detective."

Before she put the phone down, I said, "I'm a police officer, ma'am. Things have changed up here in the past few days."

"What's happened?"

"I'd prefer to tell you face to face," I said. "Could we meet?"

Mrs. Westlake gave me their address and promised to be at home that afternoon. I hung up and collected a handful of car rental company leaflets from the reception desk; if Willard couldn't get my Jeep going, I'd have to improvise. I tried not to think of how much money I'd already gone through.

I knew what I had to do next. I'd put it off for long enough. I went up to my room and found Mendez's card. When I heard his voicemail greeting, I smiled and started to leave a message. Then I heard his voice cut in. "Mendez here."

I took a breath. "It's Steve Burnett."

"Burnett? So you finally got my messages." The background sounds of conversation, laughter and ringing phones disappeared as if Mendez had closed a door. "I heard you're up in Vermont?"

"That's right," I said. "Rest and recuperation. A bit of peace and quiet."

"R and R? Long way to go for that."

I didn't reply.

Mendez said, "I noticed on Carl Shaw's statement that he has a place up in Eastham, as well as the apartment in Hoboken. I don't suppose you've run into him?"

"We had dinner together last night."

"You did? I suppose you talked about the shooting. About Tyrone Cursell."

"Not that much." I wondered how much Mendez knew, or how much he thought I knew. "Carl's still pretty shook up about it."

"I bet," Mendez said. "I called you at home because I wanted to check another weird coincidence."

I waited. I could hear the hotel maids pushing their carts down the corridor.

"I interviewed Cursell's girlfriend," Mendez said. "She shared a one-room pit in Red Hook. And she shared Cursell's liking for crack. But she stayed awake long enough to tell me that Cursell came into money the week before he got shot. And he expected to get more."

"I'm sorry, I don't see any connection."

"It's coming. Cursell still had over two hundred dollars left in his stash. He kept it in a plastic bag that the banks use. A compliments slip had been folded in with the bills. Both the slip and the bag had a bank's name and address on them."

I waited.

"Burnett, that money came from Eastham."

It was dumb; it made no sense. If you were hiring someone to commit a crime for you, to do a job, you didn't leave evidence about where the money came from. No way. Not unless you wanted to be caught.

I thought about the news as I walked into town. Before he hung up, Mendez had told me he would be up in Eastham in two days. He would have come up right away but he had to testify at a murder trial. I hoped he would take his time.

I turned things over. Someone from Eastham had paid Cursell a week before the holdup and shooting at Lazzini's deli. Through stupidity or sloppiness, they'd left a great big clue pointing back home. So far, everything pointed to Carl setting me and Sam up. But why? He had to have a motive, but I couldn't see it, not yet.

Information. I needed more information.

A car horn's beeping made me look up. I saw a dark blue, extended cab pickup pull on to the grass shoulder ahead. The chrome and paintwork gleamed. My hands clenched into fists, then relaxed as I saw Elaine leaning from the driver's window. I walked up and leaned on the sill.

"You looked miles away," Elaine said.

"Just thinking."

"Carl?"

I glanced away. "And other things."

Elaine rested her hand on my arm. "I wanted to thank you for coming over last night. It was getting harder to hide you from Carl. Sometimes, he gets paranoid."

"He seemed okay last night." I wanted to ask Elaine outright about the photograph of me and Sam, but it was tied up with too many other things. Carl's relationship to Sarah, for one. "He told me about the stalker; it sounded pretty scary."

"It was," Elaine said. "Carl started to get really worried—that's why he got the gun."

So Elaine knew about the .38. "Did he buy it around here?"

"I guess so. There are gun stores in St. Albans and Richford. I know he seemed a lot happier after he got hold of it."

I doubted that the .38 had come from a store recently. The ballistics database that Mendez mentioned would have detailed it.

"Can I give you a lift?" Elaine asked. "I'm just running into town."

I could see the roof of Willard's garage through the trees. "Thanks, but I'm almost there. If you're free later, there are a few things I'd like to ask. I could use your help."

Elaine nodded. "I'll be at the hotel bar around seven. Take care, Steve."

I watched Elaine's pickup disappear around the bend. I followed the road and found Willard in his workshop. My Jeep stood on a hydraulic ramp, making the engine bay level with my head. It didn't look like it would be going anywhere for a while.

"The part hasn't come in yet," Willard said. "I'll give the distributor a call and see what I can do."

I left him to it and walked on into town. I had a choice: Shirley's Diner, Petersen's office or Fran. I chose Fran. As I walked up Main Street, I didn't spot Elaine's truck. But I did see Petersen: he walked down the steps of the station, saw me, did a double take and waved me over.

"Where are you headed?"

"Nowhere special," I said. "I'm just waiting for Willard to get my Jeep on the road."

Petersen looked me over. "You got any news for me?"

I shrugged. I thought about Mendez and his promised visit. I could mention it later. "We had dinner at the Shaws' last night."

"We?"

"Me and Fran."

"Fran can always smell news." Petersen hesitated, then said, "Harry's ex-wife is on her way up here to identify him."

That threw me. I hadn't known he was married. Then again, the things I did know about Harry could be written on a stamp.

Petersen continued, "He had her picture and number in his wallet. She didn't sound surprised when I explained what happened."

I knew I was taking a risk, but I asked, "Could I meet her, too?"

Petersen nodded. "I kind of wanted you there. You were the last one to see him alive."

That didn't really make much difference. Maybe Petersen wanted someone else around when Mrs. Braid arrived. I could understand that. I'd seen enough families receiving bad news; sometimes, I'd been the officer telling them about their loved ones. It didn't get any easier.

"When's she due in?" I asked.

"She's coming up on the eight o'clock train tomorrow morning."

That gave me an idea. "Can I ask a favor?"

Petersen narrowed his eyes. "What?"

"Can you give me a lift to the train station?"

Petersen got me to St. Albans in time for the train to New York. After thirty-five minutes, it called in at Burlington. I used one of the concourse pay phones to tell Mrs. Westlake I'd arrived and then found a cab stand outside the station. I gave the driver the Westlakes' address.

"That's a fair way out," the driver said, turning in her seat and looking at me. "You want to do a rate?"

I agreed to a hundred, there and back. As far as I knew, Essex Junction could be just around the corner. You have to trust cab drivers in a strange city. You don't have much choice. Besides, it was probably still cheaper than renting a car.

I sat back and watched fields and trees replace Burlington's suburbs. I wondered if the locals ever got tired of the beautiful countryside. They probably took it for granted, just as Paris faded to a background for Parisians, or New York for me. Even the most impressive scenery turned to wallpaper if you stared at it long enough.

We passed signs for Winooski Park and then Essex Junction. The driver had to pull over and check her map before she stopped in front of a detached brick house set back in its own grounds behind a curving driveway. The trees and shrubs had been trimmed recently. The lawn grass had been cut by someone with a liking for stripes.

"Will you be long?" the cab driver asked.

"About half an hour."

She checked her watch. "I'll be back at four, okay?"

As the cab turned back toward the main road, I saw the front door of the house open up. A tall woman with gray hair stood waiting for me. Middle-aged, maybe fifty or so, she wore a dark gray and blue woolen suit. "Mr. Burnett?"

"Mrs. Westlake." I shook her hand. "Thank you for seeing me."

I followed her through a dark hallway and into a cold front room. The furniture looked old, heavy and expensive. I could smell beeswax polish and stale air. A loud grandfather clock counted the seconds. I wondered where Mr. Westlake might be.

Mrs. Westlake waved me into a chair and sat on the couch. "You said you had news."

I didn't know where to begin. I started with Harry: "You hired a private investigator after . . . after your daughter's murder."

"That's correct. A Mr. Braid."

I nodded. "Harry Braid was murdered two days ago in Cardford Springs."

Mrs. Westlake stared at me. Two spots of color grew in her cheeks. "You believe it was connected with Sarah's death?"

"I don't think there's much doubt."

Mrs. Westlake stood up and walked to the wide rear window. She showed me her back as she gazed out at the rolling lawns and trees behind the house. Strong floodlamps had been switched on and coated the gardens with a cold white light. I thought I could see a tree house in an old oak. At the bottom of the garden, or at least the edge of the lawn, stood a man with a golf club. I saw the top of his swing and the flash of silver as he swung the club down.

"Harry met me in Eastham on the night of his murder," I said. "Then he drove out to Cardford, probably to meet someone. Someone who had information Harry could use."

A pause, then Mrs. Westlake turned and said, "He gave us nothing, Mr. Burnett. Nothing."

I waited.

"When we saw the police investigation going nowhere, we wanted—no, needed—answers. We hired Mr. Braid to help us find them. After four months and five thousand dollars, we knew little more than when we started. The money is unimportant, you understand; we just had to know."

As with all families, they had wanted closure. Harry hadn't been able to provide it. I wondered how hard he'd tried. "How did you find Harry?"

Her smile didn't reach her eyes. "We found him in the phone book. Can you believe that? We didn't have much choice: there aren't that many investigators around here."

I wondered if they'd asked for references or checked with the local police. There wasn't much point; it wouldn't help either of us right now. "You said he worked for you for four months?"

"Perhaps a little over; from mid-December until the start of May."

"What did he tell you, Mrs. Westlake?"

She sat down and curled her hands in her lap. "He said that Sarah had been afraid."

"Of what? Or who?"

"Braid couldn't say, or didn't want to," she said. "He told us that he'd interviewed many of the people in Eastham, and Sarah's friends at the University. She had been due to work for the Shaws until January but she decided to leave early. That made us wonder."

"You think she was afraid of the Shaws?"

"Perhaps. We had expected Mr. Braid either to confirm or deny our suspicions. He did neither."

So Harry had been fishing around the Shaws. "Did Sarah tell you anything? Did she write or phone?"

"Sarah phoned us every week or so." Mrs. Westlake looked at the floor for a moment, then back to me. "In hindsight, Mr. Burnett, we weren't very good parents. Both David and I concentrated on our careers while Sarah was growing up. You'd think a lawyer and a surgeon would know about quality of life, but . . ."

Another flash of silver told me that the golfer was still practicing his swing. I wondered how many balls Mr. Westlake had driven into the distance. How many hours he'd spent down there repeating the same movement until it numbed him.

"She never hinted that she was scared?" I asked.

"No. She told us how beautiful Eastham was, how well her work was going . . . perhaps she wanted to protect us, stop us from worrying."

"Did you know why she went to work for the Shaws?"

Mrs. Westlake nodded. "To study them. Well, Carl Shaw, I suppose. She met him while observing recovering alcoholics and drug addicts. She wanted a good case study to complete her thesis. And she had read his novels, I think."

That tied in with Professor Crosby's comments. I shifted in my chair and asked, "Were you worried that Sarah and Carl might . . . that is . . ."

She smiled. "Sarah preferred the company of women, Mr. Burnett. We were surprised when we first found out, but it wasn't a great problem. To be honest, we rather thought it was a temporary thing, just a phase."

I must have looked skeptical, because Mrs. Westlake blushed and said, "I know, it's a naïve and old-fashioned attitude, but we hoped one day we might have grandchildren."

Just for a moment, there, I thought Mrs. Westlake was going to crack. Her shoulders slumped, her eyes glistened and her face slid. Then she tightened her hands into fists and regained control. She sat up straight on the couch and stared at me.

I tried to remember what Alison, Sarah's roommate, had told me. "Sarah kept all her notes on her laptop, didn't she?"

"I imagine so. It never left her side."

If I was right, then that laptop hadn't moved too far from where Sarah had died. Harry had returned to Cardford on the night of his death with one idea: to get the laptop before I did. "Do you know if she kept backups?"

"I'm sorry?"

"Backup copies of her data, in case anything happened to the laptop. She might have saved her notes to disk or CD."

Mrs. Westlake shook her head. "She sent nothing back here."

Harry had asked Alison the same question and gotten the same answer.

"Can I ask you something?" Mrs. Westlake said, leaning forward.

"Sure."

Her eyes drilled into me. "Do you know who killed Sarah?"

I hesitated. I had some ideas but I didn't want to get her hopes up for nothing. I glanced at the golfer in the garden and said, "I think I know, yes. But I don't know why. I have to work a few things out."

She nodded. "You know that the Shaws put forward a reward?"

"I heard that," I said, although I didn't see how that

would work out if Carl himself was the killer.

"We'd pay out ten times that reward if you find her murderer."

I shook my head. "Even if I could take it, I wouldn't."

"You're sure?"

"I'm sure." I have my own reasons for this one, I thought. "Is there anything you could tell me that might help? Anything."

Mrs. Westlake got up and paced the carpet in front of the empty stone fireplace. "I don't know. Sometimes it seems like it happened so long ago, sometimes only yesterday."

I let Mrs. Westlake think.

"The University isn't so far away, but we saw her only occasionally, every three or four weeks, but—" Mrs. Westlake stopped in front of the fire. "Thanksgiving."

"I'm sorry?"

"Sarah promised to come home for Thanksgiving, but she cancelled three or four days before. I know it's not much, but I remember thinking that she sounded stressed. I even told her to slow down and relax."

"Stressed—overworked?" I asked. "Or stressed—scared?"

Mrs. Westlake nodded. "More scared, I think. It's hard to tell, over the phone, but she sounded nervous. If I remember correctly, she called from a pay phone that time; usually, she just called from the Shaws'."

A car horn beeped outside the house. I stood up. "That'll be my cab."

Mrs. Westlake held out her hand. "I'm afraid I haven't been much use, have I?"

"You've helped a lot," I said. "Really."

She didn't let go of my hand. Instead, she covered it

with both of her own. She stared into my eyes as if trying to hypnotize me. "Mr. Burnett, please find out who killed her."

I nodded and promised that I would. On the way out, I looked through the rear picture window. The floodlamps pushed the early evening back. The golfer had a small wire basket beside him, with only three or four golf balls inside it. I wondered what would happen when the basket was empty. Maybe he'd just start all over again. I didn't want to be around to find out.

10

In the cab on the way back to Burlington, I thought about Mrs. Westlake. I could understand her and her husband wanting answers. Especially if they felt they hadn't been as close to Sarah as they could have been. I remembered my own dad's passing. I'd wanted closure, then. Not to forget, but to move on. You had to move on eventually.

According to Harry, Sarah had been scared. And Mrs. Westlake had the same impression when Sarah cancelled Thanksgiving. From what had happened, it looked like Sarah had good cause. But what had scared her? Top of the list had to be Carl, but Mathers came a close second.

I tried to imagine life for Sarah in that remote house. Since the stalker had appeared, Mathers had moved in. That meant four people living on top of each other, up close and personal. Sarah had wanted to study Carl; I wondered if she'd discovered more than she could handle. The answer to that could be on her laptop.

As the cab entered the outskirts of Burlington, I checked my watch. I had an hour before the train back to St. Albans. I leaned forward and asked the cab driver to drop me off at the University. The receptionist at the Psychology building told me that Professor Crosby was giving a lecture but I could wait if I wanted to.

I sat on the foyer's tired couch and tried not to check my watch every two minutes. I'd just about decided to call it quits and go for my train when I saw Crosby. Dressed for the journey home, and carrying a battered leather briefcase, he made for the exit. He saw me and walked over. "Mr. . . . Burnett, wasn't it?"

"Sorry to ambush you."

Crosby smiled. "What can I do for you?"

I asked him whether Sarah had ever sent in any backup disks or notes.

Crosby pulled me to one side. "You know that I can't discuss Sarah's work with Shaw: it's confidential."

"I understand that, but it was a more general question. I've been told that Sarah used her laptop to record her notes. The laptop was never found, so I wondered if she ever took backups . . ."

Crosby nodded. "I see what you mean. No, she sent nothing back to me. We discussed the situation, of course, and kept in touch."

"So you know what was going on in the Shaws' house?"

He grimaced. "Please. It's like a doctor with her patient."

"But Carl wasn't Sarah's patient."

"We could argue about that," Crosby said.

I could see his point of view but it didn't help me. I said, "What if the State Police or the local Chief asked you for information?"

"If they had a subpoena, then I'd have to comply. Until then . . ."

I nodded. "Thanks for your time. I don't want to hassle you."

As we walked outside, Crosby said, "It's not that I enjoy being obstructive, you understand. I want to see Sarah's killer prosecuted as much as anyone."

I thought about Mrs. Westlake, and her husband driving golf balls into the night.

"Where are you going now?" Crosby asked.

I checked my watch. "I need to get to the station and make the St. Albans train."

He pointed his briefcase toward a car park at the side of the building. "I'll give you a lift."

Thanks to Crosby, I made my train and settled back for the short journey. Without trying, I fell asleep and woke up as we pulled into St. Albans. I'd dreamt about the night me and Sam left Lazzini's and rescued the girl from the crack-house fire. It had seemed so real: the smoke tearing at my throat, the crack of burning wood, the heat. The girl totally silent in my arms, staring up at me with huge, deep eyes. I often wonder what those eyes had seen. Too much already for a little girl.

I'd forgotten about all the publicity at the time, and the *New York Times* photograph. Marie had wanted me to keep a copy, but I'd refused. It hadn't felt right. Now I wondered what the reporter had written about us.

I used a station pay phone and called Sam's number. I heard Donna, his wife, pick up.

"Steve, how are you doing?" Donna asked. "How's the ribs?"

My hand went automatically to my side. "Not too bad, Don. How's Sam?"

"He's getting there. You know he's improving when he starts complaining. I bet the nurses will be glad to get rid of him."

I smiled. "I need to ask a favor."

"Sure."

"Remember when me and Sam got photographed for the *Times*? Did you keep a copy?"

"I framed it," Donna said. "It's on top of the TV, between photos of our Denise's youngest. Why?"

"I need to know what they wrote about us, in the article under the photo."

"Sorry, babe, I cut the rest of the newspaper off." Donna paused, then said, "I might have kept another copy of the paper, though. I can't promise anything, but I could take a look. You want me to call you back?"

I gave Donna the number of the Mill Hotel.

"What are you doing all the way up there?" she asked.

"It's a long story. Say hello to Sam for me."

I couldn't see any cabs outside the station. I ate a sandwich in a greasy diner across the street and called for a ride as I finished my coffee. The driver's radio played some kind of weird, hybrid Cajun music turned down low, all accordions and disjointed drums. It reminded me of the eighties, when that music seemed to be everywhere for about six weeks before disappearing. The darkness beyond the cab's foggy windows looked total and uninterrupted. I started to doze on the back seat.

As the cab pulled up in front of the Mill Hotel's main doors, its beams swept across the car park. I paid the driver and walked over to my Jeep. It stood parked off to one side, clean and shiny. Plastic covered the driver's seat. In the lobby, the desk clerk gave me my room key and a heavy envelope with my name on the front. I found the Jeep's keys and a note from Ross Willard saying the car was running fine now. No bill, though. And no mention of his trashed pickup. I didn't look forward to that final total.

"Steve?"

I turned around and saw Elaine. It took a moment for my brain to slip into gear.

"I said I'd meet you here at seven." She stepped forward. "Remember?"

"I'm sorry, it's been a long day." I slipped the keys into my pocket. I'd forgotten about meeting Elaine on the road into Eastham that morning. It seemed like days before, not hours.

"You look beat; do you want to leave it for tonight?"

"Tonight's fine," I said. I didn't have that much time: Mendez was due up, and I didn't know if Chief Petersen would hold me to the deadline he'd given. "Can I buy you a drink?"

The middle-aged bartender, Bob, wasn't on duty in the Wheelhouse; instead, a young girl in a blue shirt and black bow tie smiled at us and poured out a white wine and a beer. I carried the drinks to a booth and sat opposite Elaine.

She said, "First off, thanks again for coming to dinner last night. Carl doesn't get out much these days. It's not healthy for him, but he's a very stubborn man."

I had plenty of questions to ask her but I didn't want to rush. I sipped my beer and waited.

Elaine ran her finger around the rim of her wine glass, making it hum. "I think that stalker didn't help. For a while, last year, we felt like prisoners in our own home. Carl imagined he could see people watching us from the forest. He was afraid to open the mail or pick up the phone."

"How about you?" I asked. "Were you worried?"

She nodded. "I was. You only have to watch the TV news or read the papers to see what people are capable of. There are plenty of weird characters out there."

I had to agree with that. Sam had told me stories about the call-outs he'd seen over fifteen years. Even in my short time on the force, I'd seen enough to make me realize that "normal" wasn't as common as I'd thought.

"So you hired Mathers as security?"

"Leon was already working for us," Elaine said. "He'd looked after the house and grounds, did odd jobs, fixed anything that went wrong. He seemed capable."

"He could look after himself?"

Elaine thought for a moment. "Put it this way: we

preferred him on our side."

I remembered Patti's description of Mathers: the Hulk. His reputation as a hard man went before him. But I guess that's what the Shaws had wanted.

"It seemed to do the trick," Elaine continued. "The letters gradually stopped, and the phone calls. Mathers patrolled the grounds with a shotgun and put warning notices up. If anyone had been watching, they soon got the message."

That might tie in with one of my suspicions: what if Mathers had been the stalker? It was a possibility but he'd need a hell of a motive. Maybe he'd come on to Elaine? That would be too obvious, but I had to ask. "Did Mathers ever make a play for you?"

Elaine smiled and said, "Leon? I think he was slightly afraid of me, to be honest. When he first started working for us, he'd blush every time I met him."

That didn't answer my question completely, and it didn't tie in with the image in my mind, the image built up by Patti and by my experience as a puck in a game of truck-hockey. "How about Sarah and Mathers? Anything there?"

"Not as far as I know," Elaine said. "But Sarah kept herself to herself. She was always in the background, watching, observing."

I thought I picked up a trace of bitterness there. "You weren't happy about her staying with you?"

"I wasn't consulted." Elaine drained her wine and signaled for another. "You know how she met Carl, don't you?"

I nodded.

"Well, I was the one that pushed him into rehab," Elaine said. "I told him straight: get better or get out. So it was my fault he met Sarah. Oh, there wasn't anything between them, don't think that. All innocent and aboveboard. At least . . ."

She paused and thanked the waitress, then took a sip from the fresh glass. "Sarah studied everything we did, everything we said. She'd got close to Carl during his rehab and used that leverage to work her way deeper into our lives. Can you imagine having someone record and analyze your every word?"

It didn't sound attractive. Privacy is important to everybody. I wondered if Carl had regretted inviting Sarah up to Eastham. I asked Elaine.

She said, "Not at the start. Then the novelty wore off. But Carl doesn't have good . . . people skills, if that's the right way to put it. He keeps things bottled up until he just blows."

"Is that what happened with Sarah?"

Elaine looked away. "They had a few arguments. I don't think Sarah took them as seriously as she should have done. Not until the end."

I leaned forward. "What happened before Thanksgiving?"

"You know about that?"

I waited.

Elaine said, "They had a fight. A big one. Carl wanted Sarah out. He said he was fed up with being under a microscope. She said she'd been honest, that she'd explained exactly what she'd wanted right from the start. It got ugly."

"How ugly?"

Elaine took a drink. "I had to pull them apart. Carl . . . he had his hands around her neck. I knew then she'd finally realized then what she'd got herself into."

It all fitted together. "She packed up and left?"

"Not right then. The next week."

The week they found her at Cardford Springs. "How did Carl take the news of her death?"

"Not good," Elaine said. "He locked himself away for two days. I thought he'd gone back on the whisky but he'd been writing. That's his new addiction, to replace the drugs and alcohol: his writing. That's how he works things out of his system. He's lucky."

I wondered how Elaine could still live in that remote house with a possible murderer. Was she scared, too? Or did she think, like battered and abused wives, that things would get better one day? That their partners wouldn't really hurt them.

"Who was the last to see Sarah?"

Elaine thought for a moment. "Me, I suppose. I drove into Eastham with her and we had a coffee at Shirley's. Sarah set out for Burlington, as far as I knew. I stayed in town; there was a meeting of the Volunteer Fire Department fund-raising committee at the Church Hall. After the meeting, I had dinner and stayed over with Barbara Stevens and her husband; he's Eastham's ex-mayor. I never saw Sarah again."

So Elaine had a solid alibi while Carl had none. It didn't look good for him. But I couldn't ask Elaine if she thought her husband had killed Sarah; Elaine must have asked herself that question many times over the previous year.

"Have you any idea why she went to Cardford Springs?" I asked.

"To meet someone, I suppose."

"She knew nobody there?"

Elaine shook her head. "She'd hardly left our house since she came up to Eastham."

"How about her laptop PC?"

"What about it?" Elaine stared at me.

"Did she have that with her when she left?"

"I presume she did," Elaine said. "We never found it in the house."

I finished my beer and hid a yawn. I'd discovered a lot of new information in the last twenty-four hours. I didn't know how it all fitted together yet, but it was beginning to make a pattern. I needed to sleep on it.

"Long day?" Elaine asked.

"The traveling takes it out of me."

"Traveling?" She tilted her head to one side.

"I visited Sarah's parents outside Burlington. And Sarah's boss, Professor Crosby."

"Really? Were they any help?"

I hesitated, then said, "They backed up what you've told me tonight, and what I'd heard off other people. The Westlakes were disappointed that Harry hadn't been able to find the murderer."

Elaine looked down at the table top. "I can understand that. I'm sorry they've been through all this. I wish it hadn't happened."

I didn't have anything to say to that. "Would you like another drink? Have you eaten yet?"

Elaine looked at me and smiled. "Thanks for the offer, but you look beat. I'll let you relax."

As we stood up, she asked, "When are you going back to New York?"

I thought of Mendez and Petersen. "In another couple of days, I think. It depends."

"Well, take it easy." She stopped in front of the lobby's main doors and rested her hand on my arm. "It's not worth dying for."

Before I could say anything, Elaine slipped through the doors and into the lot. I watched her pickup's lights disappear into the darkness.

I yawned again and rubbed the left side of my chest. I thought of a hot bath and then sliding into bed. It sounded good. Instead of making for the stairs, I found the Jeep's keys in my pocket and grabbed my coat.

Cardford Springs looked deserted in the darkness. Distant house lights, from across the bay, rippled on the lake's surface. I parked next to Ed Petchey's house and climbed out of the Jeep. Apart from the wind pushing the trees' branches around, the only sound came from a distant boat somewhere out in the bay. I listened to the engine's regular heartbeat until it faded.

Either Petersen or the State Police had locked Petchey's house up tight. I didn't expect to find anything in there anyway. The guy that had battered Petchey had ransacked the place. And I doubted that he'd found what he'd been searching for.

As I walked along the shore, my eyes adjusted to the night. I could see pale stones and driftwood at the water's edge. The jetty showed up ahead as a dark, skeletal bridge to nowhere. When I climbed up, I couldn't see where Harry's body had lain. No police tape, no outline. Just the rough wood.

No lights shone in Louise's store. I knocked at the glass. Silence. I knocked again and again. A man's voice called out from behind the door, "We're shut."

"I need to speak to Louise," I said.

A pause, then, "I've got a shotgun up against the door, pal. You want me to use it?"

I stepped to one side, just in case. "If you don't talk to me, you'll be talking to the police in the morning. Or maybe to Leon Mathers."

I waited and listened. After a minute, I heard bolts drawn back. The door opened. I slipped into the dark room and moved away from the door as fast as I could. I crouched, my hands loose in front of my body.

The light blinded me. I saw a pot-bellied man in jeans and checked shirt standing behind the door. He had a baseball bat in both hands. He blinked at me and half-raised the bat.

"Oh, put it down, Derek." Louise stood by the light switch. Her right hand drew the front of her frilled dressing gown together. Curlers pulled her hair tight against her head and made her look old. She looked at me and said, "What do you want now?"

"The laptop."

"We don't know nothing about that." Derek looked between me and his wife.

I ignored him and said, "You found Sarah's body before Petchey did. You took her suitcase, purse and laptop. You let someone else report the murder."

Derek licked his lips. "You can't prove it."

"I'm not interested in the case or purse," I said. "I don't even have to bring them into this. But the laptop is important. If the police find out you've been hiding it . . ."

Louise looked at me, then nodded. "Derek heard the shot from his boat. He'd dropped a cargo off at Swanton—"

"He doesn't need to know that!" Derek said, stepping forward.

Louise ignored him and continued, "He heard the shot and pulled in to shore. Someone must have heard his boat and drove away."

Derek nodded. "I heard his truck, too."

"You're sure it was a truck?" I asked.

"Sure. Big one, V6 or a V8."

"So what did you find?"

Derek looked away. "She was in a mess. Whoever done it, they'd done it real close. I didn't bother checking her pulse nor nothing. I could see."

"So you searched the car?"

"I found her purse on the back seat. The suitcase and computer was in the trunk. I figured, why let them go to waste? We could use the money, maybe get a good price for them. Been a bad year, this one. Don't get as many people up here as we used to."

Did scavenging run in Derek's blood? Maybe most of the people in Cardford had a loose attitude to the law. I would guess that smuggling people or goods across the border paid good money, but Derek and Louise didn't look rich, or even comfortable.

Louise said, "We used to get by with the store. If things were slow, Derek would bring back cigarettes or liquor, machine parts, stuff like that. We never got into anything heavy; no drugs nor people."

I nodded and asked Derek, "So what did you do next?"

He scratched his neck. "Well, I brought her stuff up here and we started going through it. It was mostly clothes, nice ones, expensive. Nothing people up here could use."

"You must think we're evil," Louise said, "going through the poor girl's clothes while she was still warm."

I let that pass. "Think back: when you opened the suitcase, had it been packed neatly?"

Derek said, "No, the things were all thrown in one on top of the other. Messy."

So Sarah had left in a hurry. "Go on."

"Well, I left the store and went back to the car—"

"What for? Afraid you'd missed something?"

"No, it wasn't like that. I'd forgotten the license plate number; I was going to call it in, anonymously. Swear to

God I was. Anyway, I'd started walking back when I saw the car's inside light on, and someone else half in and half out of the door."

"Petchey."

"I didn't know that then, but, sure, it was Ed."

"So you panicked and threw the suitcase and purse into the lake."

Derek looked away. "Two days later. I got scared. I thought maybe the cops or the one that killed her would come looking for her stuff."

I rubbed my eyes. It had been a long day and I didn't enjoy hearing Derek's confession. But I had to go through to the end. "Okay. You dumped her luggage. What did you do with the laptop?"

Derek glanced at Louise, who said, "We hid it. We wouldn't know to use it, not even to turn it on. So . . ."

I stood back as Louise brushed past me. She reached up onto the shelves at the rear of the store. The lower shelves held large bags of flour, rice and sugar. Above them, canned food and boxes of pasta and cereal. Louise removed a section of cereal boxes and reached into the crevice. She brought out a thick square of dark gray plastic about fourteen inches across. As she stepped back, the laptop slipped from her hand.

I leaped forward but Louise had caught the laptop before it shattered on the floor. I let out the breath I'd been holding.

"There you go." Louise held out the laptop. "You're lucky we still have it; we were going to get rid of it tomorrow."

"Why tomorrow?" Then I remembered Harry's body tethered to the jetty. "You saw the warning?"

Derek ran a sleeve over his nose. "We didn't want to end up like that investigator guy."

I carried the laptop to the counter and opened it. I couldn't see any damage. "Where's the power cord?"

Derek stared at me. "The what?"

"There should be a power cord."

"That's all there was."

I reached out for the recessed power switch and then stopped. I guessed if it hadn't been powered up in a while, the battery would be dead. And I didn't want to risk losing anything. "I need a bag for this."

Louise rooted beneath the counter and produced a thick plastic bag from a Canadian supermarket chain. "What are you going to tell the Chief? About us, I mean."

I told her the truth. "I don't know."

"I didn't kill her," Derek said, clutching my arm. "I swear, I found her like that."

I looked him in the eyes. "I believe you. But you should have told the Chief when you had the chance. I can tell him you cooperated by handing this over, but after that . . . I don't know."

"Do what you can," Louise said. "Whatever we got coming, we deserve it."

I slid the laptop under my jacket and left the store. Outside, in complete darkness, I imagined figures hiding behind tree trunks or shrubs, just waiting to jump out. I hurried back to my Jeep, certain I could hear footsteps on the jetty and the rough road. When I climbed into the Jeep, I thrust the laptop under my seat and locked the car doors. Much good that would do against a bullet.

I started the Jeep and left Cardford Springs behind. Paranoia made me drive too fast. I eased my foot off the gas and told myself nobody was following me.

With luck, the notes on the laptop would be able to tell me why Sarah had been so scared. They should at least give me an idea of life in the Shaw house in the months before Sarah died. And I needed an insight into Carl's state of mind.

No lights showed in my mirrors. Nobody forced me off the road. I pulled into the hotel lot and hid the laptop under my jacket. I hurried across the lot and into the lobby. Along with my room key, the desk clerk gave me a folded slip of paper with Donna's name and number on it.

I'd started to turn away when I remembered the power cord for the laptop.

The desk clerk took a look at the back of the laptop and said, "Sure, no problem. Standard size."

She disappeared into the back office for a few minutes and returned with a black plastic cord. I thanked her and made for my room.

I double-locked the flimsy door and set the laptop on the credenza, next to the TV. I hesitated. I held Donna's message in one hand, the power cord in the other. I dropped the cord and walked to the phone. "Donna? Sorry to call so late."

"That's okay, honey. I was just watching TV. Let me get the remote . . ."

I heard the background sound of the TV, blaring music and a scream, suddenly stop. The sound of plastic hitting a table top.

Donna said, "That's better. Now. The photo. Good news."

My hand tightened around the phone.

"I did have a couple of old copies of the *Times*," Donna said. "I put them at the back of the closet, thinking maybe I'd show my sisters when they came around, not to brag, you know? Just to show them what you and Sam have to do every day, what you have to go through, you know . . ."

I resisted the urge to hurry Donna along.

"So I found the article you said you needed. You want me to read it out?"

"Please."

"Okay, here goes." Donna cleared her throat.

> The photograph shows the Commissioner with two police officers commended for bravery for their part in rescuing a three-year-old girl from a burning drugs haunt on Leicester Street. Patrol officers Samuel Hollis and Steven Burnett entered the burning building before Fire Crews arrived and dragged the girl to safety. Officer Hollis explained, "We'd just grabbed a coffee at Lazzini's around one-thirty, like usual, when a guy ran up and told us about the fire. We were just in the right place at the right time, I guess."

"And that's about it, Steve," Donna said. "Just like Sam to put his foot in it and tell them about the deli, right? Steve?"

I let out the breath I'd been holding. "Thanks, Don. You've helped."

"Any time. You keep in touch."

"I will." I set the phone down and stared at the dark window. I hadn't expected that much from the *Times* article. When it first came out, I'd hardly glanced at it. I'm not big on fanfares.

Donna was right: Sam had given a lot of information away. Anyone reading that article would know where we'd be at one-thirty in the morning; he could place us at a certain time and a certain place. Creatures of habit, me and Sam. Most officers were the same. Walking into Lazzini's like ducks into a blind.

That night, Tyrone Cursell hadn't been waiting for just anyone; he'd been waiting for Sam, Carl and me.

11

After I got tired turning over Donna's news, I powered up the laptop. Nothing happened. Maybe Sarah's killer had sabotaged it; maybe Derek and Louise had damaged it. I reached out to check the power cord. Then the screen came to life, cloudy blue. It didn't ask me for any passwords.

I used the small touchpad on the laptop and found lists of directories. I waded through them, looking for a meaningful name. After ten minutes I found Sarah's notes on the Shaws. I pushed a chair in front of the hotel room's door and opened the files.

By three o'clock in the morning I'd read maybe half of the documents. As I stretched in my chair, I caught a glimpse of my face reflected in the mirror above the credenza. The laptop's milky light made me look like a ghost. I left the machine on and threw myself on top of the bed.

Plenty of Sarah's comments didn't mean that much to me. She hadn't used medical or psychiatric terms too often, but she had liked abbreviations. Maybe Professor Crosby could help me decipher them. Then I remembered his professional code, his ethics. He wouldn't be too impressed to see me wading through the Shaws' private lives.

Sarah had been scared. Not at the beginning, when she started working for Carl; her notes from then gave a picture of quiet family life. Carl had returned from rehab in Burlington and immediately settled down to work. Sarah had noted his medication and his progress. For Carl, no great mood swings, no return to the bottle or the pills.

But life had changed. Sarah noted arguments between Elaine and Carl. Some of her notes mentioned adoption, but didn't give any details. Had Carl and Elaine seriously been trying to adopt a child? Why? Sarah mentioned the stalker, and the effect on Carl. She hadn't seen him return to drink or drugs, but she'd listed dates when Carl had disappeared into his study for days at a time. He'd been withdrawn and occasionally aggressive. I wondered what life had been like for Elaine. Not easy.

Sarah had started locking her door at night: she thought someone was going through her belongings. She became convinced that someone had started following her; she stopped taking walks through the Shaws' land and the forests. Mathers' name appeared again and again.

From being the observer, Sarah had become the observed.

Gradually, her notes shifted from focusing on Carl to focusing on the relationship between Carl, Elaine and Mathers. Then I noticed a problem: Sarah had dated all her observations, but there were gaps. I'd have to go through every document, just to be sure, but I could see missing dates here and there. Either Sarah had wiped them from the laptop or I wasn't the first to go through her notes.

But why would someone want to edit her records?

When I woke up, I couldn't remember where I was. I lay on the hotel bed, staring up into darkness. Then I remembered the laptop. I bolted upright, winced and hugged my ribs. The laptop still sat on the credenza but the screen had switched itself off. It flickered to life when I pressed a key.

I opened the room's drapes and stared out. Pre-dawn light made everything gray and flat. A few birds arced down and landed on the lake, black commas against the hard water. Cold air drifted from the window panes and made me shiver.

In the shower, I went over Sarah's notes in my mind. Given enough time, I would have gone through every entry and really taken it apart. But time was one thing I didn't have. Mendez would arrive the next day. Chief Petersen had said he wanted me back in New York as soon as the Jeep was fixed. But he'd told me that before Harry had been murdered. To me, that changed everything.

The hotel cleaners had left my pressed clothes hanging up behind the door. I dressed, then powered down the laptop. I held the machine in my hands and hesitated. I didn't want to leave it in my room and I didn't want to carry it with me all day. Then I remembered the hotel safe. Downstairs, the yawning night clerk promised to lock the laptop away for me. I waited until I'd seen him do just that.

I still had plenty of time before Harry's ex-wife arrived in Eastham. Gary said her train would be in at eight. I wondered how she'd react, whether she'd blame me for his death. I could understand it if she did.

I used the lobby pay phone and left a message on Fran's answering machine. I hadn't forgotten my promise, to give her news as I found it. I should have called Petersen. I decided to tell him in person. Before I set the phone down, I hesitated, ready to tap out Alison's number in Boston. She said she worked weird shifts; I might be lucky and find her at home, or I might wake her up and get her mad at me. I decided to call her at a more respectable hour.

As I drove into Eastham, mist and fog floated in the roadside ditches. The forest stretched away into shadows either side of the road. I wondered where Mathers was right at that moment. Not Canada.

A light shone in the police station but I parked outside the diner. A lone man in coveralls and baseball cap sat in one of the booths, a mug and a newspaper before him. I sat at the counter and smiled at Shirley. I was beginning to feel like a regular.

Shirley tilted her head to one side and examined me. "How are you getting along with the girl's murder?"

"I think I'm getting somewhere."

"Well, don't keep Gary out of it." Shirley poured coffee into a mug and pushed it toward me. "He's about the best Chief we've had, even better than his dad before him. You can trust Gary."

I nodded. I'd already decided as much for myself. "Fran said you pretty much knew everything that happened in Eastham."

"I hear things, sure," Shirley said.

I thought about Sarah's cryptic notes. "Did you hear anything about the Shaws adopting a child?"

Shirley stared at me. "How'd you know about that?"

I didn't answer.

"Way I heard it," Shirley said, leaning close to me over the counter. "Elaine Shaw asked County Social Services to consider them, her and Carl, for a placement last year. Nothing came of it."

"Any idea why?"

"You'd have to ask them."

Sarah had obviously found out about the Shaws' request. From her tone, Sarah had sounded against the idea. She must have had a good reason.

I asked, "Couldn't the Shaws have kids themselves?"

Shirley looked away. "Maybe they could, at one time."

I remembered what Fran had told me about Elaine's visit to hospital. "I heard that Elaine had to go to the ER in St. Albans . . ."

Shirley hesitated, then said, "About eighteen months back. Damn near died that night, I got told. Patti's mom was on duty, said she never saw so much blood from someone that didn't die. Poor woman."

"What happened?" I asked. "Did she fall? Early delivery?"

Shirley crossed the diner and poured coffee into the other customer's mug. When she returned to the counter, she said, "There's lots of reasons someone can lose a child like that. Lots of well-known medical reasons."

"But this wasn't one of them?"

Shirley wiped the counter with a cloth and concentrated on the wet circles it made. Just when I thought she wouldn't answer, she said, "All I know is what Patti's mom said: Elaine looked like she'd gone ten rounds with Sonny Liston. But Elaine told Gary she wouldn't press charges."

I shook my head. Me and Sam had been called out to similar cases plenty of times, to apartments and to hospital emergency rooms. We'd seen women beaten with fists, feet and the nearest household object. Only a small fraction of them wanted to press charges and give a statement. Most of the time, they withdrew the statement a few days or weeks later. But I hadn't seen a woman lose a child before. Maybe Sam had.

"Fran might know more about it," Shirley said. "I just get the gossip."

"You've been a great help to me."

Shirley gave me a brief smile.

"What time does Fran reach her office?"

Shirley glanced at the wall clock behind the counter. "Not for another hour, maybe more."

I could see another light burning in the police station. I knew I should tell Petersen about the laptop, but I wanted to question Fran first. "Could you tell me where Fran lives?"

Armed with Shirley's directions, I drove out of Eastham and headed north, toward the Canadian border. After fifteen minutes, I saw the turning for Lake Carmi State Park. Fran lived on the northern border of the Park. The road changed from asphalt to gravel. I followed it and saw Fran's green sedan parked next to a low clapboard house.

I pulled up next to the sedan and skidded a little on the gravel. As I climbed out of my Jeep, something caught the early morning sunlight. I caught a flash of chrome and looked into the trees behind Fran's house. The truck had been reversed into the woods. I saw chrome roll bars dotted with big spotlights. The front grille and bars were dented. The truck looked like a monster with a broken smile.

I heard a movement behind me. I spun around. I was too late. A squat, wide guy that had to be Mathers fell on me in a whirlwind of fists. I did my best to block the blows but Mathers knew what he was doing. He concentrated on my damaged ribs; each punch sent a starburst of pain exploding through me.

We rolled back through drifts of leaves. I kept my elbows close to my body and used my head, butting Mathers' face. It didn't seem to slow him down. I didn't know how much more I could take.

The gunshot made us freeze. Mathers hesitated, then jumped up and ran for the cab of his truck. I had time to roll out of the way before the truck skidded past. Mathers aimed the truck between my Jeep and the side of the next house. He skidded onto the gravel road and disappeared eastward, taking my side-view mirror with him.

Fran stood on the top step of her back door. Her right hand held the edges of a pink chenille robe together. Her left hand held the small .22 automatic I'd seen in her glove compartment. The barrel pointed to the floor.

When I tried to sit up, Fran ran down the steps and helped me. I leaned against her, sucking in air. Each breath brought a hot knife through my ribs. I couldn't speak. Fran took me up the stairs, one step at a time, and helped me into a kitchen chair. She set the gun on the table between us.

I watched her pour out two glasses of whisky. Half of the liquor ended up on the floor. I left my glass untouched on the table.

Fran sat opposite me. "I'm sorry."

I shook my head and leaned forward with my arms wrapped around my ribs.

"He appeared last night," Fran said. "I didn't know what to do. He swore he had nothing to do with Sarah's death."

"How about Harry?" I asked, my voice sounding like something out of a rusty can. "And Ed Petchey?"

Fran looked at the table top. She laid one hand on top of the other and clenched them until they turned white. "He told me he'd lost his temper with Petchey. It's difficult . . ."

She looked up and continued, "He never used to be like this. I knew him for years before we . . . He could control his temper, control himself. You don't know the type of family life he left behind, the beatings and the arguments. He did well just to survive and keep out of prison."

What could I say to that? I had to wonder how women like Fran got together with men like Mathers. Maybe they thought that they would be the one to change them. Maybe that's what Elaine believed when she trusted in Carl. The men looked different through their eyes.

"What about Harry?" I asked.

"Leon said he didn't kill him."

"Do you believe him?"

"I don't know." Fran stared at me. "I want to, but who else would have done it?"

I didn't answer her. Instead, I asked, "Could I have a glass of water?"

Fran crossed to the sink and let the water run. The kitchen reminded me of my grandmother's: clean, neat, comfortable. Wooden units and everything in its place. The opposite of the chaos in Fran's office.

Fran set the glass in front of me. "Are you going to tell Gary?"

"I don't think we have much choice, do we?"

Fran looked at the phone. "I guess not."

I searched my pockets and found a single remaining painkiller. I washed it down and asked, "When did he start to change?"

"Leon? That's easy." Fran sat down and pulled her robe tight against the cold. "When he went to live with the Shaws."

"He'd worked for them for a while, hadn't he?"

"Sure, but it was different when he lived there. We were still friends, but I saw less and less of him. And he seemed . . . darker, in a way. More unhappy. He got into a few fights at the Tavern. Gary hauled him in a couple of times. He changed for the worse, definitely."

I thought of the Shaw household: Elaine, Carl, Mathers and Sarah. "Who do you blame?"

Fran gave a thin smile. "Blame? What's the point?"

"But something there changed him . . ."

"It was too intense, there." Fran pushed a wisp of hair out of her eyes. "Carl was getting over his addictions, Sarah was studying them and Elaine had her own demons."

"The baby?"

Fran nodded. "I don't know how she survived that.

Mentally and physically. She's a strong woman."

"But you don't like her, do you?"

Fran focused on me. "I admire her, but no, I don't like her."

I remembered dinner at the Shaws'. Fran had been extra polite and friendly toward Elaine. That might be one way of dealing with the situation. Another might be to push your hatred deep down and hide it until you needed it. "You wanted me to find out the truth there, didn't you? You used me."

Fran left the table and poured herself another drink. "I knew something was rotten in that house, but I couldn't find out what."

"And you thought I could?"

"I hoped so." Fran leaned on the table and stared into my eyes. "Tell me the truth: did Leon kill Sarah and Harry?"

I returned her gaze. "I think he was involved in their deaths. I just don't know how deep."

Fran emptied her glass into the sink and looked through the window. "I guess I should call Gary."

I braced my hand on the chair and table and got to my feet. "I'll do it. You go and get ready."

She turned to me. "You're sure?"

I tried to smile. "I'm sure. And thanks for scaring Mathers off."

From the doorway, Fran said, "He wouldn't have hurt you, not really hurt you."

I pretended not to notice the waver in her voice. When I heard a shower running in another room, I called the police station and told Evie a version of what had happened. As Fran returned to the kitchen, dressed and pulling a brush through her hair, a car pulled up outside. Fran opened the back door and let in Petersen.

He looked at my face and clothes and said, "So, Mathers wasn't in Canada."

"Looks that way."

Petersen asked Fran, very quietly, "Did he hurt you?"

"No, Gary. He's not like that. At least . . ."

Petersen glanced at me and shook his head. He leaned against the stove and said, "Fran, I have to haul Mathers in. You know that."

Fran nodded.

"Do you have any idea where he's gone?"

Fran hesitated. She looked at me, then at Petersen. "He still has keys to all the cabins he used to look after. There's a few up by the border, Carllin and around that way."

Petersen used the hand-held radio from his belt to give instructions to his men; I heard him tell the sergeant to collect Mrs. Braid from the train station. When Petersen slid the radio back into its holder, I said, "I've got some news for you both."

Fran and Petersen listened while I told them about the laptop waiting back at the hotel. I didn't mention Louise or Derek. I hadn't promised to keep them out of it, but some part of me held their names back.

"That laptop is State evidence," Petersen said, his face hard and cold. "You should've told me soon as you found it. Stanton, too."

"In the middle of the night?"

"Even then."

I knew he was right. But I would have appreciated some thanks for finding the laptop. Stanton and Petersen could have done the same. Perhaps they were too busy defending their own territories like terriers.

"Where did you find it?" Fran asked.

I said nothing.

"You can tell me, Stanton or a judge," Petersen said. He folded his thick arms. "It's up to you."

"One of the locals found the laptop and stored it away," I said. "They didn't have anything to do with Sarah's murder."

"You know that for a fact, do you?"

I nodded. "Petchey found Sarah a few minutes later."

Petersen glanced at Fran. "And saw Mathers, too."

I shrugged. "Or Mathers' truck, at least."

Fran smiled at me. A brief, fleeting smile of thanks.

"Did you look through her files?" Petersen asked.

"A little," I said. I hated admitting it, but what could I do? "I wanted to make sure I had the right one."

Fran leaned forward. "What did you find?"

"Not much; Sarah started off as an observer but she got scared. She thought someone was following her."

"Who?"

"I didn't find out. But I think some of the notes were missing."

"Sounds like you had more than a little look at the laptop," Petersen said.

"I skimmed through it. Enough to know that there was trouble in the Shaw house."

"From Carl or from Leon?" Fran asked.

"We can argue about that later," Petersen said, heading for the door. "I'll follow you back to the hotel, Burnett. Fran, are you going into the office? I don't want to leave you alone—"

"I'll be fine, Gary." Fran touched the Chief's arm for a moment. "Can you give us a minute?"

Petersen looked between us, then pushed the back door open. "I guess. I'll call Stanton and give him the good news. And don't forget, Burnett: Gillian Braid will be here soon enough. I want you there."

When Petersen left, Fran told me, "I noticed needle marks on Leon's arms. He never used hard drugs before. And the marks were fresh."

I remembered Carl attending rehab in Burlington. Had he gone back to using, too? "What did Mathers say?"

"I didn't ask him," Fran said. "I saw the marks when he was asleep on the couch."

I didn't know where Mathers' habit fitted in, but I knew it was important. "Can you tell me something about the Shaws?"

"I'll try."

"How did Elaine lose the baby?" Shirley had already given me an answer but I wanted to hear Fran's version.

Fran stared at me. "You know, don't you?"

"Why didn't you tell me at the start that Carl beat his wife?" I asked.

"It was just rumor."

"Rumor? Elaine almost died on the way to St. Albans' ER, didn't she?"

Fran nodded. "But she wouldn't press charges. Women don't, most of the time."

Not until it's too late, I thought. "You didn't want me to make up my mind too early? About Carl Shaw?"

"I didn't want you jumping to conclusions," Fran said. "Like I said, something stank in that house."

A car horn sounded from outside. I moved toward the door. "One last thing: why didn't the Shaws adopt? Did Social Services find out about the beatings?"

"I don't know. I suppose I could try to find out."

"Please. I'll call around later."

Fran reached for my hand. "Be careful."

At the side of the house, Petersen leaned out of his patrol car window. One hand rested on the wheel. "What was that all about?"

"Just Fran warning me to be careful," I said. I climbed into my Jeep and spun the car around.

All the way back to the Mill Hotel, I could see Petersen's patrol car in my mirrors. After I'd parked, he walked with me into the lobby and waited while the clerk went to the safe. Petersen slid the laptop into a clear plastic evidence bag. He pulled me to one side and said, "You're making a habit out of getting there before me."

"It's not deliberate."

He stared at me. "Maybe. Maybe not. But I'd appreciate you keeping in touch; if you think you've got something, for Christ's sake call me. Your luck's running out."

I walked with him to the lobby doors and asked, "What about my deadline? You wanted me back in New York . . ."

"Yeah, I guess I did." Petersen looked out across the lake, then back at me. "You know you'll have to stick around for now. Too much has happened, what with Braid and Petchey. And we're not finished with Sarah's murder, either. Not by a long shot. I'll see you in my office at ten."

I watched Petersen climb into his patrol car and drive off. I should have asked if he knew that Mendez would be arriving the next day. My time, like my luck, was running out.

I went up to my room and changed into clean jeans and sweatshirt. I examined my chest and ribs in the mirror; fresh red weals had joined the fading blue-green bruises. My skin looked like it had been tenderized. One last strip of painkillers waited on the bathroom shelf. I slid the strip into my pocket for later.

I called Carl's number. As I listened to the rings, my heart beat a little faster, a little harder. I was just about to hang up when I heard Elaine's voice. "Hi, it's Steve Burnett."

"Is everything all right?"

Instead of answering that, I said, "Could I come over and speak to you and Carl later today? It's important."

"Why . . . yes, of course. Can you tell me what it's about?"

"I'd like to explain in person."

Silence for a moment, then, "We'll be expecting you."

Downstairs, another coffee stopped my eyes from wanting to close. I walked along the shore for a minute to clear my head, then drove into Eastham. Evie, sitting on the police station's front desk, waved me through. Petersen nodded to me from his chair but didn't get up. "Mrs. Braid, this is Steve Burnett."

Gillian Braid sat opposite Petersen. Even sitting down, she looked tall but not heavy; what my mom would have called "big-boned". Her blond hair had been cut into a short bob that didn't suit her. I remembered the smashed photograph I'd seen in Harry's rented apartment; Gillian hadn't changed too much from that smiling girl on the beach.

She looked up at me from green eyes set in a tired, round face. "You saw Harry before he died?"

"The night before."

She stared at me. "But you didn't kill him. Right?"

That threw me. I worked my mouth until something intelligible came out. "I didn't. We got into an argument, but that's all it was. Harry thought I was muscling in on his case. I wasn't, not deliberately."

Gillian nodded and reached into her scuffed leather purse for a disposable plastic lighter and cigarettes. She lit one and crossed her legs to reveal low shoes worn at the heels. I guessed she had been doing about as well as Harry had.

"He was a loser," she said, looking past Petersen and through the window. "But he was a pretty nice guy with it. When he was flush he'd share the wealth, take me out and buy me stuff I didn't need and hadn't asked for. Generous, you know? As if he wanted to make up for lost time, for all the shit we'd been through together. But that didn't happen too often, the past few years. He'd kind of lost his way."

I waited. Petersen relaxed in his chair, still and calm.

Gillian stared at the window as if Harry's life had been written on the glass. "First time we were married, eighty-eight, Harry was a salesman, everything from chainsaws to toys. Then he started up his own company making specialty clothes and collars for dogs. That lasted five minutes. We got back together in ninety-six. He'd got his license by then. He liked the job, liked meeting people and helping them. Always a smile and a handshake. He did okay for a while. Even lost some weight."

Petersen asked, "Do you know why he came up here?"

"Sure: to find out who killed that girl, Sarah Westlake."

"He told you?"

"He kept in touch." Gillian's smile etched fine lines around her mouth and eyes. "He always said we'd get back together when he made it big. He expected to get rich soon. He always did."

I asked, "He thought this was the one? His big chance?"

She nodded. "I guess. He'd call me up every few weeks to tell me he was onto something, to pack and get ready because we'd have to leave in a hurry. And not just over the border to Canada, either. No, it had to be somewhere warm: Acapulco or Guadalajara. Maybe Mexico City. As if! The heat would have killed Harry. Wouldn't have done much for me, either. Poor guy."

I watched Gillian grind her cigarette out in the ashtray

on Petersen's desk, then asked, "Did he tell you what he was on to? Any hints?"

She looked between Petersen and me, then shrugged. "What the hell. You've figured it out for yourself by now. He reckoned he'd found information he could sell, information that someone would pay a lot for. A hell of a lot."

"Blackmail," Petersen said.

"Harry preferred to call it a business deal."

"What about the Westlakes?" I asked. "Didn't he owe them something?"

Two spots of color appeared high in Gillian's cheeks but she didn't reply.

Petersen asked, "Did Harry say who he was trying to blackmail?"

Gillian shook her head.

"No names? Nothing?"

"I guessed it was someone local," she said. "Harry rented himself an apartment up here and asked me to forward his mail. All he got were letters from the repo outfits and bailiffs, credit card companies and the IRS. Some mail."

Petersen leaned forward. "But he never told you who it might be? Who killed Sarah?"

"He never came right out and said; he told me he wanted to protect me. But, one night he was drunk, he let slip that he almost had his hands on some computer. It sounded important."

I exchanged a glance with Petersen.

"Did he tell you about the reward?" I asked Gillian. "The ten thousand dollars?"

"Sure, but he expected a lot more than that. Whoever it was that he pinned down, Harry said they'd have to sell a hell of a lot of books. Does that make sense?"

It did to me. And to Petersen. So Harry had been trying to blackmail Carl. It made a lot of sense. Suddenly, I wanted to hear what Carl had to say about this. "Do you need me?" I asked Petersen.

"I guess not. But don't go far. And remember what I told you: keep in touch. We need to talk about this."

"I know." Before I left, I told Gillian, "I'm sorry about Harry."

She gave me a slow smile. "So am I."

I hesitated, then asked, "Would you have gone away with him if he'd come through?"

She went to speak, then turned away and stared through the window. I closed the office door without a sound as I left.

12

I left Petersen's office and headed for my Jeep. When the fresh air hit me, it knocked me a little dizzy. I leaned against the etched stone sign outside the police station. Exhaustion pulled at my thoughts and made them hazy, difficult to pin down. More than anything, I wanted to lie down and rest. I could still feel Mathers' fists in my ribs. It wasn't far to my hotel; I could go back to my room, hang a sign on the door and sleep for maybe the next twelve hours. That sounded pretty damned good.

Instead, I climbed into the Jeep and set off for the Shaws' house. I went through what I planned to say. Like the Westlakes, I needed closure: I wanted to see the look on Carl's face when I explained about Mathers and Harry, and about Sarah and Cursell. Petersen wouldn't appreciate me going to see his main suspect, but he hadn't warned me against it. And I promised myself that I wouldn't give too much away.

I just needed to prove to myself, one way or another, whether Carl had killed Sarah.

It didn't look good for him. Harry thought he'd found something incriminating on Sarah's laptop, something he could use as leverage against Carl. Then Harry ended up dead. That meant that Carl could be tied to three murders. I didn't want to make it four. Maybe it already was, if you counted the baby that Elaine had lost.

I thought about Gillian, married twice to Harry and still having a connection to him despite their separation. Maybe third time would have been the charm. Harry must have thought so. I couldn't agree with blackmail, not for any reason, but I could understand Harry's logic, his trying to make one last big deal. To make everything all right.

The Shaws' electric gates slid back and I followed the drive up to the house. Sunlight coated the wood and brick. The heat of the sun drew a thin mist from the roof. I parked beside the porch and saw Elaine waiting for me at the open door.

"Thanks for seeing me."

"How could I refuse? You sounded so mysterious." She tried to smile but it didn't work.

I followed her into the living room. "Is Carl around?"

"He's just finishing up in the study. Sit, please. Would you like some coffee?"

"Not right now, thanks." I lowered myself into a chair and ignored the pain in my side. I waited. I didn't want to start without Carl.

Elaine lit a cigarette and blew smoke away from me. "How is the investigation going?"

"Which one? Sarah's or Harry's?"

"Both, I suppose."

"They're moving," I said.

"What does Gary say? Does he think they're linked?"

Before I could answer, a door opened and closed somewhere in the house. Footsteps sounded on the varnished floor. I pushed myself up and stood waiting.

"How are you?" Carl nodded to me but didn't offer to shake hands. He wore faded jeans and a padded plaid shirt. He hadn't shaved that day. He looked like a lost logger. "Elaine said you had some news."

I hesitated. I had to tread carefully. "The laptop has been found."

Carl stepped forward. "Sarah's laptop?"

"Where?" Elaine asked.

"Over in Cardford Springs. Someone found it after Sarah had been murdered. They kept hold of it."

Carl looked at Elaine and then at me. "Why didn't they hand it in to the police?"

"They found the body first, didn't they?" Elaine said. "They found it before Ed Petchey."

I nodded.

"Did they take the luggage and purse, too?" Elaine asked.

"They did, yes."

"And then they threw her suitcase and purse in the lake. Wonderful." Carl shook his head. "Has Gary taken them in?"

"He doesn't know who they are."

Carl stared at me. "But, you said—"

"I sort of promised to keep them out of it," I said, although the promise had been mainly to myself. "Otherwise that laptop would have disappeared. I'm surprised they kept hold of it for so long."

"The reward," Carl said. "They wanted to hold out for the ten thousand."

Elaine crossed to the wall cabinet and poured herself a drink. She turned to me with a glass in her hand. "You obviously negotiated with them. Did they see anything or anybody before Sarah's murder?"

"Not that they told me. I think Petchey was the main witness."

Elaine swallowed half of her drink. I looked at Carl; if he'd noticed his wife drinking, he didn't show it. He folded his arms and stared out of the window, south, back toward Eastham. For a married couple, Elaine and Carl orbited each other like acquaintances; not quite strangers, but not too far from that.

I wondered what life had been like here before Sarah had arrived, before Carl had gone in for rehab. Two damaged people, one recovering from losing her baby, the other suffering from long-term addiction and taking it out on her. And then it had gotten worse: the stalker had started. Phone calls in the night. Abusive letters and threats.

These two had done well to survive at all. They must have reached some sort of compromise, but it appeared to be working. Had Sarah and Mathers disturbed the balance?

I moved toward Carl. "There's more: Harry Braid's wife arrived this morning."

If that meant anything to Carl, he didn't show it.

"She thinks Harry was trying to blackmail someone," I said. "Harry thought the laptop contained evidence. He was killed trying to buy it."

Carl tilted his head to one side. "What evidence?"

"The only information I found on it were Sarah's notes about you."

Carl blushed. "You think Braid was blackmailing me?"

I didn't reply.

"So that means you think I had something to do with Sarah's murder," Carl said. "Is that our illustrious Chief's opinion, too?"

"Calm down, Carl," Elaine said.

Carl took a step toward her. "Calm down? They're accusing me of murder and you tell me to calm down."

I stood between Carl and Elaine. Even with my bruises and cracked ribs, I could drop Carl. He stared at me, wide eyed, his hands loose at his sides.

"Steve's trying to help us," Elaine said. "Aren't you?"

Carl looked between us, then shook his head and walked

to the window. "I thought this was all over."

"It will be, soon enough," I said. "The police are going over the laptop. If there's anything on there, they'll link it with the rest of the evidence."

"I've nothing to hide," Carl said, without turning. "I had nothing to do with Sarah's murder. Nothing."

I glanced at Elaine, who stood like a statue, the glass clutched in both hands. I asked, "Did Harry ever try to blackmail you?"

"No," Carl said. "We co-operated with him because we wanted to help the Westlakes. For Christ's sake! We even offered a reward!"

"It's true," Elaine said. "We really did want to help."

I rubbed at my eyes. This hadn't gone the way I'd expected. I began to realize that I shouldn't have come.

Carl turned to me. "Okay. In hindsight, maybe some of Braid's comments could have been hints at blackmail. But at the time they meant nothing."

"What did he say?"

Carl shrugged. "Just that he was making progress at Cardford; generalities, nothing specific. It meant little to me."

I wondered how much to reveal. "Did Sarah leave any disks here when she left?"

"What, floppy disks? No. Why?"

My mouth let the words out before I could stop it. "I think that some of her laptop notes are missing. The dates don't make sense. If she made backup copies—and I'm pretty sure she did—then they should have the full story."

Elaine touched my arm. "Have you tried anyone else?"

"Her family and her old roommate; nothing so far, but I'm going to ask them again."

"I don't know what you expect to find," Carl said. "She

wrote about my recovery, and just my recovery. Those were the terms of the deal. She swore she wouldn't deviate from them."

I went to contradict him, then asked, "Why was Sarah scared?"

Elaine looked away.

Carl said, "Scared?"

"It runs through her notes: she thought someone was following her, going through her stuff. She finished her job early; she was due to work for you until January, wasn't she?"

Carl stared at me. "She had nothing to be scared of. Not from me."

I saw Elaine start to speak, then freeze. I'd have to talk to her separately, away from Carl. I knew I should leave the house; I'd said too much already. But it was like giving up in the middle of a race: I was in the zone and I just couldn't stop pushing.

"Why don't you go ask Mathers?" Carl said, stepping toward me. "Run up to Canada and ask him what he got up to with Sarah."

"He's not in Canada," I said. I told them about the attack out at Fran's house.

Carl licked his lips. "He's around here?"

"He could be. Petersen is checking all the cabins Mathers has keys for."

"Did he hurt you?" Elaine asked.

"A few more bruises to add to my collection," I said, then turned to Carl. "Did you know that Mathers was using drugs?"

"Here? No. No, I didn't."

"How can you be sure?" Elaine asked.

"Fran saw needle tracks up his arms."

"It wouldn't surprise me," Carl said. "And it might explain a lot."

"You think Mathers killed Sarah?"

He stuck out his chin. "It was his truck someone spotted out there that night, wasn't it?"

"He claimed he wasn't driving it."

"He would, wouldn't he? And look what happened to the one and only witness, Petchey."

Carl had a point. Mathers could have killed Sarah and rigged an alibi. But everything pointed toward Carl being the murderer. All I needed was a motive. "You say you got on well with Sarah? No arguments? No rows?"

Carl looked down and said, "I don't think I want to answer any of your questions. I'm pretty damned sure I don't have to."

"That's true, but Petersen will come around looking for the same answers."

Carl stared at me with small, hard eyes. "Unless he's got proof, I'll tell him the same as I'm going to tell you: get the hell out of my house."

I nodded to Elaine and made for the door. She followed me; as she opened the door, she leaned close and whispered, "I'll talk to you later."

"Be careful."

She gave me a brief smile. "I always am."

I turned the Jeep around and headed back to Eastham. I hadn't found closure after my interview with Carl. In fact, I'd blown it. He'd got more from me than I had from him. At least we knew where we stood. But I'd have to watch my back from now on in.

Did I really think Carl had killed Sarah? It looked that way. The gun, the blackmail, the notes on the laptop: all circumstantial but all pointing to Carl. But why? What had been his motive? Had Sarah discovered that Carl used to beat Elaine? Perhaps she'd found out about the baby.

Would Carl kill her for that? Maybe so, if he was drunk enough and afraid she'd broadcast the information outside Eastham; Carl had a lot of fans out there, and I doubted they'd welcome the news. Sarah could have brought him a lot of unwanted attention.

I had plenty of questions for Elaine. I just hoped she'd be okay, alone with Carl. She must know how to handle him by now; she'd had enough practice.

Every answer that Carl had given me had to be treated as suspect. I had to filter everything through the prism of accumulated facts. For instance, Elaine had told me Sarah and Carl had a violent argument before Thanksgiving; Carl said they never argued. Carl said Sarah hadn't been scared; Sarah's laptop notes said the opposite.

But Carl had seemed sincere. If he was acting, he was doing a good job.

I used a pay phone on Eastham's Main Street and called Alison's number. She picked up on the fourth ring. "Mr. Burnett? Of course I remember you."

"Is this a bad time?"

She yawned. "Not too bad. I just got off my shift. What can I do for you?"

"I'll keep it quick: did Sarah ever send you any disks?"

"You know she didn't." Alison's voice had a sharp edge. "I already told you that."

"I know, but this is really important. I wouldn't pester you if it wasn't. I wonder if she could have sent it to an old address or to—"

"I have moved around a few times, this past year," Alison said. "My mail was forwarded, but I guess I could check . . . it's that important?"

"Yes, it really is."

Alison took the number of my hotel again and promised

to get back to me. I stepped out of the phone booth and looked up and down the street. There were no patrol cars outside the police station. I guessed that Petersen would probably be taking Gillian Braid to her train. The local officers would be searching the remote cottages and holiday homes for Mathers. Instinct or cynicism told me that they wouldn't find him.

Thoughts of Mathers brought me to Fran. I walked up to the *Courier* office. I found her talking over the counter to a young couple in jeans and padded ski jackets. I waited, listening to the couple trying to decide the wording of a wedding announcement. When they left, hand in hand, I smiled at them; the boy scowled and pushed his future bride out ahead of him.

"How are you feeling?" Fran asked, raising the hinged counter to let me through.

"Like I've been through a washing machine on full spin."

She looked away. "I'm sorry."

"It's not your fault. It just goes with the territory."

"Even so." Fran sat on the edge of a desk. "You wanted me to find out why the Shaws didn't adopt. Well, I called a friend of a friend, or a contact of a contact, and eventually talked to someone who works for County Social Services. They couldn't give me everything, but she said the department denied the request after the intervention of a medical professional. That's how she phrased it; I guess she was reading from the screen."

"Did she say what kind of medical professional?"

"I just assumed it was a doctor. Did you have anyone in mind?"

I wondered if Sarah could have been called a medical professional. If anybody knew of a good reason why they shouldn't adopt, it would have been her. But would she tip off Social Services? "Was the tip-off anonymous?"

Fran shook her head. "Everything's on their system, including the doc's name, but they wouldn't tell me. I'm kind of glad, in a way. I wouldn't like to think they'd give out too much information to just anybody. Even if it's me."

Could it have been Sarah? Maybe Petersen could find out. He'd carry some clout with the County, but I wasn't sure if it would be enough. I didn't feel like asking Detective Stanton.

Fran continued, "They didn't know about Elaine losing the baby when she arrived in St. Albans' ER."

"Shouldn't they?"

"Maybe not, if Elaine never pressed charges," Fran said.

I wondered if one of the doctors or nurses from the ER could have tipped off the Social Services. I didn't think it was likely. That would be the sort of stunt that could lose them their jobs. But they might be tempted; I would be, in their shoes.

"So, how about you?" Fran asked. "Did you give Gary the laptop?"

I told her everything that had happened that morning, from Petersen collecting the laptop to Gillian Braid and then my interview with the Shaws.

"Did you think that was a good idea?" Fran asked.

"Going up against Carl? I did, at the time. Now, I'm not so sure. But I needed to see how he reacted, and I'm running out of time."

Fran stared at me, her head tilted to one side.

For a moment, I thought about telling her the truth, and about the arrival of Detective Mendez. Instead, I asked, "How did Carl get hold of his drugs?"

"Sorry?"

"When he was still using; who supplied him? Who was his pusher?"

Fran thought for a moment. "There can't be that many opportunities up here."

"Exactly."

"Don't get the wrong idea," Fran said. "This is no paradise. We still have the same problems: murders, violence, sex crimes and drugs. Everything that the cities have. There's just a lot more daylight between our statistics. They stand out more."

I had to agree with her. Pack a few million people into any one city and, statistically, you'll get every type of crime you can imagine. Certain times of the year, the patterns will change: more random violence and murders in the hot summers, more robberies and muggings in the dark winters. Sam had his own theory, based on the laziness of criminals. Like rivers, they took the path of least resistance, the easiest route.

"What about Mathers?" I asked. "Would he know people?"

Red blazed in Fran's cheeks. "You're just like Gary and the others; you've already made up your mind about Leon, haven't you?"

"Look, Fran, I—"

"Just because he doesn't fit in with everybody else. Just because he's been in trouble a few times, you think he's the one to blame. Why bother with anyone else, right? Just blame Leon!"

Maybe she was right. Maybe I had jumped to conclusions. But it was a reasonable conclusion to aim at. After all, Fran's ex-boyfriend had worked me over and possibly tried to kill me with his truck. Still, I took a deep breath and said, "Fran, I'm not sure that Mathers is the killer. But I do think he's mixed up with this, and in deep."

Fran closed her eyes and leaned her head back.

I continued, "I have to wonder how Carl got hold of his supply, that's all. It's possible that Mathers knew someone; it's more likely than Elaine or Carl having a connection, isn't it?"

"I suppose so." Fran let out a breath and opened her eyes. "I suppose so. But I think you're heading in the wrong direction. Remember, Carl was an addict well before Leon showed up. So Carl must have organized his supply already."

I nodded. "You're right."

"The gun is something else, though."

I waited.

"It's not registered," Fran said. "I found out from Gary: Carl doesn't have a permit."

"You think Mathers helped him get it?"

"I don't know. But it's possible. Leon picked up some weird friends, acquaintances, whatever you want to call them. Maybe one of them . . ."

It made sense. Fran reminded me of the mother of a suspect me and Sam had questioned: the woman swore her thirteen-year-old son couldn't have broken into the store, it didn't matter that two people had recognized him, it couldn't have been him, no way. Then when the boy arrived home, the mother had tried to beat the crap out of him. We'd had to pull her off him.

So Fran wouldn't be the first, or the last, to be able to hold two different images of someone she loved.

"Has Mathers tried to call you since . . ."

Fran shook her head. "If he did, I'd tell him to give himself up to Gary. It's his best chance."

"I know. I hope he does, too." I made for the counter. "I'll keep in touch."

"Steve."

I turned, with my hand resting on the glass door.

Fran twisted her hands. "If you do find something . . . if it is Leon . . . tell me. Okay?"

I promised that I would. I left the *Courier* office and headed back to my Jeep. I could see someone leaning back against the hood. Even from a distance, I recognized Petersen. Arms crossed, feet planted on the sidewalk, he waited for me.

"Chief. Everything okay?"

Petersen stared at me. "I've just been up to the Shaw place."

I waited. I ignored the glances of the people passing us by, the locals and a few tourists.

"I dropped Mrs. Braid off at St. Albans," Petersen said, "and drove up to speak to Carl, who sounded a little worse for the bottle. Only Carl won't tell me anything; he won't see anyone. He mentioned your name. He didn't much like it."

I cleared my throat. "Chief, I—"

"What did I ask you? To keep in touch, I said. We needed to talk about the case. So what do you do? You race up to the Shaws and tip them off."

I looked away.

"What's the matter, son? You trying to screw this case up?"

I breathed out slowly. "I needed to see Carl's reaction to the news."

"What news?"

"That the laptop had been found," I said. "And that Gillian confirmed that Harry was trying to blackmail someone."

Petersen dropped his hands to his side and stood up. By instinct, I let my hands go loose, ready to block. My heart accelerated.

"You just out and told them all that?" Petersen said. "What the hell were you thinking?"

"I didn't mean to give that much away . . ." I rubbed my eyes and wished I hadn't taken so many painkillers. It was getting harder to string two thoughts together. But I couldn't blame them alone for my mistake. "I'm sorry I went up there without telling you. I needed to see how he'd take it. It seemed to make sense to me right then, but he got more out of me than I got out of him."

Petersen shook his head. "You got a lot to learn, son. One hell of a lot."

Before I could reply, the radio at Petersen's belt crackled. He hesitated, then tore it from its holder and turned away. "Petersen. Go ahead. Where? I'm on my way."

"What is it?" I asked, struggling to keep up as Petersen headed for his car.

"Phil's found Mathers' truck."

"Can I come with you?"

Petersen jabbed a hard finger in my chest. "You are staying right here. We need to talk. And this time I want the truth. Not just pieces of it; I want the whole thing. You owe me."

I looked into Petersen's eyes. "Okay. The whole truth and nothing but."

I watched Petersen's car roar up Main Street and turn north. I could go back to the hotel and sleep; I could go tell Fran that Mathers had probably been sighted; I could try to contact Elaine, who had promised to come see me. I had plenty of choices. But I'd told Petersen I'd wait around for him. And the booths in the diner looked warm and comfortable.

I found Patti, Shirley's waitress, behind the diner's counter. I ordered coffee and a piece of pie I didn't really want, then sat in a booth facing the street. I watched the few pedestrians. Everyone wore heavy, padded clothes, hats and gloves. The sky had a flat gray sheen and looked low enough to touch. It sucked all color from the storefronts and passing cars.

"Coffee, apple pie, there you go." Patti slid the plate and mug onto the table and asked, "How are you doing? Find that girl's killer yet?"

I shook my head. "Where's Shirley?"

"Lying down for a few minutes. Her apartment's out back, so she's kind of sleeping over the store."

"Is she all right?"

"Shirley? She'll bury us all," Patti said, smiling. "Says she needs her beauty sleep, though."

I looked around. Only three other customers. One guy reading a book, two talking over their bowls of chili. I waved Patti into the opposite bench seat of the booth and said, "I need to ask you something."

She hesitated, then slid her pad into her apron pocket and sat down. "Shoot."

I leaned forward. "You worked for the Shaws for six months, right?"

"Just on, sure."

"Did they get many visitors?"

Patti shook her head. "Hardly any. Mrs. Shaw would go out a lot, especially if they were arguing all the time, but he just stayed in his office, writing."

"You say hardly any; what about the few that did?"

Patti shrugged. "Deliveries, mostly. Food and booze, office supplies, that kind of thing."

I waited while Patti got up to refill one of the other customers' cups. When she sat down again, I asked, "Did you ever see Carl hit his wife?"

Patti looked away. “Mom says I shouldn’t gossip.”

“It’s important,” I said. “And I don’t think it’s gossip.”

“Well . . . I saw bruises on Mrs. Shaw’s arms one time, and another time I had to clear up a load of broken crockery that they’d hurled around the living room. I didn’t see Mrs. Shaw for a few days after that, so maybe . . .”

I nodded. The debt that I owed Carl had been almost eaten away.

“How about kids?” I asked. “Did you ever see them around children?”

“Sure. Mrs. Shaw asked me to bring my nephews and nieces up to the house a few times. She loved fussing over them. You could tell, just watching her. She would have made a good mom.”

I remembered Fran telling me that Patti’s mother had been in the ER when Elaine had been brought in. I wondered if Patti’s mother had told her what happened. “Did you know about Elaine and what happened?”

Patti looked up at me, then away. “Mom told me; that was one of the things that made up my mind for me. I didn’t want to work for a guy that would do that, you know? I mean . . .”

“So you never saw Carl with kids?”

“Shaw? No way.” Patti snorted. “He looked at them like they’d just puked on his shoes.”

Patti moved away when another customer walked into the diner. I picked at my pie and drank my coffee. I kept glancing over to the police station. I had two more cups of coffee. Still no sign of Petersen. The daylight bled away and yellow streetlights glowed.

I decided that Petersen wouldn’t be returning for a while. I waved to Patti for my tab and reached into my pocket for my wallet. Then I saw a car I recognized:

Elaine's pickup. But if she was driving it, she had a problem. The pickup veered all over the road, narrowly missing an oncoming RV and a station wagon packed with kids. The RV driver blew his horn and skidded to a stop. The traffic behind the pickup kept a healthy distance.

As the pickup drifted under a streetlight, I thought I saw the pale, lean face of the driver hunched over the wheel. It didn't look like Elaine.

I paid Patti and strode out of the diner. Another car horn sounded ahead of me. I walked up Main Street and wasn't surprised to see the pickup parked outside the Tavern. Parked wasn't the right word: abandoned would be better. The front tires had chewed up the pathetic flower bed in front of the Tavern while the pickup rested across three parking spaces. No sign of the driver.

I crossed the street and paused. Petersen might not be back for hours. I took a deep breath and opened the Tavern's door.

13

I found Carl in the Tavern's second room, the room where I'd sat down with Harry in what seemed like months ago but had in fact been days. At first glance, Carl didn't look drunk. He stood straight at the bar. He didn't lean or slump. Only the white knuckles, clenched on the edge of the counter, gave a clue. That and spots of red high in his cheeks.

Carl wore a baggy wool jacket over his jeans and shirt. I couldn't see his waist or under his shoulders. He might be carrying a fistful of guns and I wouldn't know. Hell, he could have an Uzi jammed down the back of his jeans and I wouldn't know.

Two middle-aged customers in coveralls sat by the window, talking. Another man sat alone, sipping a beer and reading a newspaper. There had been more people in the first room I'd walked through; younger people, probably students, laughing and sharing pitchers of beer.

I stood next to Carl. He didn't acknowledge me. He kept staring ahead. A shot glass of whiskey stood on a coaster in front of him.

The bartender walked over. "What can I get you?"

"Beer, thanks," I said. I watched him pour it and set it down. I didn't want a drink, but I needed to stay close to Carl. I took a sip and watched our reflections in the pitted mirror behind the bartender. The Tavern had the same smell I remembered, the smell of old bars and saloons in every city: spilt beer, stale food, sweat. The shaded lights made the room's shadows appear even deeper and thicker, almost solid.

Laughter, high and clear, cut through from the first room. Then Carl said, "I saved your life, you bastard."

I didn't reply. My heart upped a gear.

Carl still stared straight ahead. He downed his drink and signaled for another. When the bartender walked to the side, Carl continued, "I knew what people were saying, when Sarah died. I could hear them talk about me, blame me, whisper just loud enough for me to hear. But I thought all that was over. Then you kick it up again. Why persecute me?"

"I didn't mean to target you."

As if he hadn't heard me, Carl continued, almost to himself, "A hell of a life: struggling to go through rehab—God knows why—and the police sniffing around, going through the house, not asking me too many questions, no sir, not with my lawyer ready and waiting, but you could see what they thought . . . They knew what they knew. Mathers made sure he had an alibi, he's not stupid. He's a lot of things, but you could never call him stupid."

Carl swayed at the bar, then gripped the edge tighter. "And Sarah, drifting around like some ghost, always watching, waiting, listening. Taking down everything you said, every little comment and word, blowing it up and analyzing, always frigging analyzing. Sometimes a word is just a word; you don't always mean what you say. Try telling that to Sarah!"

The words came out like water from a burst dam. I knew Carl spent most of his days alone, working. Either the drink or the shock of my news had turned a switch in him. He had to talk. He had to talk to me.

"You're just as bad as that PI, Braid. He thought he had

something on me, I'm sure of that. Poor bastard. Like watching the fattest kid in school trying to keep up with the jocks. He just didn't have it."

Part of me wanted to shut Carl up. Another part wanted to get as much out of him as I could. Neither part enjoyed listening to what was pouring out.

Carl said, "Everyone wishes they could go back. I wish I'd never met Sarah, never gone on rehab. I wish I'd never gone to New York and saved your worthless ass. But it's all done now. All water under the bridge. You can never go back."

"What about Elaine?" I asked. "What would she change?"

He threw back his head and laughed, making the customers turn and stare. "Jesus! What wouldn't she change? She's probably got a list ready and waiting. All she needs is the opportunity."

"Where would kids be on that list? Near the top?"

He turned to me. His eyes, cold and glassy, stared into mine. "Why? Why drag all this up again?"

I could have lied. I could have hinted at the connections between Cursell's death and Sarah's murder. But I'd had enough. The time had come. I said, "I'm up here because of the .38."

He blinked. "My gun?"

"Ballistics showed a match," I said, quiet and calm. "The gun that killed Tyrone Cursell was the same one used on Sarah."

It took a few seconds to sink in. I could almost see the train of thoughts crossing Carl's face. His jaw dropped a little. His eyes opened wide, then narrowed. "And you think I killed her?"

"I needed to find out."

I couldn't guess exactly how drunk Carl was. He'd been

off the bottle for over a year, as far as I knew. Maybe it would just seep through his system. Maybe it would hit him like a cartoon anvil falling from the sky. Maybe nobody could predict his reaction.

He shook his head. His right hand tightened around the empty glass. Then he threw his left at me.

I ducked in time. The punch grazed my left cheek. From the corner of my eye, I saw the bartender reach under the counter. Then Carl came for me.

The drink and adrenaline must have pumped him. I blocked most of his punches but a few made it through. One caught me on the chin and sent me back two steps. But I didn't want to hurt Carl. So I kept blocking and waited for the rush to die down.

Carl's red face wore a rictus grin. Spittle dotted his lips. As the adrenaline began to fade, so did the color. His arms slowed. His breathing sounded ragged and hoarse. Unlike Mathers, he didn't know what he was doing; his arms windmilled in my direction. I knew it was just a matter of time.

Then the bartender jumped over the bar with a blackjack in his hand. He distracted me. Carl grunted and sent a good right hook into my left eye. The room exploded with white splinters. I staggered back.

I couldn't help it. Instinct took over. My left arm went up to block Carl. My right fist sank into his stomach. As he folded over, I drew back my left fist. I had a sudden image of Harry laid out on the rough wooden planks of the jetty at Cardford Springs. Then I slammed my fist into Carl's chin.

His head snapped back. He fell onto the wooden floor, his arms splayed out at his side.

"I saw it all, man. He hit you first." The bartender stood beside Carl. The blackjack hung forgotten in his hand. "I saw it all."

I knelt down beside Carl and checked his tongue wasn't blocking his throat. When I put my ear to his chest I heard a hard heartbeat and then a wet bubbling sound. I managed to turn Carl on his side before the vomit spilled out. His eyes opened for a moment. He puked again, spattering my clothes, then passed out.

"Some men shouldn't drink," one of the other customers said. The three men stood around like witnesses at a road accident. More curious faces filled the doorway between the Tavern's two rooms.

"You want me to call Doc Samuels?" the barman asked.

I hesitated. Petersen would find out sooner or later, but I doubted Carl needed any treatment except a night's sleep.

Elaine saved me from answering. She pushed through the people at the door and spotted me. "I saw the car outside and . . ."

She knelt down beside her husband and felt at his neck. "Is he all right?"

"He'll be okay, once he sleeps it off," I said.

Elaine looked at me. In the bar's yellow light, her face appeared to be swollen on one side, just under the left eye. "Can you help me get him home?"

"Sure."

I ignored the stabbing pains in my chest and sides and gripped Carl around the shoulders. His knuckles grazed the wet floor. One of the other customers, a wide man in Power Company coveralls, lifted Carl's feet. Together we carried Carl through the Tavern like a funeral procession. As we left the first room, I heard Elaine apologizing to the bartender and offering to pay for the mess.

The doors to Elaine's pickup hadn't been locked. We wedged Carl onto the extended cab's back seat, on his side. The man who'd helped me carry him looked at Carl, shook his head, then spat into the gutter and went back inside the Tavern. I leaned against the hood and dragged in cold air. Fatigue replaced the adrenaline. Someone had poured lead into all my muscles. I wanted to sleep, but only for a day or two. Not too much to ask.

Elaine left the Tavern and laid a hand on my arm. "Thank you."

I smiled and opened the passenger door. "No problem."

"Shall I drop you at the hotel?" she asked, climbing into the driver's seat.

"I'm coming back with you."

"You don't have to." Elaine looked at me. The cabin's overhead courtesy light threw her face into relief. The cheekbone under her left eye swelled out. She had the makings of a fine bruise.

I slammed the car door. "I'm coming with you."

Elaine reversed onto Main Street and turned around. When she passed the police station, I couldn't see any patrol cars in the parking spaces. I wondered how it had worked out with the search. If Mathers was holed up in some remote cabin, Petersen might have a siege on his hands. I could see that happening.

Elaine concentrated on her driving. We didn't talk. Carl made no sound from the back seat, not even a whimper. I reached back and checked his pulse and breathing.

The Shaw estate's electric gates rolled back as the pickup approached. Elaine parked close to the front door and came around to help me lift Carl from the back seat. A security light, probably keyed to a sensor, flooded the area with white light. The rest of the house looked as dark as a sewer.

I climbed down and looked at Carl. It's no fun trying to haul a dead weight in a confined space. Me and Sam had

had plenty of experience shifting drunks, tramps and druggies, some of them a hell of a lot bigger than Carl. Sam could have done it with one hand. But Sam was a long way away, and in no shape to lift anything for a while.

I dragged Carl out by the legs. He lay on his back along the bench seat, his arms behind him.

"Should I lift him from inside?" Elaine asked.

"No, let me think for a minute." The doctors had told me not to lift anything for a month. But they'd also told me to relax and take things easy.

I tried to remember my training at the Academy. I reached for Carl's arms and pulled him into a sitting position. Then I squatted down and got my shoulder in his stomach. His head lolled against my spine. I braced my back and legs and then straightened into a fireman's lift. As I turned, Carl's head thudded into the edge of the car window.

"Here, I'll get the door." Elaine ran ahead and fumbled at the front door.

Step by step, I followed her. I heard a low rumbling sound, then a bubbling and a thick splash. I didn't need to look to know Carl had puked down the back of my legs. I stood there, my legs braced, my arms wrapped around his thighs.

Elaine turned from the door and stared at me. She bit her top lip, then started laughing. She leaned against the door and clutched her stomach. "Oh, I'm sorry . . ."

I let her finish; it would be good for her. "It's okay. But he's getting a bit heavy."

She wiped her eyes and pushed the door open. With Carl draped over my shoulder, I took a deep breath and followed Elaine into the house. I tried to ignore the hot needles digging into my chest and ribs. As I turned into the living room, Carl's unconscious body swung around and knocked a handful of photographs to the floor.

"Can you put him on the couch?" Elaine asked, already moving cushions.

I knelt on the floor and unrolled Carl's body onto the couch. Elaine caught his head and settled him down. I helped her turn Carl onto his side with his slack mouth pointing to a waste basket. I stood up, rubbing my sides and feeling the sweat on my back grow cold.

Elaine looked at the back of my jeans and coat. "Carl's clothes wouldn't fit you, but Leon left some old jeans and a couple of shirts behind . . ."

"Thanks." Now that I wasn't concentrating on hauling Carl's body around, I could smell his vomit, a sweet and sour bile that caught at the back of my throat.

Elaine disappeared for a few minutes. I heard doors opening and closing in the house. I looked down at Carl. Greasy beads of sweat dotted his gray skin. His eyes moved under their lids as if he was deep in REM sleep, dreaming of God knew what. He didn't look much like a killer. But I guess that even killers dream.

Elaine returned with an armful of clothes. She gave me a sad smile. "I'm really sorry about this. I am. But these are clean and dry. There's a bathroom down the hall."

"These will be fine." I left her with Carl and found the bathroom. I stripped off my puke-spattered clothes and dumped them in the tub. Mathers had left a pair of dark jeans, a white tee shirt and a plaid shirt criss-crossed with blue and green stripes. I washed my face and arms before I pulled on his clothes. In the mirror, I saw my left cheek swelling up just like Elaine's. Carl seemed to have a favorite target.

I didn't know what to do with my clothes. I collected my keys, wallet and money and was just about to roll the dirty clothes into a ball when someone tapped at the bathroom door.

Elaine, muffled by the door, called out, "Just leave your clothes there; I'll wash them out."

I opened the door and saw that Elaine had changed, too; she wore a loose track suit kind of outfit in fine blue wool. It had probably cost a fortune. When she saw me wearing Mathers' clothes, her eyes opened wide. "They fit?"

"Where they touch," I said, smiling. Mathers must have a good forty or fifty pounds on me. His jeans were too short and his shirt ballooned out. "How's Carl?"

"Sleeping. He won't wake up for the best part of a day. It hits him hard, drinking after he's been clean for so long."

The harsh light of the bathroom caught the swelling beneath Elaine's eye. She saw me looking and reached up her hand to cover it. "Let's go into the kitchen. I don't want to sit listening to Carl snore."

I followed her to the back of the house. The kitchen looked new and well-designed, with wooden units and stainless-steel appliances. An enormous wooden table, at least six inches thick and scored with age, stood in the center of the room. I sat down and watched Elaine pour white wine into two glasses. I waited until she sat opposite before asking, "What happened?"

Her story was simple: after I'd left, Carl had reached for the bottle. He'd disappeared into his study and locked the door. Elaine, worried and trying to help, had tried to talk him out of it. He hadn't listened. When she said this, her hand once again went to her swollen face. After finishing the best part of a bottle of bourbon, Carl had taken Elaine's keys from her bag and driven into Eastham. The rest I knew.

"I'm sorry you got mixed up in all this," Elaine said, staring down at the table.

"It was my choice. I didn't have to come up here."

She finished her wine, then tilted her head up to me. "You know . . . you think Carl had something to do with Sarah, don't you?"

I didn't reply.

"It isn't anything I haven't gone through a thousand times in my own mind," Elaine said. "I go back to that night, wondering, analyzing. Could I have changed things? Could I have helped? It's difficult."

I nodded. "Maybe I did the wrong thing, coming here, raking up the past. I don't think I've done you any favors."

Elaine smiled. She reached over and laid her warm hand over mine. "Trust me, the past wouldn't have stayed buried. You just happened to get in the way."

I smiled. "Don't shoot the messenger, right?"

She squeezed my hand and went to speak. At that moment, a buzzing cut through the air. I followed Elaine's gaze to a small metal box set on the wall beside the door. She crossed the room and pressed a button. "Who is it?"

"Elaine, it's Gary. Are you okay?" Petersen's voice sounded like a movie robot's, sharp and metallic.

"Sure, Gary. Come on up." Elaine pressed another button and walked over to me. "Looks like we have company."

The track suit material showed off her slender body. The top zip had been pulled down to just below her throat. The pulse in my own throat beat just that little bit harder and faster. I said, "Maybe we should check on Carl?"

Elaine nodded and smiled. "Maybe we should."

We walked through and saw that Carl hadn't moved. A thin dribble of mucus had leaked from his mouth and onto the couch. He snored.

We heard tires on the gravel outside. Elaine came back into the living room with Petersen and the sergeant I'd seen in Cardford Springs. Both men carried their hats in their hands. Their crumpled clothes bore streaks of mud and grass. Petersen nodded to me, then crossed to the couch and knelt beside Carl. He lifted up one of Carl's eyelids and grunted. When he stood up, he asked Elaine, "He hit the bottle?"

She gave a smile that didn't reach her eyes. "So hard he bounced."

"How about you?" Petersen turned to me. "Joe, the bartender at the Tavern, said you and Carl had a set-to down there."

"He took a dislike to me," I said.

"To you or to your ideas?"

"Maybe both."

Petersen stared at me for a few seconds before telling Elaine, "I'll have to see Carl when he's sober; there's a trail of traffic violations to be sorted out, and maybe a charge of assault on Mr. Burnett here . . ."

I shook my head. "Not from me."

Elaine touched Petersen's arm. "I'll call you when he wakes up. I promise."

"You want me to leave Phil here to keep an eye on him?"

"There's no need."

Petersen didn't look as though he believed her, but he didn't press the point. He asked me, "What are you doing now?"

"Well, I'd hoped for a shower and a few hours sleep back at the hotel," I said. "Apart from that, nothing."

"Good. We can carry on where we left off today."

I followed Petersen and his sergeant out to their patrol cars. As I turned to say goodbye to Elaine, she kissed me on the cheek and said, "Thank you."

I saw Petersen watching me. I smiled at Elaine and

climbed into the Chief's car. As he swung around the gravel drive, I looked back and saw Elaine waving from the doorway.

"What was all that about?" Petersen asked.

"Just saying thanks."

"For knocking out her husband?"

I shook my head but didn't reply. At the bottom of the road, where it joined the main route into Eastham, Petersen turned west instead of east. I saw the sergeant's car take the turn into town.

"I thought we were going into your office."

Petersen glanced at me. "I've had a bitch of a day; I need a shower, clean clothes and something to eat. Then you can tell me the real reason you're up here, and just what the hell's going on."

I let him drive for a minute, then said, "You didn't find Mathers?"

"No, we didn't find Mathers. But we will. We will."

Petersen lived in a squat wooden house northwest of Eastham. At the end of a rough dirt track, the house looked like it had been put together by a child: in the headlights' beams, one side of the house seemed taller than the other. Brick and clapboard fought for space. The porch ran three-quarters the length of the front but ended as if chopped by a chainsaw.

When I climbed out of the car I could see the lights of the Mill Hotel about two miles away. Darkness covered the rest of the countryside, split occasionally by clusters of streetlights or car headlights. I could hear the rush of water over rocks nearby. "Remote."

"It was, when my grandparents built this place," Petersen said, leading the way to the front door. "But we have less and less real country now. There's talk of building vacation homes in the field over the river."

I'd expected someone waiting for Petersen, a wife or relation, maybe a girlfriend. But nobody called out hello. Nobody ran to meet us. Petersen flicked on lights as he walked through the silent rooms. I saw old, high-backed couches and worn rugs over polished floorboards. Pale wooden chairs. A dresser and roll-top desk in wood so dark it looked black. A boiler clicked and wheezed somewhere below us, exhaling hot air through vents.

In the kitchen, Petersen opened an old fridge roughly the size of my first car. He rooted around inside. I heard the clink of bottles and jars, then, "Can you cook?"

"Not too well," I said. "But I can reheat."

"Frozen pizza it is, then." Petersen dropped two frozen boxes rimed with frost on the table. He crossed to the cast-iron stove and turned a dial. "Put those in for a couple of minutes. Coffee and tea are over there; mugs in the cupboard. Give me fifteen minutes."

I heard his boots on the stairs. I ran water into the kettle and searched out mugs, tea, milk and sugar. The kitchen looked neat and clean, with pots and pans set on top of the units and plates stacked behind glass doors. No trash lying around waiting to go out. No crumpled cans of beer. Nothing like the apartment I'd shared for the past few years. If I'd had to guess, I would have said Petersen had someone to look after him.

I could have disappeared and walked back to the hotel. Petersen didn't have the right to ask me anything. In theory, neither did Mendez, once I gave him the basic statement about Cursell's shooting. I could take my Jeep and head back for New York, putting the past few days down to experience. An expensive, painful, frustrating lesson in how not to get involved.

But I'd given Petersen my word.

I put the pizzas on to warm and sat at the table. I wondered what Elaine was doing at that moment. Probably watching Carl lying comatose on the couch. Would anyone blame her if she grabbed a cushion and pressed it over his face? From what I'd seen and heard, she'd have good reason. But I couldn't see her doing it.

My back and side cramped suddenly. Pain sliced through my ribs. I started checking my pockets for painkillers. Before I remembered I was wearing Mathers' cast-offs, I found a smooth nugget of metal in the plaid shirt's pocket. I reached inside and found a small key, slightly rusty. It could have fitted a small suitcase or vanity case. Or maybe a left-luggage locker. I held it under the bulb. It had the number forty-two stamped into the metal.

It didn't make sense. Elaine had told me that Mathers' clothes had been cleaned. The key would have appeared in the wash. Unless someone had slipped it into the pocket afterward.

I heard Petersen coming down the stairs. I slipped the key into my pocket and crossed to the mugs and kettle. I poured hot water onto the tea and turned to see Petersen in jeans and sweater. His wet hair stuck up in tufts. I said, "I thought about running off with the family silver but I couldn't find it."

Petersen almost smiled. "Don't think there's anything here worth taking. Not to anyone else, leastways."

"That's what everyone says, until they've been ripped off."

Petersen crossed to the stove. "You could have a beer with your pizza but I don't have any in the house."

I remembered my visit to his office, when he'd added bourbon to my coffee but not to his own. "You don't like to drink?"

He smiled. "I love to drink. I think it's the best damn thing in the world, better than eating, sleeping and just about anything else you can name. So I avoid it. Life's easier that way."

We ate the pizzas in silence. Petersen seemed happy to wait. He slid the dishes into the sink, sat down and said, "Now. From the start."

Petersen knew most of what had happened to me in Eastham. I filled in the rest. I told him almost everything: Carl riding patrol with me and Sam; Carl shooting Cursell; ballistics matching the bullet to Sarah's murder. I told him about Harry and the laptop, but I left out Derek and Louise. I still wasn't sure why. Maybe because they looked like they always ended up with the dirty end of the lollipop.

When I finished telling him about my evening with Elaine and Carl, Petersen just sat there and stared at me. I waited for him to yell, to erupt. Instead, calm and quiet, he said, "You should've told me about the gun."

"I owed Carl," I said. "He saved my life. And my partner's."

Petersen shook his head. "All the same. If you'd told me, Harry might still be alive."

I rubbed my eyes and didn't reply. What could I say? Petersen was right. Me and Sam did owe Carl, but that didn't make it right. Harry had paid a price, too.

Petersen said, "I have to tell Stanton."

"I know."

"It doesn't look too good for Carl Shaw."

I had to agree with that. Everything pointed to Carl for both Sarah and Cursell. Maybe Harry, too. "You think Mathers is in this with Carl?"

Petersen looked through the kitchen window, into darkness split by the Mill Hotel's lights. "I don't know. Stanton always figured Mathers for Sarah's murder."

"What about his alibi?"

Petersen shrugged. "Three buddies in a bar off Route 89. Two of them have done time, the third just missed the penitentiary. Would I trust them? About as far as I could throw them."

I nodded. "And Petchey spotted Mathers' truck at the scene."

"Mathers said his truck might have been there but he wasn't in it," Petersen said. "And then Petchey withdrew his statement."

I thought for a moment. "That makes no sense. Everyone thinks Mathers beat up Petchey to make the guy pull his statement. But Mathers had an alibi; why beat up Petchey?"

"Insurance? Maybe Mathers wanted to make sure he wouldn't see a courtroom."

I wasn't so sure. "What if Mathers' alibi was real? What if someone else killed Sarah and then arranged for Mathers to beat up Petchey?"

"Carl?"

"It would make sense."

"I guess," Petersen said, leaning forward. "But I still don't see a motive for Carl killing Sarah."

I leaned on the table and rested my head on my upturned palm. My eyes wanted to close. I had to chase thoughts of Carl, Mathers and Elaine through my tired mind. "There's sex . . . maybe Sarah slapped Carl down so hard he cracked . . . maybe she just plain pissed him off . . . or she knew he went back on the drugs . . ."

Petersen stood up. "I'll give you a lift to the hotel. I think you've just about had it for one day."

I yawned so hard my jaw cracked. I rubbed it and said, "Will Stanton need to know about this tonight?"

Petersen hesitated. "Tomorrow's soon enough. He's been sitting on Sarah's case for the best part of a year. Another few hours won't hurt. But he'll roast you for not telling him right at the start. And I mean roast."

I nodded. I was looking forward to seeing Stanton about as much as seeing Mendez. But it had to be done. I realized I was lucky that Petersen had taken my story so well; he could have run me in for withholding evidence, obstructing an officer, the whole list. Maybe he still would, when this was all over. He had that right.

"What time is your Detective Mendez getting in tomorrow?" Petersen asked.

"I don't know. Afternoon, probably."

In the hallway, Petersen passed me my coat and shrugged into his own. "I'll pick you up at eight in the morning. We've got someone to see."

That woke me up. "Who?"

"Carl Shaw's ex-pusher."

14

Eight-fifty on an icy Vermont morning. I sat in the passenger seat of Petersen's unmarked Ford Explorer, parked in a turn-off by at the side of Interstate 89, just south of St. Albans. Across the road, the squat horseshoe of rooms that made up the Fall Splendor motel. It didn't look all that splendid. Even from this distance I could see brown paint peeling from the walls. Weeds grew through fissures in the parking lot. One of the rooms showed the writhing black smoke trails of a recent fire; smashed windows still hadn't been boarded up, and yellow tape fluttered in the breeze. It reminded me of the little girl in New York.

According to his latest arrest record, Mike Gregory, Carl's ex-pusher, lived in the rougher suburbs south of St. Albans. But when we'd called there, a little after eight that morning, a young woman with a squalling baby on her hip told us she'd thrown Gregory out. She gave the name of the motel on I-89 and said Gregory could go screw himself. She said a few more things beside that. I didn't think Gregory would be going back there anytime soon.

"You're sure Gregory supplied Carl?" I asked.

Petersen nodded. "We didn't have that many people pushing hard drugs around Eastham. Gregory was one of them. Last December, we pulled him in for possession with intent; with his record, that would have been five to seven. So he dumped on just about everyone he knew, most of his contacts."

"Including Carl?"

"Kind of: Sarah's murder was in the newspapers around then, and her connection to Carl; Gregory told us he used to supply him. Gregory would have told us anything we asked. I've never seen anyone so keen to avoid jail. He practically wet himself."

I wondered how many other pushers and users Gregory had informed on in the past. There might be more than a few guys in prison who'd be happy to see Gregory walk through the gates. Some welcoming committee. And there would be plenty waiting to get out and visit Gregory, from what Petersen had said. If I was Gregory, I'd move further away than the motel.

Petersen leaned forward. "Here we go."

I looked through the blurs of passing cars and trucks. A battered sedan pulled up in front of the motel manager's office. The car door opened wide and a wide, pale man squeezed out like Jell-O from a tub. Despite the cold, he wore shorts and a tee shirt. He collected an armful of supplies from the back seat and unlocked the manager's door.

I climbed out of Petersen's Explorer and followed him across the road. We dodged traffic and walked up to the office. The motel didn't look any better up close. The vivid green and brown of the trees behind it made the rotting woodwork and paint look like something that crawled into the woods to die. Of the three cars in the lot, two had flat tires.

Petersen pushed open the glass door. We saw the manager behind the counter, which held the brown paper sack and the coffee he'd just collected. The smell of fried grease filled the cold air.

Petersen smiled and leaned on the counter. "Morning, Frank. How's business?"

"We're clean, Chief," the manager said. He had sugar in

his beard and a bitten cruller in his left hand. "All nice and quiet. No trouble."

"I'm sure." Petersen nodded and turned the register around. "How many guests?"

"Four." The manager licked his sugared lips. He glanced at me.

Petersen said, "We're looking for a Mr. Mike Gregory but I don't see his name down here."

"I just go by the names they tell me."

"You mean you don't check?" Petersen asked, smiling.

The manager looked at the cruller in his hand. I could see that he wanted to take another bite. He could wash it down with coffee and start on the rest of the paper sack's contents. Even as I watched, grease stains grew on the side of the sack like mold on a wall.

"Guy in number three," the manager said. "I didn't like the look of him. Small, gray face, all pockmarked."

Petersen nodded. "Blond hair in a ponytail?"

"That's right."

"Thanks, Frank." Petersen made for the door.

"Is there going to be any shooting?" the manager asked, already grabbing the sack of donuts and heading for the back of the office.

"No, Frank. Enjoy your breakfast."

Outside the office, I saw a painted number three on a room to the left.

"You go around the back," Petersen told me, "just in case he gets shy."

While Petersen crossed to the room's front door, I stepped through the weeds and broken glass at the side of the building. I counted windows until I stood behind number three. Even though Petersen said there'd be no shooting, my heart speeded up and my throat tightened. I curled my hands into fists and then made them relax.

Petersen's quick knock and voice carried through the cold air. "Gregory? It's Gary Petersen. Open up."

Silence, then a muffled voice: "One minute."

I moved back against the wall of number two. Each room had a small window at the back. I saw the top half of number three's window slide up. A hand emerged, followed by a greasy blond head. The man had his thin body halfway through the window when he saw me. He froze like a deer caught in headlights.

I stepped forward and smiled. "Hey. How's it going?"

Gregory tried to smile. "Oh, shit."

I waited until he'd slipped back into the room and I heard Petersen's voice calling me from inside. The motel room looked like a hundred other cheap dives I'd seen. The carpet stuck to the soles of my shoes. Gregory, wearing leather pants and a jazzy blue silk shirt, sat on the stained bed. Petersen leaned on the credenza, beside the TV. I stayed on my feet.

"This is harassment," Gregory said.

Petersen smiled.

"You're just fishing; you know I'm straight." The scowl on Gregory's face made him look older than the thirty-eight years recorded on his arrest sheet. The sallow skin and pockmarks didn't help.

"We called on your girlfriend," Petersen said. "She didn't seem too happy with you. Why's that?"

Gregory looked at his hands washing each other in his lap. "I wouldn't know. Women's stuff."

"Could it be because you've gone back to your old habits?"

Gregory said nothing. I didn't know whether the smell came from him or from the room: sickly-sweet and dank, like chocolate cake left to rot.

"Carl Shaw," Petersen said. "Remember him?"

Gregory glanced up. "Sure. I told you all about him. I *volunteered,* you know that."

Petersen nodded. "You *volunteered* plenty of names. But we're interested in Shaw."

Gregory looked at me.

"This is Officer Burnett," Petersen said. "He's come all the way from New York."

It might have been my imagination, but when Petersen mentioned New York I thought Gregory's eyes opened wide. In fear or surprise. Maybe both.

"So, Carl Shaw," Petersen said.

"Coke, mainly." Gregory stared at me while he spoke, as if he had to convince me of something really important. "He started off with weed, then ludes, speed, bennies, your basic shit. But he settled on coke."

"Any crack?" I asked.

"I didn't move that," Gregory said.

I didn't believe him, but I said, "When was this?"

"Dates? Jesus." Gregory stared out of the window. He chewed his bottom lip with his yellow teeth. "I got it. About two years ago I started seeing him regular. I mean, it's pretty hazy, but I think it was two years . . ."

I glanced over at Petersen, who nodded once. I guessed that Gregory had been using his own stuff for a long time. Dates probably meant very little to him, just like night or day, cold or heat. He'd rolled his sleeves down but I could imagine tracks and scars.

Gregory continued, "I met him through friends of friends, college guys that wanted weed. Shaw started off small, every week or so. Then he moved up the ladder. It got to be two, three times a week. At the end, every day. Sometimes twice a day."

"Then he went into rehab," I said.

"That's right."

"Didn't that piss you off?" Petersen asked. "Losing one of your best customers . . ."

Gregory smirked and shrugged his shoulders. "I had plenty of others."

I saw Petersen straighten up. His hands hung loose at his sides.

Gregory must have seen it too, because he cowered back on the bed and raised his hands. "Hey, Gary. Come on, man. I'm co-operating here, right?"

"When was the last time you sold anything to Shaw?" Petersen asked, his voice hard and flat.

"Fourteen, sixteen months, something like that," Gregory said. "I swear!"

I had an idea. If Carl had gone back to drugs, he might not want to be caught collecting them. "How about Leon Mathers? You sell anything to him?"

Gregory looked at Petersen, then me. "Okay. Someone I know—not me—sells to Mathers, regular. But don't tell him, man, he'll hurt me—"

"What does he buy?" Petersen asked.

"Coke. The good shit. Expensive."

"Since when?"

"Last fall. October, November."

That tied in. It looked as if Carl had gone back to his old friend. Had Sarah found out? Had Carl killed her because of it?

"Did Carl ever ask about buying a gun?" I asked.

Gregory didn't hesitate. "Sure, he asked if I knew anyone. I told him I couldn't get one but I gave him a number he could call."

"Who?" Petersen asked.

"Tony Proulx," Gregory said. "He's out of circulation: the State Police put him away for eight this year. I don't know if they got it together, Shaw and Tony. I didn't want to know."

So we could see how Carl had got hold of the .38. Then I remembered Mendez saying that Cursell had numbered bills from Eastham's bank. It would be a hell of a connection, but I asked, "Did you ever hear the name Tyrone Cursell?"

Gregory winced as if I'd slapped him. "I heard it."

Petersen stepped forward. "So?"

Gregory took a deep breath, then said, "My second time inside, I shared a cell with Cursell for a few months. We got on okay, I guess. We were both into the same shit. Anyway, back in July, maybe August, someone asked me if I knew anyone in New York. They needed a job done. I pointed them to Ty."

"Who was it?" I asked. My hands clenched into fists. "Who wanted the job done?"

Gregory shook his head. "No way. He'd rip me apart."

I took a step forward. Petersen held up his hand to stop me, then knelt in front of Gregory and looked him in the eyes. "This is important. So important that you'd disappear into prison for years. With the people you've sold down the river, you might not see daylight again. You might not even see the end of your first day in a cell."

Gregory closed his eyes. His skin looked even grayer than before. He said, "Mathers asked me. Leon Mathers."

I hung on to my seat as Petersen drove too fast back to Eastham. He gripped the wheel as if it had done something personal to him. He stared at the road ahead as he talked. "All this time, Shaw's been screwing us around. Shaw and

Mathers. They killed Sarah and then went for you."

"But why?" I asked. I'd been turning it over in my mind from the moment Gregory gave us Mathers' name. "Why the hell would they want to kill me and Sam? I hadn't even met Carl—or Mathers—before that night."

Petersen glanced at me. "Are you sure?"

"What do you mean?"

"Maybe you pissed him off without knowing it. Maybe you arrested him or someone he loves. Let's face it: if he's psycho, it could all be down to one lousy speeding ticket."

How many people had Sam and me pulled over or arrested? Sam had twenty years against my three, but we were looking at thousands of cases. We'd have to sift through every incident and search for coincidences and connections back to Carl.

"It doesn't need to be you or your partner," Petersen continued, overtaking a slow minibus. "He might want to get back at the police in general, not you in particular."

"He wanted us," I said. "Evans, our sergeant, told us that Carl's people asked for me and Sam. He wanted to ride with us that night."

He had targeted us, but why? Why make it so difficult for himself? He'd set up Cursell, got himself placed with me and Sam, traveled down from Vermont . . . Why?

It didn't make sense. Not yet.

Petersen took the right lane to Eastham. "I'm going to drop you off at the hotel."

"Where are you going?"

"Waterbury," Petersen said. "Stanton needs to know all this."

"You don't need me with you?"

Petersen didn't answer until after he'd parked in the hotel lot. He left the engine running and turned to me. "I might have done what you did, if I'd been in the same situation. I'm not saying I would, just that I might. You thought Carl Shaw had saved your life; you thought you owed him. But Stanton won't see it that way."

I hesitated. "I got myself into this. It's down to me."

Petersen gave a brief grin. "Don't worry: there'll be plenty of opportunity to get your ass kicked. You won't have to volunteer."

I climbed out of the car but didn't close the door. "Thanks. I appreciate this."

"Yeah. Well." His grin faded. "I just want to get the guy that killed Sarah. Everything else is just static."

I watched Petersen roar off toward the main road. I didn't envy him his interview with Stanton, but I knew I should have been there with him. But, as Petersen said, there'd be plenty of time later for blame.

I stood in the cold lot and wondered what to do with myself. A new minivan with New York plates had been parked close to my Jeep; a family of four, including two boys maybe eight or nine, bustled about loading luggage and bikes into the car. The boys wore matching ski jackets, gloves and hats, although they weren't twins as far as I could tell. With the blond woman and man, and the sunlit lake and forest in the background, the whole thing could have been an advertisement in a Sunday newspaper supplement.

For a moment, a mixture of regret and envy cut through me like a dull knife; I remembered my own childhood and my missing father. I thought those feelings had gone away or at least subsided. I guess they never went away.

Then one of the boys tried to imitate his dad and load his bike on the carrier at the rear of the van. As he lifted the frame, he lost his balance; he swayed for a few seconds, long enough for his face to turn red with the exertion and for me to take a step forward. Then he fell back with the bike across his chest and stomach.

It was over in seconds. His father picked up the bike and the boy's mother hugged him. I could see the boy fighting the urge to cry. I wondered how I'd feel about my own kids if I ever had any. I'd been successful at not thinking about that so far.

I left the lot and walked into the hotel lobby. Nobody sat waiting for me on the couches, no Fran or Elaine. But the desk clerk called me over. "Mr. Burnett? We had a message for you about an hour ago."

The note told me that Alison, Sarah's roommate, had tried to contact me. I thanked the clerk and made for the pay phones at the back of the lobby. As I dialed, I wondered what time Alison started her next shift. Whatever time I called, I always seemed to miss her.

This time, she answered on the third ring. Sleep weighed down her voice. "Hello . . . Alison Tate."

"Hi, it's Steve Burnett. I got your message."

"Steve . . . oh, yes, sure. Give me a minute."

I heard rustling and movement at the other end, then, "I did what you asked: I called up the apartments I'd rented over the past year. I asked if they'd received any parcels or letters for me."

"And?" My heart hammered against my sore ribs.

"I interned in Oakland last year, and one of my old landlords remembered he found a note in the mail," Alison said. "Back in October, the local post office in Oakland had a delivery that needed signing for; I'd already moved on to Boston so they just kept the package and waited."

"Have you any idea what's in it?" I asked. It could be anything: junk mail, free shampoo, trash. "Is there anything written on it?"

"Sure, or I wouldn't have bothered calling you," Alison said. "It has Sarah's name as the sender."

It didn't have to be Sarah's backup disks but we had to find out. "Can you get it?"

"From Oakland?" Alison asked. "Are you serious?"

I told her I was.

"It's probably too late, anyway," she said. "I asked them to forward it to my address in Boston. They figured I should receive it tomorrow or the day after. But—"

"As soon as you get it, ring us," I said. "The police here have Sarah's laptop. If your package does have her backup disks in it, the police need to see them."

"I'll let you know," Alison said. "You really think these will help find Sarah's killer?"

"I think so."

A pause, then, "Soon as I get it, I'll call you."

I thanked Alison and hung up. I had no guarantee that Sarah had mailed her disks to Alison, or to anyone. But it looked as if all the separate pieces were coming together.

I thought about Carl and Elaine. I dialed their number and waited. Just before I hung up, Elaine answered. "Hello?"

"It's Steve."

"Oh, Steve, I'm glad you called."

"How is he?"

"Carl's still fast asleep. Doc Samuels came over last night and gave him a shot. I think Gary asked him, just in case."

I switched the phone from one hand to the other. "How about you?"

Elaine didn't answer for a moment. Then, "I'm okay, Steve. This is nothing new. But I'm disappointed; I thought we'd left all this in the past."

Disappointed. It looked like her husband had killed one woman, arranged two more attempted murders, and returned to drugs. I thought disappointed was the understatement of the year. Elaine was one hell of a woman.

"Have you got any news for me?" she asked.

I hesitated, then told her about my visit, with Petersen, to Mike Gregory.

"My God, is he still alive?" Elaine asked. "He looked like a walking corpse."

"You knew him?"

"I saw him around. He came up to the house regularly when . . . when Carl was still using. But that was more than a year ago."

I said, "Gregory said Mathers had started buying off him again."

"When?" The word came out fast and hard.

"Recently."

Silence at the other end of the line. I could imagine Elaine looking over at Carl, weighing him up and trying to figure out how much he'd lied. "What else did Gregory say?"

I didn't know whether to tell her about the gun. She'd said that Carl had bought it when someone started stalking him. She probably thought he'd bought it legally. What reason would she have to think any different?

Instead of bringing up the gun, I said, "Gregory made the connection to Tyrone Cursell for us."

"What connection?"

"Apparently, Mathers asked Gregory for the name of someone in New York who could do a job. Gregory gave him Cursell's name."

Elaine sounded louder, as if she held the receiver close. "Did Mathers say anything about the kind of job?"

"I don't think so," I said. I didn't tell her it had to be Carl setting up me and Sam. Elaine had probably figured that out for herself.

The phone line went so quiet I could her background static. Then Elaine said, "I think I might know where Mathers is hiding."

"Where?"

"There's a cabin on the northern edge of our land," Elaine said, the words spilling out of her. "We used to rent it out for vacations. It hasn't been used in a year and it's pretty secluded, hidden at the end of a dirt track. Leon used to look after it and I'm sure he's there. I'm sure."

Part of me wondered why she hadn't mentioned this before. "I'll get onto Petersen."

"You'll have to hurry," Elaine said. "The Canadian border is close and Leon won't stick around if he hears that Gregory has talked."

That made sense but Mathers would have to find out first. Of course, Gregory might try to warn him, as a way of fixing things between them. We should have taken Gregory in. "How do I find this cabin?"

Elaine, breathless, said, "Steve, don't be a hero; Leon is dangerous."

"I'll be careful," I said. I'd already decided to head up there; Petersen would still be at Waterbury. His officers might be closer, but I couldn't count on it. And Elaine was right: Mathers wouldn't hang around. "But I'll need to give Petersen directions when I tell him . . ."

Whether Elaine believed me or not, she told me how to find the cabin. "Steve, Leon took his shotgun."

"Great."

"There's more," Elaine said. "He always carried a handgun in the glove box of his truck."

"Then you better tell Petersen to come prepared."

"But what about you?"

I hung up after telling her to lock her doors and windows and sit tight. Then I rang the police station and told Officer Evie the news. She promised to radio Petersen and sergeant Phil and get them there as soon as she could. But Phil was over at Richford, checking out cabins. And Waterbury was southeast of Burlington.

I stood in the lobby, ignoring the guests and staff around me. Mendez would be in that afternoon. I'd dropped myself into enough trouble already. I should wait for Petersen or Phil to get back and take Mathers. But panic cramped my stomach; adrenaline made my tired muscles burn. I could see Mathers heading for that border. We'd be too late.

I ran to my Jeep and swung it around toward the main road. I'd screwed up enough since Cursell's shooting. I wouldn't let Mathers make it any worse.

15

I followed Elaine's directions and drove north, toward the Canadian border. Snow weighed the trees down and lined the road; the Jeep's tires hissed through meltwater. My right foot wanted to sink the gas pedal but I held back. I wouldn't do any good if I plowed the Jeep into a ditch.

The main road became a minor one, then a deserted single lane of blacktop under an interlocking arch of branches. The sun didn't reach down here. The steering wheel moved too easily in my hands, letting me feel the black ice.

I drove past the entrance and had to turn back. It looked just like Elaine said it would: a faded wooden sign hanging from a leaning post. No mailbox, not out here. A five-bar gate, once painted white, closed and padlocked. A rough dirt track disappeared into the forest's shadows. Elaine said they'd rented the cabin out to hunters in the fall and spring. It didn't look like anyone had done any hunting for a long time.

I parked the Jeep about twenty yards from the track and walked back. A rusty wire fence curved into the trees either side of the entrance. The gate's white paint had curled up to reveal wet wood. Mathers hadn't been keeping up his caretaking duties. Maybe he'd had other jobs to keep him occupied.

Fresh snow had fallen, but not enough to cover the deep tire marks. A heavy vehicle had passed through the gate recently. Mathers' truck. I put one hand on the gate, ready to climb over, then paused. Petersen would be along soon. But would it be soon enough?

I climbed over the gate and dropped into the snow on the other side. My left foot found a deep, cold puddle. I zipped up my jacket, pulled on my gloves, and started walking. I kept to the grass growing between the track and the forest. I didn't want my footprints to be too obvious. But the snow had drifted here, and lay maybe a foot thick. I had to lift and place, lift and place, like a kid's robot.

After five minutes, I had to unzip my jacket. After another five, sweat trickled down my back. My breath hung in the air. I leaned against a tree trunk and listened. A bird's cry split the silence. I could have been a hundred miles from civilization, or a thousand. Only the rough track promised some kind of life.

Then, when I turned a corner, I saw the cabin. I stepped back so fast I almost fell. I caught a branch and hoped Mathers hadn't seen me flailing around. Snow fell from the branch and dusted my head and arms.

The cabin looked like something from a children's picture book, maybe a farmstead from the Old West. Notched logs had been slotted together to form a box. Cedar shingles covered the steep, snow-shedding roof. A plank door and two windows faced the track; condensation fogged the glass. This, and the lazy smoke curling from the brick chimney, told me someone was inside. Waiting.

My heart raced and the pit of my stomach curled tight. I couldn't just walk up and knock on the door, and I couldn't kick it in like some cop from a TV show. Even on cheap apartment doors, that hardly ever worked. Then I remembered I was supposed to be watching, just watching.

I stepped back even further into the trees. I crouched down. My body began to cool. Soon, I started shivering. I stood up and rubbed my arms and legs, hoping the trees' shadows would hide my movements.

Nothing happened. The cabin stayed quiet. Smoke still drifted from the chimney. I could imagine the fire, dull red embers throwing out heat. I could almost feel it.

After what seemed like hours, I had to move. Stiff-legged, I started walking around the cabin. I kept to the trees and took my time. I saw the side of the cabin, then the back. Another window faced me, this one glowing yellow through the condensation. Another plank door opened out into a small yard. A big cruiser axe, just like the ones the Fire Department used, jutted from a wide chopping stump. The axe's blade had bitten deep.

As I turned, something caught my eye: a flash of chrome. A level stretch of ground led from the front of the cabin, deep into the trees. You couldn't even call it a track. But Mathers had driven along it and parked his truck out of sight. Snow covered the hood, windscreen and roof. The chrome bars had been dented but still looked as if they could do plenty of damage.

I froze. The truck's headlights and spotlights glared at me. I made for the truck and felt the hood. Cold. I glanced back at the cabin, then reached for the driver's door handle. As slow as I could, I tried the door; it opened with a click, letting snow trickle inside.

Daylight filtered through the snow on the windscreen and gave the inside of the truck a strange glow. The gun rack behind the seats was empty. I remembered Elaine's advice and reached for the glove box. As I opened it, the courtesy light showed the blue-gray surface of a Colt .45. I grabbed it and checked the clip. Full. I slid the gun into my jacket pocket and looked back at the cabin. I couldn't see any change.

I went to close the driver's door, then stopped. I didn't know much about cars. I'd realized that when Harry trashed my Jeep's electric wiring. But there must be plenty of ways to slow Mathers down.

Raising and closing the hood would make too much noise. I reached under the steering column and searched for wires. Blank plastic. It wouldn't stop a thief, but I couldn't risk shattering the casing. Then I remembered my uncle's old Volvo sedan; he loved that car but the fuses were always blowing. But they were easy to replace: you just reached down beside the passenger door . . .

The truck's fuses lay behind an oblong plastic cover. I twisted it open and took out every fuse. I threw them into the forest and gently closed the driver's door. As I walked toward the cabin, the back door opened.

I crouched down and reached for the Colt. Mathers must have heard me at his truck. I waited for the shotgun blast.

Instead, Mathers strolled out empty-handed. He took one last drag on his cigarette and threw it into the snow. Then he reached for the axe and a chunk of wood from the pile. He set the wood on the stump and stepped back. The axe sang through the air and bit into the wood. I heard the clean thwack of the blade.

In five minutes, Mathers had an armful of kindling. He left the axe embedded in the stump and started walking back to the door.

I let myself breathe again. I slide the heavy Colt into my pocket and stood up.

Suddenly, Mathers froze. I saw his head snap to the right. Whatever he saw made him drop the kindling and run for the door. When he came out again, he had the shotgun ready in both hands. In one smooth move, he raised the gun, sighted and fired. The blast shook snow from the branches. Birds cried out.

Mathers ran for his truck. I had time to dive to one side. He didn't see me. If he'd looked down, he should have spotted my tracks. But he was too busy.

The truck's driver's door slammed shut. Silence. No engine turning. No roar of exhaust. Nothing. Then a bellow of rage and the door flew open. Mathers stood there, his face scarlet, the shotgun ready. He spun around, searching for his enemy. This time he saw my tracks.

My hands stopped shaking. The cold didn't matter any more. I had the Colt ready, safety off. I knelt down with the barrel pointing up.

Mathers ran forward, scanning the snow and the forest. He saw my prints, then me. He was quick. He let momentum carry him forward as he dropped into a roll. The shotgun fired before he hit the ground.

Time slowed for me. I fired out of reflex but hit fresh air. As if I floated above the scene, I saw myself moving. My legs, bunched under me, threw me to one side. I slammed into snow banked behind a wide tree trunk just as the shotgun pellets tore its bark apart.

Then everything moved too fast. Ten yards away, Mathers let rip with the shotgun. I pushed my body into the ground and tasted snow and dirt. Slivers of bark filled the air above me and landed on my back and head. I could feel the roar of the shotgun, waves of sound.

I saw Mathers on his feet again and running toward me, the gun held at waist level, his mouth screaming like some forties' Hollywood soldier charging a bunker. I fired the Colt twice, deliberately wide. I wanted Mathers alive.

My shots made Mathers think again: he veered off and ran through the trees. It took me a few seconds to stand up.

I sheltered behind the tree trunk, dragging air into my lungs, with the echoes of the shotgun still in my head. I couldn't believe the forest would ever be silent again.

I didn't know what or who had spooked Mathers, but I could guess where he was headed. If Petersen and his men got here fast they might be able to block Mathers. But that border was too damn close. I switched the Colt to my right hand and set off.

A drunk could have followed Mathers: his tracks showed as deep gouges in the snow crust. Broken branches hung loose. The splintered wood showed fresh and clean and wet, like exposed bone. I could smell sap.

This was the easy part. Once Mathers slowed down, once he started thinking instead of running on reflex, he'd be a hundred times more dangerous. Daylight hardly reached back here. Mathers could sink into a nice pool of shadows and just wait. I wouldn't see a thing until it was too late.

I followed the steps, placing my feet exactly where Mathers had placed his. I tried to make no noise. Gradually, the distance between steps began to shrink. Either Mathers had got tired or clever. I leaned against a tree trunk and tried to make myself small and invisible.

Even though my eyes had adjusted, the forest still seemed like ninety-percent shadow. Small scurrying sounds rattled the shrubs and branches. Birds cried out to each other. If Mathers still moved, he was quiet with it. Not good for me. I took a deep breath and stepped out from the tree trunk. As my foot snapped through the fragile crust, I staggered.

That small movement saved my life. The tree trunk behind me exploded. Splinters sliced into my neck and cheek. I lay face-down, sure I'd taken a shot, waiting for the next blasts. Silence. Not even the bird cries. My right gripped the Colt. My left hand found warm blood on my face.

"Mathers!"

No reply. Snow drifted down through the leaves above me but I felt sweat on my back and chest. I had a pretty good idea of how a deer must feel during hunting season. I didn't enjoy it.

"Mathers! Petersen's on his way! You'll never make it!"

I didn't believe that but I had to say it. I crawled forward and risked looking over a thick log. Darkness, shadows, then a quick movement to my left. I sighted the Colt but saw only snow falling from swaying branches. Then a flash of color as Mathers ran through a shaft of light, the shotgun held across his body. He didn't look back.

I ran after him, not caring about noise now. I tried to keep him in sight. Maybe a shot would slow him. More likely it would make him jump for cover and fire back. It looked like a Winchester pump in his hands. That meant eight shots. I tried to remember how many he'd fired, but it didn't really make much difference. I figured a man like Mathers would keep a few extra shells close to hand. I wouldn't like to bet my life on the alternative.

The ground rose ahead of me. Slivers of hot pain squeezed my sides, sending me images of broken ribs puncturing my lungs. My feet slipped on branches and moss hidden under the snow. I almost lost the Colt when I tripped, but managed to stay on my feet and keep the gun. It wasn't elegant. I wouldn't win any medals.

Mathers had led me onto some kind of slope, a hill or bluff. As the slope steepened, the forest ahead thinned out to allow in more daylight. I focused on Mathers' swaying figure and tried not to slip. Just for a moment, I heard water. Not just a stream or a brook. This had to be a river, deep and wide. It sounded like water slamming into rocks from a great height.

I saw Mathers maybe a hundred yards ahead and above me. He stepped out and seemed to look down at me and then away to his right. I wondered if I could hit one of his legs from that distance, maybe knock him down. Before I could try, he slid back into the trees. I ran up through the forest until I stood just about where he had. I took a chance and stepped out from the forest for a moment, then moved back under cover.

One look had been enough. The ground to my side fell away as if cut by an axe. Thirty yards separated left and right banks; a hundred feet below, the river's surface churned and bubbled. A waterfall upstream fed the boiling rapids with a torrent of gray and white—the vertical wall of water hit the rocks below and evaporated in a plume of spray and noise.

Unless he could fly, Mathers was going nowhere.

As I tracked him, I realized he'd screwed up. He must have made a wrong turn somewhere. That helped me. It made me think I had a chance of stopping him.

The rising slope turned to rocks and snow dotted with trees. It became forty-five degrees, then something steeper. I could see Mathers way up ahead, climbing the slope and using his free hand for grip. That shotgun was getting in his way but he wouldn't let go of it.

I jammed the Colt into my coat pocket and started climbing. The cooling sweat made me shiver. I thought about the log fire in the cabin, a fire I'd never seen but could imagine. Or maybe the one in the bar at the Mill Hotel. I could stretch out my legs, drink in hand, and toast my feet.

My hands slipped from an icy rock. Before I toppled

back, I threw my body forward. My chin hit the slope and I tasted blood. I shook my head and started again, this time focusing on every move. That way, I was able to dodge the shotgun as it tumbled past. It hit the bottom of the steep slope but didn't fire. When I looked up, Mathers was using both hands to scramble up the slope. He was eating into the lead I thought I'd had.

I moved faster, trying to catch up. The world shrank to me, Mathers, the cold rock in my hands, and the taste of cold mountain air. Nothing else existed. New York, Carl, Elaine: all vanished. It was just me and Mathers. And I had the gun.

As Mathers reached the top and clambered over the edge, I veered to the right. I didn't want to appear in the same place he had. I freed the Colt from my pocket; it almost slid from my numb fingers. I chose my last few moves with care. I had plenty of time. No need to rush. At the rough edge marking the crest of the slope, I hesitated; I braced my legs, took a deep breath, then threw myself over the top with the gun already searching for a target.

Mathers had disappeared. Between the crest of the slope and the higher forest lay a white plateau. The wind made quick snow devils that sank back. In time they would cover Mathers' tracks, but for now I could see his footprints heading along the river bank. I followed them. It didn't take a genius to figure he wanted to cross the river. On the other side lay Canada.

With the river frothing to my left, I strode along Mathers' prints. The ground dipped. Just like Mathers, I sank into drifts and had to scramble out. But I held the Colt ready. Then I saw Mathers maybe twenty yards ahead. His tracks made for the river bank. Mathers lay at the end of them, stretched out and gulping air through his mouth. But he struggled to his feet when he heard me call his name.

I stood close enough to see the thoughts dart across his face. He looked at me, at the Colt, then across the river. The opposite bank waited fifteen yards away, maybe less. But the swollen water swirled in deep, vicious eddies.

It didn't matter. Mathers dived in.

I ran to the river bank, cursing. Mathers dug at the water with both hands but the current pulled him downstream. His head disappeared; he came back to the surface choking and spluttering, his arms flailing like a child learning to swim. He wouldn't make it.

I flicked the safety on and shoved the Colt into my pocket. I took three or four running steps and dived into the river. With luck, my momentum would take me most of the way to Mathers. That was as far as my plan went.

The cold hit me like a wall. I thought my heart had stopped. No sound beneath the surface, no sensation. Then my head broke the surface and I saw Mathers two yards away. I gulped air and kicked my legs, trying to bridge the gap. Mathers disappeared again; only his arms jutted from the water like broken trees.

I thought I could hear the rush of the waterfall. As I swam closer to Mathers, one of his arms touched me. Instantly, the other swung around and he tried to wrap himself around me. He wasn't trying to attack me: it was panic, reflex. Drowning men can drag their rescuers down with them.

I avoided his arms and reached for the neck of his shirt. At the third attempt, I caught it. Most of the feeling had gone from my hands and fingers. I managed to pull Mathers up and out of the water. He spat water like a whale and thrashed the water. His weight tugged at me but I didn't let go. I kicked and twisted and used my free hand to haul him back to the bank. When pebbles and rock crunched beneath my feet, I dumped Mathers and collapsed on the bank. I lay back and dragged air into my frozen body.

On all fours, Mathers crawled out of the shallows. A rock or floating branch must have caught him: blood trickled from a wound over his eye. When he looked at me, he had no color in his eyes or face. He knew how close he'd come to death.

Mathers took another step and tried to kick me in the head. I rolled aside. His boot caught my shoulder. I tried to free the Colt from my pocket but Mathers fell on me. He had little strength but plenty of mass. He knocked the air out of me and tried to punch me.

I didn't have much energy, either. I blocked his punches and threw him off. I got to my knees, but before I could stand, he caught my legs and brought me down. I elbowed him in the face and saw blood stream from his nose. He came at me like a bear that doesn't know it's shot. His hands scrawled at my eyes; his knees dug into my ribs. I could hear his breath keening in my ear.

I drove my fists into his body but every blow felt weaker than the last. My strength faded. My vision blurred. Then I saw my opportunity: Mathers slipped on the snow and fell away from me. I clawed at the Colt and dragged it from my pocket. It fell from my frozen hands and landed on the snow between us.

Mathers saw the gun. His eyes opened wide. He reached down to grab it.

I kicked his arm away and fell on the Colt. I rolled away, seeing images of the gun going off and blowing me in two. On my back, I had time to raise the gun in both hands and yell, "Stop!"

Mathers knelt above me. The Colt's barrel touched his

shirtfront. His mouth twisted and his hands curled into fists.

"Don't do it," I told him. "You're coming back with me. It's over."

For a moment, I thought he was still going to try. Then his whole body relaxed. He sat back on his heels, still staring at the gun.

I stood up without dropping the Colt from Mathers. Every movement took ten times as long as it should. I didn't trust myself to make it down the hill in one piece, but I had no choice. If we waited up here, we'd freeze. "On your feet."

Mathers dragged himself upright and stared at me. Miserable and angry, like a child caught stealing cookies, he said, "It wasn't just me."

"I know."

He stared at me. Something moved behind his eyes, some spark. He opened his mouth to speak. The words never came out.

The shotgun blast blew Mathers into the water. Blood spiraled from his body and tainted the clean mountain river. Face-down, he drifted toward the fall.

I stood up from the half-crouch that reflex and the blast had thrown me into. I stared at the trees to my left. I let the Colt fall to my side.

Elaine stood at the edge of the trees. She wore muddied jeans and a padded green jacket too big for her. She held the shotgun out in front of her body as though she'd never seen it before. Her eyes followed Mathers.

Very slowly, I walked up to her. She never moved. As I got near, she said, "I thought . . . I mean, he usually carried a gun . . ."

The wind had risen. Cold knifed through my wet clothes

and straight into my bones. My limbs trembled and I wondered if I would pass out. Not yet; I still had too much to do.

Elaine let me take the shotgun from her hands. She turned to me, her head tilted to one side as if she couldn't quite remember my name. I stowed the Colt in my pocket and let Elaine lead me through the trees and down the slope. The river roared and rumbled beside us. The water churned white, except where the sun coated it with red.

16

I sat in front of the fire in the Shaws' rental cabin, waiting for Petersen to arrive. My legs stretched out toward the flames. I rubbed my knotted thighs and calves and thought about a long soak in a tub. My body ached as if I'd just finished a marathon, but I knew I was lucky: without all the years of running, I couldn't have survived what I'd been through over the past few days. Even so, it was a close thing.

Mathers hadn't left many signs of his stay in the cabin other than a well-stocked woodpile, a bottle of bourbon and some worn clothes. Not for the first time, I'd swapped my own clothing for his; a thick wool shirt and creased jeans helped me recover from my swim.

The sounds of dishes clashing and drawers opening and closing came through from the kitchen. Elaine carried two mugs into the living room. She set hers down by the fire, then offered the other to me, handle first. The smell of coffee and hot bourbon joined the wood smoke. The liquid burned a path down my throat. I hoped the coffee would wake me up. I needed it.

"I left your clothes to dry in the kitchen," Elaine said. "I didn't know if Gary might need to examine them."

"I doubt it."

Elaine sat on a low stool by the fire. The shotgun leaned in the corner of the rough log walls nearby. I'd pulled the Colt from my waistband under the oversized shirt; it lay on a table near the door. I could still feel the cold metal against my stomach.

Everything ached: my legs, arms, ribs, chest. I felt like I'd been through an industrial washer or a cement mixer. It would be a miracle if my ribs had survived unbroken. And I could still feel the cold water and the knifing wind that had torn at Elaine and me on the trek down the mountain. I doubted I'd ever be warm again.

Elaine stared into the flames without speaking. She sipped her drink and balanced the mug on her knees. She didn't look like a woman who'd been through the mill, who'd lost a baby and would soon lose her husband, a double murderer. But then, survivors look just the same as the rest of us; inside, they're different. Stronger.

"I need to thank you," I said.

Elaine didn't reply.

"I couldn't have made it down without you."

"You would've made it," Elaine said, with a brief smile.

I wanted to say something supportive, something to help her. But what? Her life was about to change: Petersen now had enough to nail Carl. Gregory, Carl's pusher, linked Carl to the .38 that had killed Sarah and Cursell. Petersen or Mendez could trace the connection between Cursell, Mathers and Carl. Sarah's laptop hinted at her fear of Carl, who had no alibi for the night of Sarah's death. I'd seen him shoot Cursell.

Some of it was circumstantial and some of it could be twisted around by a good lawyer. But not all of it. Enough of the guilt would stick to Carl.

And Elaine would have to go through hell again.

Only one thing still troubled me: Carl's motive. Either he'd killed Sarah or he'd arranged for Mathers to do the job. Why?

I set my coffee down. "Things are going to get tough for a while."

Elaine nodded. "I know."

"Petersen has enough to link Carl, now," I said. "Carl killed Sarah as well as Cursell, didn't he?"

Elaine looked at me without expression. She waited.

I chose my words with care: "I don't know if anyone could pick out Carl's reasons . . . what he had against Sarah . . ."

Elaine turned back to the fire and I thought she wasn't going to answer. Then she said, "It was the drink, mainly."

I waited.

"Carl did so well, going into rehab," Elaine said. "He worked hard; he wanted to get clean. I could see that. I knew he felt guilty about . . . some of the things he'd done in the past. Some of the things that the alcohol and the drugs had made worse."

I thought about the baby that Elaine had lost, but I said nothing.

Elaine continued, half-turning toward me, "He met Sarah at rehab. At first, she just sat in on the group and observed. Then she singled Carl out; she said she was a big fan. She explained about her thesis and asked if she could monitor Carl's progress. She could be very plausible and friendly when she wanted something. Very persuasive."

As Elaine said this, her face twisted into some emotion I couldn't decipher. I said, "So then Sarah came up here?"

"She helped Carl with his paperwork, mail and filing and stuff. Carl seemed happy to have her around. Then . . . I don't know how it began, but Carl started to get paranoid. He decided that Sarah had other motives for coming up here: he thought Sarah was using him, us, to get her thesis noticed, maybe get some leverage. Toward the end, he became convinced she was manipulating him; he called her a parasite."

I could hear the wind picking up outside. The screen

door on the back of the cabin slammed shut. "Toward the end?"

Elaine threw another chunk of wood onto the fire. "He started drinking again. I warned Sarah; I told her she should leave. But she was stubborn. Or maybe naïve. She wanted to finish her thesis. For someone who studied human nature, she couldn't see what was coming."

With Elaine's testimony and all the circumstantial evidence, Carl didn't stand a chance in court. But we hadn't reached the end: something must have made Carl finally flip.

Elaine continued, "It happened just before Thanksgiving. Mathers brought Carl a package; I didn't know it was drugs, but I had my suspicions. I guess Sarah did, too. She'd finally decided to go home. I left her packing in her room. Carl was locked in his study. The whole house felt like a valley before a thunderstorm.

"Carl came out of his study and just erupted. He blamed Sarah for his writer's block, for making him drink again, for everything. I'd seen it before—in the past, he used to blame me. I couldn't handle it: I went into Eastham, late afternoon. I had the charity dinner in the evening. Mathers was still there, and I thought Sarah would be okay. I didn't expect Carl to . . .

"I came back the next morning. There was no sign of Sarah. I found Carl hiding in the kitchen, squatting on the floor, surrounded by beer cans. He had blood on his hands and face. He was just rocking backward and forward, his eyes wide. Mathers had disappeared. When I heard the news about Sarah being shot at Cardford Springs, I realized what he'd done."

"But you didn't tell Petersen?"

She turned to me. "Carl's my husband. He didn't know what he was doing."

I shook my head. Whatever the bonds between Elaine and Carl, they had to be strong. How could she protect the man that had made her lose her baby? What hold did Carl have over her?

The coffee hadn't helped me. I just wanted to curl up on the floor and go to sleep. But I pushed Elaine's story around my mind, trying to square it with the other facts. "Why did Carl set me and Sam up in New York? Why did he use Tyrone Cursell?"

Elaine shrugged. "You'll have to find that out from Carl. Maybe it was something to do with the gun."

It didn't make sense. I covered my mouth as I yawned. Loose ends would have to wait for another day. "I guess it can wait. Maybe we can find out from Sarah's backup disks."

Elaine sat a little straighter. "What disks?"

"Well, Sarah's laptop had been edited. I guess Carl deleted some of the notes Sarah made while she was up here; they must have pointed to him, marked him out as a good suspect. But Sarah made backup disks of her work and sent them to one of her old roommates, Alison. I should get them in the next few days."

Elaine stared at me. I saw the same mix of emotions I'd seen on Mathers' face before he jumped into the river: fear, anger and calculation. Even before Elaine reached over for the shotgun, all the loose pieces of the story clicked into place in my mind. The realization surged through me like current and slammed me between the eyes.

"Carl didn't kill Sarah, did he?" I said. "You did."

Elaine pointed the shotgun at my chest. "I'm sorry, Steve, really I am. I liked you."

I gauged the distance between us. I'd never make it, not tired and battered as I was. The mouth of the shotgun seemed as wide as the Queens tunnel. "What's on those disks, Elaine? What don't you want us to find out?"

"The truth," Elaine said. "Sarah recorded every word, every argument. She didn't miss a thing."

My mouth had gone dry. Sounds seemed louder; the crack of burning wood, the rising wind, the beat of my heart. "She saw you setting Carl up?"

Elaine stood up. The shotgun zeroed in on my stomach. "Let's go for a walk, Steve."

I hesitated. I could just sit there and wait for the shot; Petersen might have his suspicions but I knew Elaine would think up some explanation for him. Outside the cabin, I'd have some leeway, some room for maneuver. Inside, I had none. And I wasn't ready to give up just yet.

I got to my feet. "Petersen will be here any minute."

"I know."

"So how will you explain my murder?"

Elaine collected the Colt from the table and nodded toward the door. "I guess I'll tell him that you and Mathers died together in the struggle."

"You think fast."

"I'm used to it." Elaine stowed the Colt in her waistband; she didn't check the breech. She reached behind her and opened the cabin's front door, then waved me through with the shotgun.

As I walked past Elaine I thought about making a move. She knew it, and stepped back. Outside, the cold made me draw a breath. The wind slapped my face. Most of the daylight had gone.

"Head right," Elaine said, "up to the river."

I did what she told me. I didn't have much choice. My tired feet slipped on the ice and snow. I had to wrap my arms around my chest and ribs to stop the shivers. I could hear Elaine's footsteps crunching on the snow behind me.

I could see her logic: she'd kill me at the river's edge, downstream from where Mathers had died. It wouldn't really matter where my body ended up; she could blame the river's currents. A good pathologist might notice a slight difference between when Mathers died and I was shot, but there wouldn't be much in it. Maybe the Crime Scene Technicians would spot something missing at the head of the waterfall. But they'd probably take Elaine's word for it.

History is written by the winners.

"What happened?" I asked, speaking over my shoulder. If I could keep her talking, Petersen might interrupt. And I was honestly curious. "Why did you set Carl up for Sarah's murder?"

From behind me, Elaine said, "Because he killed our child and stopped me from ever having another."

I remembered Fran telling me about Elaine's visit to the Emergency Room. "He hurt you that bad?"

No answer, then, "She would have been sixteen months old, now. I was going to give her my grandmother's name. But he took her away from me."

The cold had worked through my borrowed clothes. I could hardly feel my feet or hands. I imagined I heard a car's engine from behind us, and risked a look. Nothing.

"Why didn't you tell Petersen?" I asked. "They would have put Carl in jail."

I didn't like the sound of Elaine's laugh. "For how long? He would have been out in six months, if that. With a good lawyer he would have walked free. No. I knew there was a better way. I wanted to see him suffer, see him lose everything. I just had to be patient."

The cold ate away at me. I tried to think. "Was someone really stalking him? Or was it you?"

"No, he really had a weird fan." Elaine sounded a little out of breath. "But when Carl got the gun, I saw I could use it."

"And Sarah gave you the opportunity?"

No answer.

"Why her? What had she ever done to you?"

"Apart from spy on us?" Elaine said, her voice hard and sharp. "She was too damned good at her job; she would have made a fine psychiatrist. She sat there, watching, observing, listening. I thought I could hide my feelings, but Sarah realized. And she tried to warn Carl."

That's why Sarah had been scared, I thought. She'd fathomed the undercurrents in Elaine and Carl's marriage. Had she seen how far Elaine was willing to go to destroy Carl? Probably not until it was too late.

No wonder Elaine had edited Sarah's laptop, leaving in those notes that pointed to Carl. And no wonder Elaine had panicked at my news. "You can't stop Petersen and Stanton reading Sarah's backup disks."

"Maybe, maybe not," Elaine said. "But if I get to them first, I stand a chance. I bet you got them sent to your hotel, right?"

I didn't reply. I was too busy tramping through the snow and trying to stay upright. I couldn't do it; my foot slipped and I crashed to the ground.

"Get up," Elaine said.

"Why should I make it any easier for you?"

She nudged my leg with the shotgun. "I don't want you to suffer any more than you have to. Please."

Hell of a time to show some compassion, I thought, and struggled to my feet. I wondered if Elaine would use the shotgun or switch guns and try to use the Colt. I staggered toward the sound of running water. We walked between dark gray trees linked with shadows. I didn't have to pretend to slow down. "Why . . . why didn't you just walk away from Carl? You didn't have to stay . . ."

"He owed me, Steve," Elaine said. "At the start, he was easy to be around, easy to fall in love with. Then his books sold. The more success he had, the more he drank. Some people, when they drink, get happy; some get horny. Cal started to get angry. And that's the worst. But he needed me around. He couldn't function without me. And then Sarah appeared."

I could imagine the mess of emotions and contradictions in the Shaws' house: Elaine, hating Carl but unwilling to let go of him; Carl, ashamed of what he'd done to his wife and wanting to get off drink and drugs; Sarah, watching, analyzing, waiting. Sarah, the catalyst.

"Oh, Carl couldn't wait to confess everything to Sarah." Elaine practically spat out the words. "Men love a good listener, someone who won't judge them. Or maybe they just love the sound of their own voice. Either way, Sarah slotted right in."

I tried to keep Elaine talking. "Why didn't you just send Sarah away? Why did you have to kill her?"

"Because she guessed that something would happen to Carl," Elaine said. "And because she stopped me from adopting another child."

I wondered if Sarah really had been the one to tip off Eastham's Social Services. Maybe Elaine just thought she had. The end result had been the same.

Elaine continued, her words almost falling out of her. "If they'd let us adopt, it might have been different. I might have forgiven Carl, especially after he cleaned himself up. But once Sarah blocked me . . . there was nothing left."

"Only revenge."

"I call it justice."

I listened out for Petersen's car but heard only the wind in the trees, and the rushing water nearby. I needed time. "Where did Mathers fit in? How did you control him?"

"With sex, first," Elaine said. "Then drugs. I don't think I set out to use him. Somehow, it came together. Like it was meant to be."

Suddenly the ground fell away in front of me and I tumbled down the slope. My head and arms splashed into the running water. I tried to stand, but slipped to my knees and looked up into Elaine's face. She took the Colt from her waistband and set the shotgun on the snow. She probably thought she could tell Petersen that Mathers used the Colt on me as I fired the shotgun into him. It would all make sense.

My heart beat in my throat. Had Elaine checked the Colt's breech?

"Why set me and Sam up?" I asked, breathing hard. I didn't enjoy the edge of panic to my voice.

"I saw your photo in the *Times* when I visited New York. Like I said: it all came together. Carl's pusher, via Leon, put me on to Cursell. I suggested to Carl that he needed some background for his novel. I made all the arrangements with your Press Office."

"You asked for me and Sam?"

"I knew where you'd be, and what time you'd show up."

I moved my legs beneath me, bracing them. "So Cursell would shoot Carl?"

Elaine tilted her head as if listening, then said, "Maybe. It didn't really matter. Cursell was supposed to wing you and your partner. Then either he'd shoot Carl or Carl would shoot him with the .38. Either way, Carl would suffer. The police would trace the .38."

"The same gun that you used on Sarah," I said.

"Yes, the same gun." Elaine stepped forward, holding the Colt in both hands. "Do you know something? It wasn't difficult. I thought it would be. But I just held the gun to Sarah's head and didn't hesitate. Because she'd robbed me."

"No, Elaine. You just needed someone to blame."

In the darkness, I thought I saw Elaine smile. "Thank you. You've made it easier for me."

Even as she raised the Colt and pulled the trigger, I was moving. I thrust my legs into the snow and ice. I charged forward. My left foot slipped but I had enough momentum to slam into Elaine.

I had time to see the look of surprise on Elaine's face as the Colt clicked empty. Relief washed through me, but only for a split second. Then we crashed onto the ice and snow in a tangle of limbs. The Colt skidded away into shadows.

With my face level with Elaine's stomach, I tried to wrap my arms around her and keep her down. She used her elbows on my back and head, savage, powerful blows that brought explosions of pain. She slithered out of my arms and made for the shotgun.

I caught her ankles and pulled her down. Her hand fell a few inches short of the shotgun's breech. She kicked out and drove her heel into my face. I wouldn't let go; I clawed my way up her body. The world shrank to Elaine, me and the gun. No sound except our harsh breaths.

Elaine's hand inched toward the shotgun. I could see the tendons standing out like steel cables, and the gold ring on her third finger. I didn't know how much energy I had left in me. Every muscle ached and burned. I strained to reach past Elaine.

She dropped her head and then snapped it back into my face. Pain erupted in my cheek and jaw. I loosened my grip for a moment, long enough for Elaine to fasten her hand on the shotgun.

As if in slow motion, I saw the barrel of the gun swing around. I reached to block it. I'd be too late.

The ice saved me. Elaine moved so fast, she slipped. The shotgun barrel twisted up into the air as Elaine lost her balance. The shot ripped past my cheek; I knew I'd lost an eardrum. But I got my hands on the shotgun.

We fought for the gun as we tumbled down the slope to the river's edge. Elaine plunged into the water beneath me. The cold knocked all breath away. I came up for air, still trying to hold the gun above the water. The barrel pointed down between us. Elaine's face was no more than a blur. She tugged at the gun, refusing to let go.

The second shotgun blast dug into the water. Spray showered me. Elaine looked at me with total surprise. Then, very slowly, she let go of the gun. As she drifted away, I threw the gun away and reached out for her. The current pulled me away. I saw Elaine slip beneath the surface. Her eyes never closed. I think I yelled her name. Maybe I did.

I woke up on the river bank. Bright lights. Voices. Petersen standing above me. Someone draped a blanket over me although I didn't feel cold. I didn't feel a thing.

I tried to tell them about Elaine, but the idea of sleep seemed so easy, so inevitable. I closed my eyes and drifted down into the darkness.

17

I sat in a window booth in Shirley's Diner, legs stretched out, head back against the worn red vinyl. A few early commuters and tourists trickled through the town, probably heading for St. Albans or the Interstate. The rental car that had brought Detective Mendez from Burlington stood outside the police station over on the other side of Main Street. A yellow light shone in Petersen's office, which Mendez had apparently taken over.

Mendez would want to know exactly why I'd come up to Vermont and why I hadn't told him the truth right from the start. My future in the force depended on my answers. I had to work out if that mattered to me any more.

"Coffee, white, no sugar." Petersen slid the mug across the table.

I pulled back my legs to let him slide into the booth opposite me. The movement kicked off a series of sharp pains right through my back, ribs and chest. I thought about taking another painkiller but I needed a clear head for the next few hours.

As Petersen sat down, he glanced at the light in his office, then at me. "How are you feeling?"

"Like a million dollars."

I'd woken up late the night before, in the ER at St. Albans. My injuries amounted to contusions, cuts, slight concussion. Nothing serious. I'd wondered if Elaine had been in that same room two years before, battered and bruised, her daughter already lost.

As soon as I'd spotted Petersen in the ER, I'd asked about Elaine. He told me they'd pulled her body from the lower reaches of the river, not fifty yards from where Mathers lay face-down in a rock pool. During the trip back to my hotel, Petersen said the river gave up its flotsam and jetsam as it slowed. It wasn't the first time he'd found people there.

Now, in the diner, I asked, "What did you tell Mendez?"

"That the hospital ordered you to rest," Petersen said. "Which they did. He didn't look too happy about it. But I guess he knew he wouldn't get much sense out of you last night."

I wrapped my hands around the hot mug. "Thanks. I owe you."

In the next few hours, I'd have to explain everything: what happened in New York, Tyrone Cursell's death, Sarah's murder, then Mathers and Elaine. But Petersen deserved the news first.

I repeated everything that Elaine had told me the day before, or as much as I could remember. Petersen listened without interrupting, making me pause only to wave Patti over to refill our mugs. I heard my voice slowing and turning a little huskier when I came to the end; I could still see Elaine's open eyes as she drifted downstream.

"So, she planned all this?" Petersen said.

"Not planned, exactly. I just think she used what came her way. She took advantage of the stalker to make sure that Carl got an unregistered gun. Then she tried to pin Sarah's murder on Carl."

"How?"

As two tourists pushed open the diner's glass door, I leaned toward Petersen. "Elaine edited Sarah's laptop notes, removing anything that pointed to her but leaving references to Carl. On the night of the murder, she managed to rig an alibi for herself while making sure that Carl didn't. And she planted a letter from Carl, arranging to meet Sarah that night. Trouble was, someone from Cardford Springs found Sarah's body before Ed Petchey did, and took the laptop, purse and suitcase. The letter got lost in the shuffle. The laptop stayed hidden."

Petersen nodded. "So we never had anything pointing back to Carl. Except the gun, which we didn't even know he had."

I took a gulp of coffee. "I think Elaine panicked. She was waiting for you and Stanton to put the pieces together, but it never happened. You never suspected Carl."

"We wondered," Petersen said. "But it was no more than that. Most murders are committed by someone close to the victim, but Sarah's really looked like a robbery gone wrong."

I thought about Elaine, cooped up in that big house with Carl, waiting for the police to find the clues she'd planted.

"What about you?" Petersen asked. "How did she pick on you and your partner for the setup?"

"Coincidence." I looked through the window. "She saw our picture in the *Times*. From the article, she knew where we'd be and at what time. I think she probably had Cursell stake us out a few times, just to make sure; maybe she did it herself, or got Mathers involved. Either way, she set a trap, and a good one.

"Whatever happened, Carl would get burnt. If Cursell killed Carl, fine. If Carl killed Cursell, the police would want to know why he had an unregistered gun. If we didn't match the ballistics with Sarah's murder, Elaine would find a way to tip us off. After that night outside Lazzini's, Carl would be screwed whatever happened."

Petersen shook his head. "Why not just kill him up here? She could have used Mathers . . ."

I remembered Elaine's explanation from the day before. "She wanted Carl to suffer. If Cursell had killed Carl, it would have been closure for her, sure. But, ideally, she wanted her husband to go through hell. And I think she wanted to watch."

Petersen thought for a moment, then said, "I always figured I was a good judge of people, but Elaine . . . I can't believe anyone could be that vindictive."

"She had good reason."

Petersen stared at me.

"Carl killed their daughter," I said, feeling myself blush. "He hurt her enough to make sure she could never have children. Okay, he was drunk, out of his mind, but he still did it. I don't think she could forgive him for that.

"I don't have kids, but if I did and someone hurt them . . . maybe I wouldn't do what Elaine did. I'd do something, though. Maybe I'd want to make them suffer."

"I'd think twice before telling that to Mendez or Stanton," Petersen said.

"Wouldn't you do the same?" I asked.

"Maybe so, but it doesn't make it right."

"No, it doesn't." I had to agree with that. Thanks to Elaine's determination to make Carl suffer, five people had died: Sarah, Cursell, Harry, Mathers and Elaine herself. Only Carl survived. Maybe Elaine had got her revenge after all.

I continued, repeating what had gone through my mind all the previous night and this morning: "Elaine must have been amazed when it looked like Carl would get off with Cursell's shooting. As far as the New York police knew, Carl had picked up one of Cursell's weapons and used it.

Instead of connecting Carl with Sarah's murder, they connected Cursell. Sam, my partner, didn't know any better. Only I knew the truth.

"Then I came up here. Elaine worked out the reason why, and set about using me, too. Every time we met, she told me a little bit more about Carl; she dropped hints, pointed me in the right direction. She made sure I had enough information to hang Carl. All I had to do was tell my bosses the truth."

Petersen looked into my eyes. "So why didn't you?"

"Because I thought me and Sam owed Carl," I said. "I thought he'd saved our lives."

Petersen nodded. "Maybe he did."

We'd never know. Elaine had told me that Cursell was meant to wing me and Sam. But if we hadn't been wearing armor, we'd both be dead.

What if Elaine had read another paper instead of the *Times*? What if she'd spotted some other way to set up Carl? It all came down to chance, to coincidence. Somehow, that wasn't a very comforting thought.

"So, what now?" Petersen asked, glancing again at his office over the road.

"I guess it's time to speak to Mendez." I finished my coffee and took a strip of painkillers out of my pocket. I looked at the silver strip with its clear plastic bubbles, then slipped it back into my pocket without opening it.

On the way out, I stopped at the counter and said to Shirley, "Thanks for the coffee and all the help."

Shirley, gray and petite, tilted her head to one side like a bird. She smiled. "I don't think I was much help, honey."

"You were."

"Are you leaving us now?"

"Soon."

She touched my arm with her small hand. "You take care."

I left the diner and crossed Main Street. Petersen walked beside me. We paused on the steps of the station. Petersen looked up and down the quiet street, then asked, "What happened with the Colt?"

"How do you mean?"

"You said Elaine fired at you but the Colt wasn't loaded."

I nodded. "It's an old habit that Sam taught me: whenever you take a weapon off a suspect, you eject the first round or even drop the whole clip. Elaine had to feed in the next round from the clip."

"But she still had the shotgun, loaded and ready."

"That's right."

"So, if she'd decided to use the shotgun on you instead of the Colt . . ."

I looked at Petersen without expression.

He stuck out his hand. "I'm off to Waterbury to try to explain this mess to Stanton. I might not see you before the inquest, and maybe not even then."

"Thanks for your help," I said, shaking his hand. "I owe you."

"Well, maybe you do." He took a couple of steps away, then turned back to say, "I don't agree with the way you worked up here; I don't agree with what you did in New York. But you came through in the end. And that means something."

I watched him drive away. I knew he was right: I'd screwed up. If I'd acted differently, maybe Harry, Elaine, and Mathers would still be alive. But I'd done the best I could at the time. I'd tried to make the best decisions with the information I had. I could justify almost everything.

Somehow, that didn't help.

I started up the steps of the police station. At the top, I took in the view of Eastham, from the white-painted church to the brick Victorian bed and breakfast cottages at the west. A quiet, peaceful, pretty town. Nothing bad should happen here. Certainly no murders. Murders belonged in the cities, if anywhere.

Inside the station, Evie smiled at me and pointed to a rickety chair at the back of the office. A low hum of voices came from behind the pebbled-glass door of Petersen's office. The yellow light was still lit.

I had a lot to do before I left Eastham. I had to visit Fran and tell her how Mathers and Elaine had died. And I had to call in on Willard and settle my debts for the Jeep and for his battered pickup. Petersen had told me the County would pay for the pickup. I appreciated the help.

And Fran? There was nobody to help her. I liked her but I'd have to be honest and tell her everything.

I thought about calling Gillian Braid and then Sarah's parents. It probably wasn't a good idea. Mendez and Stanton would be in touch with them. The case was out of my hands; it had never been in my hands, officially.

I heard Mendez from inside the office. I started to go over what I would tell him. I saw two options: if I intended to leave the force, I could weasel my way around the truth and protect myself as much as possible; if I wanted to stay, I told him the truth. Everything. Just the way it happened. If I wanted to stay on the force, the truth mattered.

And in that moment I realized that it mattered very much to me.

The office door opened. Carl came out. When he saw me, he stopped as if someone had pulled him back.

I stood up. I wanted to say something. Nothing came out.

Carl looked ten years older. Stooped shoulders. Gray, loose skin. Hollows in his cheeks. He looked at me from eyes red with crying or alcohol, or both. He had the look of a man who can't believe what the world is doing to him, or why. He looked lost.

His life had ended when Elaine had lost their baby in the ER at St. Albans. He may as well have given up then. Instead, he'd have to stick around, waiting, thinking. Would he have the strength to survive? Or would the bottle be the first thing he saw every morning and the last at night?

He shook his head and walked away. I wondered where he'd go; back to the big, remote house? I wouldn't want to return there. I couldn't.

I eased my body back into the chair and waited. I wondered how long it would take for my collection of injuries, bruises and wounds to heal up. Years of running had given me the stamina to get through this. But as a kid, back on the Albany projects, I'd started running to escape from the things I couldn't handle; it had taken me a long time to realize you could only run so far.

But did I have what it took to stay in the Police? Could I handle other cases like this one? I'd know only if I stuck around to find out.

"Officer Burnett." Mendez stood in the doorway of Petersen's office.

As I walked past Mendez, he closed the door and said, "Sit down."

The pit of my stomach flipped over. I sat down and took a long, slow breath.

Mendez sat behind the desk and opened a file. "I have to tell you that you have the right for your lawyer to be present, or a member of your association. This is only a preliminary interview, not disciplinary hearing, but if you want some kind of advocate . . ."

"I don't need anybody right now, sir."

Mendez nodded. He leaned forward and asked, "Are you ready to tell me what happened?"

I thought about Sam, Cursell, Harry, and Sarah. I thought about Mathers and Elaine, and about Carl. I sat up straight in my chair just like I'd stood to attention on parade in my new uniform, three years before.

"Yes, sir. I'm ready."

ABOUT THE AUTHOR

TOM BRENNAN, 39, shares a house on the English coast with his wife Sylvia and many cats. He enjoys writing mysteries and speculative fiction, and watching the ships heading out to Ireland and America. His short fiction has appeared in the *Writers of the Future* series (Vol. XVIII) and in magazines in the U.S., U.K., and Canada. His fantasy novel *The One True Prince* appeared in May 2004.